THE
DISAPPEARED

THE
DISAPPEARED

THE DISAPPEARED

C. J. HARPER

SIMON AND SCHUSTER

First published in Great Britain in 2013 by Simon and Schuster UK Ltd
A CBS COMPANY

1 3 5 7 9 10 8 6 4 2

Simon & Schuster UK Ltd
1st Floor, 222 Gray's Inn Road
London
WC1X 8HB

Simon & Schuster Australia, Sydney

Simon & Schuster India, New Delhi

A CIP catalogue record for this book is available from the British Library.

PB ISBN: 978-0-85707-698-4
eBook ISBN: 978-0-85707-699-1

Printed and bound by CPI Group (UK) Ltd, Croydon, CR0 4YY

www.simonandschuster.co.uk
www.simonandschuster.com.au

Special thanks to everyone who submitted a photo for the cover image of this book.

For Bailey

'What do you think it's like to kiss a girl?' Wilson says as he scans his holocard and steps on to the metro train.

'It's not unpleasant,' I say, following him.

'Yeah, right! You've never kissed a girl,' Wilson says, in an unnecessarily loud voice.

'Shh!' I look round at the construction workers and shoppers on the train. They don't seem to be listening. 'You don't know everything about me,' I say.

'Jackson, we've been living at the same school since we were five. I do know everything about you.'

'Actually, in the past eleven years there have been a number of occasions when you haven't been present. There was that intimate evening walk with Mel Ross . . .'

'You were eight! And the only reason she wanted to talk to you was to break the news that she'd accidentally sat on your genetic mutation experiment.'

He's right of course. Wilson is my best friend, but sometimes I hate the fact that we live in each other's pockets. When the kids in our district take the Potential Test at age five, only those with the highest scores get into our Learning Community: it's one of the top schools in the country and they keep the classes small. Which means everyone knows everything about everyone.

'You're not exactly a girl magnet yourself,' I say.

Wilson waggles his eyebrows at me. 'Don't you remember my Biology project with Leela Phillips? We spent a lot of time in that lab together.'

'We all know that she only chose you for a partner because you're the biggest Science brainer in the school,' I say.

'No, you're the biggest Science brainer. Actually, you're the biggest *brainer* full stop.' He gives me a kick. Quite a hard kick.

I smother a smile. It's useful being smart. Everyone wants to be in my work group and on Fridays my name is always on the high achievers list, which means extra privileges.

The train pulls into the Business Sector and two women in suits crowd into our carriage.

'Maybe we need to meet a different kind of girl,' Wilson says. He looks around as if he suddenly expects to see a selection of teenage females. Unsurprisingly, there aren't any.

We're not likely to meet a 'different type' of girl. We're not supposed to be friendly with anyone outside of school. In fact, we're not even supposed to think about anything outside school. The children who get into top-rated

Learning Communities like ours leave home at five years old and from then on our teachers are always going on about how we're the elite and we're being trained for important Leadership work and how we need to focus on our studies. Anyone who doesn't work hard is a disgrace. I don't mind the hard work, but I do mind never being allowed out. We go home for just two weekends a year and we rarely leave the school grounds. I'd like to see my mum more. Wilson says he never really thinks about his parents, but I speak to my mother on the communicator a lot. She's cool. My dad died when I was baby so it's just us.

Wilson pokes me in my side to get my attention. Then he punches me in the arm. He's a bit wired because we're out on a trip. It's the first time in ages that we've been given a pass out. Our teacher, Facilitator Johnson, gave it to us so we could deliver a package for him.

Wilson jabs me again. 'Do you think we could get an evening pass out? Maybe we could go to an entertainment centre and meet some girls.'

'They don't like us going to entertainment centres. They're full of kids from Second Class Learning Communities.'

'So?'

'I don't know, maybe they think if we mix with average kids it will rub off on us. Anyway, do you really want to date some girl who's going to end up as a nurse or a secretary? What's wrong with the girls at our school? They're the academic elite. We're talking the finest teenage minds in the country.'

3

'Maybe it's not their *minds* we should be interested in, my friend.' Wilson lets go of the hand grip to reach out and pat me on the shoulder. The train jerks to a halt and he ends up falling on to the man in front of us.

Wilson pats him on the shoulder instead. 'Sorry! Sorry about that,' Wilson says.

The man stares down at Wilson's hand. Wilson pulls it back and folds his arms. The man eyes our school badges and tuts.

I drag Wilson a little further down the carriage. The train slows and we pull into our stop. We hop off and take the high-speed lift to surface level.

'I don't know if I'd even want to meet an outside girl. Have you noticed the general public aren't exactly keen on us?' I say.

We step out of the lift and head into the long, sheltered avenues of shops. The winter sun is shining, but the wind is biting.

'They're jealous,' Wilson says. 'They think we're living a life of luxury at a top Learning Community. They've got no idea how hard we work, or how much pressure there is on us to get into the Leadership and sort this country out.'

'Jealous or not, all this stuff about us being geniuses and the future of our nation doesn't make us popular.'

'I reckon we'd be popular with Academy girls. I heard they'll do anything you want,' Wilson says grinning at me.

4

If you don't score high enough in the Potential Test to get into a Learning Community, even a Second Class one, they send you to an Academy.

'What are you saying, Wilson? The only girl who'd go out with you would have to be too stupid to know any better? How many Academy girls do you think would understand your latest research?'

'I'm sure we'd find something else to talk about,' says Wilson, working his eyebrows again.

In a minute he'll be winking at me. I give him a shove. 'What would you have to talk to a girl about anyway?' I say.

'Just, y'know, stuff.' He shrugs his shoulders.

I don't know what I'd talk to a girl about. I can't imagine that they'd be interested in the things that Wilson and I discuss. We talk about Science. And sex. And sci-fi films. Preferably ones with sex in. And sometimes Wilson rambles on about the novel he's writing about a world ruled by dragons and gnomes.

Wilson is staring at me.

'What?' I say.

He eyes me up and down. 'That red jacket doesn't really go with your hair,' he says.

'My hair is black, how can it not go?'

'But there's so much of it.'

My mother is always telling me to cut my hair. It's thick and curly and grows quickly, but I like it when it's just starting to hang in my eyes.

'I like my hair and I like my jacket,' I say. 'Even Facilitator Johnson told me it was striking.'

'You're a bit long and skinny for it.'

Suddenly I get it. Wilson is just as long and skinny as me. He is also obsessed with finding the perfect outfit that will make him irresistible to females. I shrug off my jacket and hand it to him.

'You could have just asked,' I say.

He hands me his own plain black jacket. 'I never like to miss an opportunity to tell you that your fringe makes you look like one of those dogs with all the hair in its eyes.'

I kick him in the shins.

We walk quickly down a parade of the expensive kind of shops. The screens in the windows change constantly. They flash up footage of models or music videos or arty shots of the latest communicator. I nod my head towards the greeter at the door of one of the shops. 'That's the kind of place Second Class Learning Community girls end up working,' I say.

'Does it really matter where a girl works?'

He's trying to wind me up. 'Shut up, Wilson, don't give me all that anti-Leadership crap. Of course it matters where you work, it's supposed to be "individuals working to their potential for the good of all" remember?'

He covers his ears. 'Don't start spouting The Leader's speeches at me.'

'I'm just saying: everyone's got their place and that's why it works.'

6

'And I'm just saying I don't see why kids from different schools can't get . . . friendly.'

I shake my head at him. I don't believe he'd really go near a Second Class Learning Community girl and definitely not one from an Academy. He's just obsessed with the thought of girls full stop.

We take a right, then a left. As we approach the edge of the shopping sector the stores get shabbier and smaller. There's a row of three digital poster screens; each one is cracked but you can still see The Leader delivering a speech. It's one of his most famous ones.

'*If we want to survive, we must work. If we want to prosper, we must work. If we want to keep our enemies at bay, we must work. We must work with our minds and with our hands to build a better nation. The power lies with* you.'

Wilson likes to joke, but even he has to admit that after the Long War, when this country was in a mess, it was The Leader who got us back on our feet. He's the one that got kids doing the Potential Test and now, unlike the olden days, everyone is matched to the work they're best suited to. And that's how we've become a force to be reckoned with again.

Whenever I hear that work speech I make up my mind to do better in my next assessment. Everybody says that I'll be chosen for one of the top Leadership positions when I'm twenty-one and leave school, but I want to make sure.

Sometimes I wonder what my dad did before he died. I like to imagine he had an important job in the Leadership. My mother hasn't told me much about him. I think it makes her too sad. Yesterday, I finally got up the courage to try to hack into the National Register to see if there was anything about him on my official notes. But I couldn't fully access my records. I suppose the point is that I really want to do something that would have made my dad proud.

Wilson is watching me. 'You've gone all gooey eyed.' He looks up at the digi posters. 'You can't wait to get into the Leadership, can you? You love all that "strive to serve" stuff that Facilitator Johnson goes on about.'

'It's going to be great,' I say. 'The way I see it, we've spent the last seventeen years recovering from the Long War and now the Leadership is really getting into its stride. It's going to be our generation making the decisions that make this country great again. We're going to be so important.'

'Yeah.' Wilson grins. 'I suppose we will be, won't we?'

It's easy to find the factory workers' accommodation block we're looking for because it's in the shadows of a huge factory which towers above the other buildings. The factory and the block are surrounded by high fences. In front of the main gate we find a scanner. When I walk through it the gate clicks open for me. We pass through two more gates like this. As we approach the factory I nod my head towards it. 'And that's where Academy girls end up,' I say.

'All right, snobby, stop going on about it.'

'I'm not a snob. That's just how society works. If you want to work in the Leadership then you can't mix with Academy kids or factory workers.'

Wilson smirks at me and points at the package in my hand. 'Facilitator Johnson knows someone in a factory accommodation block,' he says.

'That's different.'

Wilson is quiet for a minute. His face is more serious now. 'Do you ever wonder what it would be like though? If you went to an Academy and ended up in a factory?'

'If your Potential Test suggested that you should be a factory worker then that's the best place for you.' I don't know why he's questioning the system. It works perfectly. Everyone has a role and everyone knows their place.

We've reached the accommodation block. Wilson looks up at it. 'I suppose so.'

'Come on, we want the fifth floor,' I say.

We make our way up the metal staircase clinging to the side of the grey concrete block and quickly overtake an old man carrying a battered shopping bag.

'Why isn't he at the factory?' I whisper.

We watch the man's quivering hand reaching for the banister. 'I don't think he's fit for work any more,' Wilson says.

'But he still gets to live here? That's nice, isn't it. See? Everyone is provided for.'

Wilson shrugs.

9

We don't see anyone else on our way up the stairs. I guess they're all at the factory.

'You can see the Wilderness from here,' Wilson says.

I lean on the rail and look out behind the block. A few hundred metres away is a familiar style of tall fence made of strips of metal and topped with barbed wire. You see them wherever the district borders the Wilderness. Beyond the fence is a wasteland littered with rubble that stretches, without a hint of greenery, as far as I can see.

'*Do your duty, do your best, or you'll be sent to the Wilderness*,' Wilson whispers in a creepy voice.

'Shut up.' I haven't heard that rhyme since I was a kid.

'Remember what happened to Facilitator Amonetti?'

Facilitator Amonetti disappeared from the Learning Community at the same time as a rebellious boy called Fisher. The rumour was that Fisher had wound the facilitator up to breaking point and that she had strangled him and then been sent to the Wilderness as punishment. 'There was never any proof of all that,' I say.

The Wilderness is a huge area of desolate land that was created by bombing during the Long War. Being sent there is worse than going to prison. They say it's roamed by packs of feral people who will tear you limb from limb. The rumours about the Wilderness are enough to keep anyone's murderous rage under wraps.

I shudder; just looking at the place gives me the creeps. I turn back to the steps.

'They should get a lift,' Wilson says. 'Imagine living

on the twenty-fifth floor. I wouldn't want to climb these every day.'

'Factory workers are trained for physical work,' I say.

'I'd like to see how "physical" a factory lady could be.' Wilson squeezes the air in the region where a very short and very wide lady's breasts would be.

When we reach the fifth floor we stop in front of a set of fire doors that lead to a corridor. Through the misty glass I can see someone.

'Hey Wilson, maybe this is your factory lady.'

We push open the door. I stop dead. Wilson bangs into me from behind.

It's not a lady.

It's a man with a gun.

2

'Don't make a noise or I'll kick your heads in.'

The man is wearing a black jacket with the hood up. He gestures us forward with the gun. I don't want to get hurt. I shuffle forward. Wilson follows, staying close to me. My heart is pounding and my mouth is dry. I flick my eyes left and right. The corridor is lined with doors leading to flats. I pray for one of the doors to open.

'What are a couple of brainers like you two doing out on the streets?' says a voice behind us.

I spin round. There's another man, in a navy hooded coat. He must have been behind the fire doors.

'I would've thought you were too precious to the Leadership to be out where you could get your throat slit,' he says, walking towards us and making Wilson and me take a step back. Under his hood I can see his wide, flat nose and a fleck of spit on his fleshy lips. 'What are you looking at?' he snaps.

I drop my eyes to the ground, but he's talking to Wilson.

'I . . . I'm not . . .' Wilson opens and closes his mouth.

We've moved so far back that now we're sandwiched between the two of them. I don't turn round but I can feel the massive presence of the man behind us.

'Give me your money,' says Navy Hood.

Wilson scrabbles about trying to pull his currency card out of his pocket. He drops it and has to bend down to pick it up. He hands it to the man.

'Thank you,' Navy Hood says to Wilson.

Wilson tries a shaky smile in return.

The man headbutts him.

'*Uhhh!*' cries Wilson and lifts his hand to his head. The man behind us brings down an elbow into Wilson's neck. Wilson crumples over, his face smashing straight into Navy Hood's thrusting knee.

'No!' I cry.

Both men turn to look at me.

'You can't . . .' I begin, but my voice fails me.

Black Hood's eyes are in shadow, but I see him bare his teeth and I wince away just as he punches me in the nose. It's like an explosion in my face. I reel backwards and Navy Hood kicks me in the stomach. As I go down I see Wilson trying to get to his feet.

The men are kicking me; raining blows on my face, my stomach, my back. I hold my arms curled over my head. I can't breathe. It feels like they're splintering my spine with each kick. Why has no one come to help us?

'Efwurding little brainer. Do you think you can tell us

what to do?' He kicks me in the stomach so hard it feels like his boot has punched through my flesh. 'Think you're better than us?'

I try to call out, but I can't get air into my lungs. I'm going to die.

'Hey!' Wilson shouts.

The kicking stops.

I gasp for breath. I retch. Keeping my arms over my head, I open my eyes. The two men are running down the long corridor after Wilson. I've got to get up. I've got to help Wilson. I roll over on to my knees and lift my head. There's a rushing sound in my ears. I try to use my hands but they're numb from where the men kicked them and my arms are shaking so hard I can't support myself. I lean against the wall while I push up with my legs, then half run, half hobble down the corridor.

I'm coughing and choking for breath and have to stop and suck in air to shout for help, but my voice is tiny in the dimly lit corridor. There's no one in sight.

I bang on the nearest door. 'Help!' I scream, straining my vocal chords. There's no answer. I bang on the next door. Nothing. 'Help!' I shout again. 'Police!' The doors stare back at me blankly like eyes that don't see.

I've got to help Wilson – where is he?

'Ahhhhhhh!' I hear Wilson screaming somewhere outside. I try to run to the end of the corridor, but it's like I'm moving in slow motion and the floor is made of sponge. I stagger through another set of fire doors out on to the

14

outside balcony at the back of the block. I twist left then right; there's no sign of Wilson or the men. They can't have just vanished. I look from side to side again and up at the balcony above. There's no one there either. The whole place is deserted. I look down over the railings on to the metal balcony below.

And there is Wilson's body.

3

Wilson is totally still in a horrible, final sort of a way. One of his arms is twisted back at a sickening angle. The drop to the balcony below is deep. They must have thrown him over. His face is white against my red jacket.

Footsteps thunder below me. The men are coming.

'I'll kill you!' one roars. I turn and run back through the doors and along the corridor. My legs feel disconnected from my body and there's a stabbing pain in my stomach, but I move faster than I ever have before. At the other end of the corridor I run back down the steps that Wilson and I were climbing only moments ago. Before everything went crazy. I keep twisting back to see if the men are following, but there's no sign of them. All I can hear is the sound of my own ragged breathing. Below me there's the metallic ring of something hitting the rail of the stairs. I look down the centre of the stairwell and see Black Hood looking up at me.

I spin round and run back up the stairs. My legs are on fire. I feel like tendons are ripping with every step I take.

Below, through the metal I can see the man getting closer. I stumble through double doors and down another corridor. This is hopeless. There's nowhere for me to go. I can't escape and, when they catch me, they'll kill me like they killed Wilson. I kick the flat door nearest to me as I listen to Black Hood pounding up the stairs.

This is it.

Then the door in front of me opens.

I'm pulled into the room, where I fall to my knees. I press my head to the ground and let my mouth hang open in a silent scream while my body shakes. As my gasping slows I'm aware of the men outside shouting. I freeze, pressing my hand over my mouth.

I turn my head to the side and look up at the flat owner. It's an old woman. Her birdlike head is cocked in the direction of the door. She's completely still, with her hands slightly raised as if she's waiting for them to come bursting in. I've got to hide. I roll over to look around the room. It's tiny. The painted walls are flaking and there's a purple-black bloom of mould across the ceiling. There's a cupboard too low and narrow for me to hide in, a stove, a table, and a rickety bed. I crawl under the bed and press myself against the wall. There's another shout from outside and the sound of the door at the top of the stairs swinging back so hard that it cracks against the wall. Then it's quiet. I watch the old woman's feet cross the room to the window. Outside, a car squeals away at high speed.

'They're gone,' she says.

I wriggle out. It's hard to get to my feet. My bones feel broken, my skin feels split open across my back, and somehow my head seems swollen to twice its size. I have an overwhelming urge to lie down on the bed and sleep for a long time.

'You've to go now,' the woman says, watching me carefully.

Go? Go out there? My mouth drops open. Everything is wrong and no one will help me.

The woman looks away. 'You've to go now,' she repeats.

I can't find the words to tell her that she can't do this to me. When she turns back I can only stare at her.

'We've been told,' she says. 'Not to be opening the door. They say sometimes one of them gets out of the Wilderness. More animal than man they say they are.' She looks me up and down. 'I'm not to be talking to you. Do you understand?'

I don't understand. Who would tell her to ignore something terrible happening outside her own front door? 'But I'm not from the Wilderness,' I say.

She doesn't answer.

'Call the police.' I realise as I'm saying it that she doesn't have a communicator in her room.

'Call the police!' she says. 'Then they'd be knowing I didn't do the thing they told me to do.'

The old woman is clearly mad. Paranoid. Prone to conspiracy theories. Who are this 'they' she keeps talking

18

about? My head is swimming. I'm too battered to try to get this straight.

'I don't want to be all unkind,' she says, putting out a hand, but dropping it before it touches mine. 'I'm an old woman. I don't want trouble now. You've best to go.' She looks at the door.

I shake my head. I find myself walking towards the door. I can't believe she won't help me.

I stop. She *has* helped me. If she hadn't brought me in here, I'd be dead by now. 'Thank you,' I say.

She gives an almost imperceptible nod, but her eyes are still on the door, so I leave.

I take a deep breath and sway my way back down those terrible stairs. The steps keep looming up into my face then shrinking away again. It's hard to make my feet land in the right place. When I reach ground level I have to stop and throw up. I want to lie down, but I need to find a policeman and tell them about Wilson.

When I reach the row of shops I almost throw myself at the first person I see, but suddenly I'm conscious of how messed and bloody I am and feel embarrassed. *Embarrassed!* It's so ridiculous that I let out a little laugh that quickly turns to a sob.

Not now. Find a policeman.

I spot a police pod on the other side of the road. I limp across and rap on the enquiries window.

A chubby policeman with sandy hair slides open the glass. 'What happened to you?' he says, eyeing me up and down.

I try to pull myself together. I don't want to sound like a babbling idiot. 'These men, they mugged us. They beat me up and my friend Wilson too . . . and they killed him. They took his currency card. They were huge, they had hoods . . .'

The policeman is frowning. 'Where did this happen?' he asks.

'In the factory accommodation block, come with me. I'll show you.' I turn to cross the road.

'Wait a minute, young man. I'm going to want some back-up if we're going to the accommodation block.'

He slides his finger across his computer screen then taps it twice. 'P.C. Wright, Pod 675 requesting back-up car for a five-niner at the East Hill factory accommodation block,' he says.

'Back-up car on its way,' replies a voice from the speaker on the computer.

P.C. Wright gets up and makes sure his taser is attached to his belt. He carefully places his hat on his head, checking his reflection in the computer screen. What does he think he's doing?

'Come on!' I say. 'They'll be miles away by now.'

'What exactly were you doing in the block, sonny?'

'We were delivering a package.'

'Who to?'

'I don't know.'

P.C. Wright raises his eyebrows. 'Do you know who it was from?'

'Of course I do! Facilitator Johnson. He's my teacher.'
I stand up straight. 'At the Willows Learning Community.'

'Where is it?'

'Where's what?' I say, feeling increasingly impatient.

'The package, where is it?'

I stare down at my empty hands. I don't know where it is. I must have dropped it when the men were kicking me.

'So you're a Learning Community boy and your facilitator sent you to a factory accommodation block to deliver a package?'

Oh great. He doesn't believe me. 'Listen,' I say. 'My friend is *dead*. You're a policeman. I think you should come and look.'

A squad car pulls up by the pod with another policeman inside. 'This is P.C. Barnes,' says P.C. Wright as he waves me into the back seat. I nod to the other policemen and finally we head for the accommodation block.

We stop at the front of the block, the side without the balconies, where Wilson and I came in. I can't believe it was only an hour ago that Wilson badgered me into lending him my jacket.

I lead the men up the stairs. These horrible stairs; it's like a nightmare where I'm forced to keep on going up and down them for ever. My whole body is throbbing. There's a screaming pain in my jaw where I've lost a tooth. My stomach feels like someone has ripped back the skin and pulled out bits of my intestines.

'This is where they came at us,' I say when we get half-way down the corridor. 'They took Wilson's currency card and started kicking and punching us, then Wilson ran further along the corridor and they chased him.' I lead the two policemen down the corridor. 'I tried to go after them, but I could hardly stand and when I got out here' – I open the far set of doors '– they all seemed to have disappeared, but then I saw that Wilson had been thrown over the balcony.' I approach the rail and screw up my face ready to look at poor, broken Wilson. The policemen draw up on either side of me. We peer over the railing.

Wilson is gone.

I can't believe it. What has happened to Wilson's body? I make the policemen go down on to the balcony to check if there is any evidence that Wilson had been there. Nothing. I make them knock on the door of number eighty-seven, where Facilitator Johnson told us to drop off the package. No reply. I almost tell them about the old woman, but something stops me. Mostly because I know she won't open her door again, but also because I've got a horrible creeping sense that maybe there's some truth in what she was saying. So we trudge down the steps again. P.C. Wright turns to me.

'Listen, son, I don't know exactly what happened to you . . .' He eyes my swollen face.

'I told you those men killed—'

'And I'm not sure that I want to,' he interrupts. 'We all know that there are some things it's best to leave the police out of.'

My mouth falls open. I bloody well don't know that. 'I was under the impression that the police were here to safeguard the people and to arrest criminals – but you don't seem to want to do either of those things,' I say.

'I've seen no evidence of a crime, smart man.'

'Urrr!' I slam my fist down on to my thigh. 'This is ridiculous.'

P.C. Wright takes a step towards me and P.C. Barnes puts his hand on his taser.

'Listen, boy,' P.C. Wright says. 'I'm sorry about your friend, or whatever it was that you think happened, but we don't get involved in factory worker fights, okay?'

Factory worker fights? *He thinks I work in a factory.* And live in an accommodation block like some moron.

'I am *not* from a factory,' I say.

He takes a step back. 'You're not . . . Wilderness are you?'

'No! My name is Jackson and, I told you before, my facilitator sent me here. I belong to the Willows Learning Community,' I say drawing myself up. 'I've got an AEP score of 98.5.'

'98.5 is it?' he says, but at least he takes his hand off his taser.

Obviously appealing to sense is going to get me further than anger.

'Officers, I appreciate that my appearance is rather unkempt,' I say. 'And I understand that you don't want unsupervised kids roaming about. But I can assure that I am a Learning Community student.'

'He can't be a worker,' P.C. Barnes says to P.C. Wright.

'They've all got security chips fitted so he wouldn't have been able to get out of the factory compound gates to come to your booth.'

'If you would just give me a lift back to my Learning Community we can sort all this out quickly,' I say.

P.C. Wright sniffs. 'Well, I suppose it can't hurt,' he says.

P.C. Wright takes me by the elbow and guides me into the car. 'What's your surname, Jackson?' he asks. He and P.C. Barnes climb into the front seats.

'Jackson is my surname. But that's what they call me at the Learning Community.'

P.C. Barnes turns round to look at me.

'Well they do,' I say. 'Everyone is called by their surname.'

'Got some funny ideas those brainer types. I heard they all wear dresses to eat their dinner, even the men,' P.C. Wright says to P.C. Barnes.

'Not *dresses*, robes. And that's only on Fridays.' I say.

'Oh, just on Fridays. Do they save the frilly pinnies for special occasions?' laughs P.C. Barnes.

'I'm sure the *Second Class* Learning Community you went to had its own traditions,' I say, coldly.

P.C. Wright coughs. 'Yes, of course. And that's quite right, isn't it, Barnes?'

He doesn't answer.

'That's how it should be,' P.C. Wright goes on. 'We all fit in somewhere, don't we?'

It's good to hear him talking sense and sounding like a proper policeman. Maybe he can stop those men who killed Wilson after all.

When we draw up at the Willows, P.C. Barnes sucks in his breath. 'Fancy,' he says.

I stare out the window and try to see it through the policemen's eyes. I suppose it's a nice enough building. It's old, grey stone with big bay windows. There's a stained-glass rose window above the door. Around the side there are greenhouses and on the left is a tennis court . . . But it's just a house really. I don't know why he called it fancy.

'Come on,' I say. I'm desperate to get inside so Facilitator Johnson can make them do something about Wilson. We've wasted so much time already.

I still ache all over from my beating and my head is throbbing, but I rush up the drive and P.C. Wright and P.C. Barnes follow behind. I notice neither of them tries to hold on to my elbow now. I dash into the entrance hall, but they stop outside the front door. P.C. Wright straightens his jacket and takes off his hat. He widens his eyes at P.C. Barnes until he does the same.

'Mrs Clark—' I say to the receptionist, but before she answers me, P.C. Wright arrives at my shoulder and interrupts.

'Ah . . . ahem. Got one of your pupils here. If it's not too much of an inconvenience, could I have a word with whoever's in charge?' He makes a weird little bob like a bow.

Mrs Clark's eyes flick sideways to me. I smile, but she doesn't smile back.

'One moment,' she says. 'I'll fetch Facilitator Johnson.' She disappears.

I jiggle from foot to foot. Why won't anyone hurry up? P.C. Barnes gives me a smile.

'Nice place,' he says. He walks behind the desk and leans over to get a closer look at the computer.

'Stand still, man,' hisses P.C. Wright.

P.C. Barnes slowly pulls up straight, but his eyes roll around, taking in the Creativity class's tapestry hanging on the wall and the wooden staircase carved with fruit and vines.

P.C. Wright is sweating. He mutters something like, 'Not really our jurisdiction . . .' and smacks down P.C. Barnes's arm when he stretches it out to touch the tapestry.

Finally, Facilitator Johnson appears with a serious expression. I wonder if he's already heard about Wilson.

'Sir, something terrible has happened,' I say, rushing up to him.

He takes a step backwards.

'Wilson and I took your package to the block and we were attacked and –' a sob escapes me '– they . . . Wilson's dead.'

Facilitator Johnson's forehead creases. He moves his lips several times before he finally says, 'Who's Wilson?' He looks up at P.C. Wright and then back to me. 'And who are you?'

My mouth drops open. 'Jackson,' I say.

Facilitator Johnson is still frowning at me.

'I'm Jackson! I only left a couple of hours ago. You gave me a package to take to the factory block, remember? With Wilson?'

'I've never seen you before in my life,' he says calmly.

I feel like you do when you miss a step on the stairs. 'Facilitator, are you joking?' I say in a small voice.

He shakes his head sadly and turns to P.C. Wright. 'This boy is obviously in a state of distress and he appears to be injured. I suggest that the most appropriate course of action would be to take him to see a doctor.'

P.C. Wright turns red. I grab Facilitator Johnson by the arm. 'I don't want to see a doctor. I just want to go to my room. It's upstairs on Curie corridor. I'm *Jackson*. I'm in your Global Philosophy session . . .'

He prises my fingers from his arm. 'Officers, I'm afraid I really am very busy.'

'Of course, of course,' says P.C. Wright. He nods his head hard.

This is insane. Has Facilitator Johnson lost his memory? I look round for someone else. 'Mrs Clark! You remember me, don't you?'

The secretary raises her head from her computer. She's biting her lip. 'I'm afraid not. I think perhaps you're not very well.'

P.C. Barnes is watching her. He narrows his eyes. P.C. Wright reaches for my arm.

'No!' I shout. 'I don't know what's happening. This is my school; I've lived here for eleven years!' I've got to think, there must be all kinds of evidence to prove who I am. 'The records! I'm on the school records! Check them – go on, check them.' I'm almost crying with relief. No one can possibly dispute computer records.

Facilitator Johnson lets out a long breath. 'Young man, if we check our records, will it persuade you that you are not a student here and you never have been?'

I nod desperately, still unable to believe he doesn't know me. 'Just check.'

'Or if you'd prefer, sir, we could just remove—'

Facilitator Johnson raises his hand to interrupt P.C. Wright and walks over to Mrs Clark's desk. No one speaks. In the distance I can hear the sound of laughter and doors opening. Overhead there's the muffled thump of feet. It must be session changeover time.

Facilitator Johnson swings the wafer-thin screen round

to face him. I move to look over his shoulder. He taps the screen and brings up a page entitled *student search*. He uses his forefinger to tick a box that says *Search all records?*

'Surname?' he asks.

'Jackson,' answers P.C. Barnes before I can open my mouth.

'Or so he claims,' says P.C. Wright, scowling at P.C. Barnes.

Facilitator Johnson's fingers move across the keyboard.

Relief floods through me. They'll find me on the records and this ordeal will finally all be over.

The screen changes to three words in red:

No record found.

How is this possible?

Facilitator Johnson turns to the policemen. 'If that will be all?'

'No . . .' I say, but no one is listening to me. How can I have just disappeared? This is my home.

P.C. Wright grabs hold of my elbow. P.C. Barnes takes my other arm more gently. He looks between me and Facilitator Johnson and back again.

'I would appreciate it, officers,' says Facilitator Johnson, 'if in future, you were able to resolve minor issues by yourself. I'm sure that *The Leader* –' P.C. Wright looks over his shoulder as if he imagines The Leader has appeared. '– expects his police force to use their initiative rather than disturbing the training of members of the future Leadership team.'

P.C. Wright grips my arm even tighter. 'Sorry to take up your time, sir,' he says. 'It's just . . . well, he talks a good talk, doesn't he?'

'Quite,' says Facilitator Johnson and he walks off down the corridor.

'What about Wilson?' I shout after him, but he doesn't look back or even hesitate. 'You've got to listen to me. This is where I belong . . .'

P.C. Wright is already turning me towards the door. It's like some horrible dream where no one understands what I'm saying. I've got to find someone who knows me. I open my mouth to plead, but I know it's no use. I simply have to resort to violence. I twist to my side and knee P.C. Wright hard in the crotch. He immediately lets go of my arm and crumples over. I try to throw a punch at P.C. Barnes, but he steps back to avoid it and trips over a potted plant. I turn and run. There's a blistering pain in my kidneys where the hooded men kicked me earlier, but I manage to stumble through the double doors on to the main corridor. I open the garden door and run across the quadrangle.

'Stop!'

I look over my shoulder. P.C. Barnes is chasing me. I run through an open door on the other side of the quad and head for my work group's study. Someone there will recognise me. P.C. Barnes is gaining on me. I open the door. The room is empty, but at this point I'm relieved just to find our study is still here. P.C. Barnes lurches through the door, but stops before he reaches me.

I stand still, breathing heavily.

'I think it would be best if you come with me,' he says.

'You can't, you can't take me away.'

'The facilitator is in charge here, son. Best we go.'

I clench my fists. 'I won't go! I live here. Look, these are my things . . .'

I twist round towards my desk.

It's gone.

All the other desks have been moved very slightly so that there is no obvious gap. My desk, my computer, my old-fashioned fountain pen, the mug Wilson made me in Creativity session . . .

All gone.

Like I never even existed.

They take me to the police station and put me in a cell. When I sit down, all the pain that I've been ignoring wells up in me. My eye is so swollen that it hurts when I blink. I can feel my blood surging round my body, throbbing in time with my waves of nausea. I'm so tired I can't hold my head up, but still I can't sleep. I'm starting to think that everyone else is right and that I must be mad. I don't seem to be the person I think I am.

I try to be logical. It's possible that I've forgotten who I am, but I remember so much that it seems unlikely. I remember my mother and how she clicks her nails across her teeth when she's thinking. I remember Wilson and I being interviewed on the Info when we won the Moritz Prize for outstanding research. I've got the trophy on my desk. The desk that's been removed from the Willows. I remember the Willows as well. I knew exactly where to find my study.

But no one recognised me. That screen keeps flashing into my mind: *No record found*.

I sit bolt upright on the bed.

I do exist. Everything I remember is true.

Facilitator Johnson typed in my name and it came up on the screen, *John Jackson: No record found*. But the computer was wrong. I know without a doubt that Facilitator Johnson knows who I am.

Because he typed in my first name without asking me what it was.

'P.C. Wright!' I call. 'I've worked it out.'

Both policemen appear at the flexi-glass window to my cell.

'Remember when Facilitator Johnson entered my name?'

P.C. Wright rolls his eyes.

'I didn't tell him my first name! But he typed it in. See?' I say. 'He must remember me.'

'Course you told him your first name,' says P.C. Wright. He walks away, but P.C. Barnes is still watching me.

'I didn't, did I, P.C. Barnes?' I say.

He screws up his mouth. 'P.C. Wright says you did.'

'But I—'

'Wait a minute. P.C. Wright says you did. If we were to ask Facilitator Johnson, I'm pretty certain he'd say you did too. A police officer is an important man. A facilitator is an *extremely* important man . . .' He raises his eyebrows at me.

My stomach contracts and something warm and acid bubbles up my throat. He's telling me that no one is going to believe my word over theirs.

'It's disgusting,' I finally say.

'Listen, son,' he says. 'You don't seem like a bad sort of a lad. I don't know what you're mixed up in at the block, or what the facilitator has got to do with you, but my advice is not to make trouble.'

'Not to make trouble?' I echo.

'It's easier if you do whatever it is that they want you to do.' He nods at me. 'Just do what they want you to do,' he repeats, and then he walks away.

Early in the morning, while it's still dark, P.C. Wright leads me out to the car.

'Are we going back to the Willows?' I say hopefully.

'Don't start that again,' he says. 'We're taking you to the local Academy.'

The Academy! This is outrageous. Just when I think things can't get any worse. Academies are full of backward, criminal kids who failed their Potential Test and can't even count on their fingers.

The passenger door opens and P.C. Barnes gets in.

'I am not going to an Academy,' I say.

'You haven't got much choice, son,' says P.C. Barnes without turning around.

I clench my fists. 'I don't know what is going on in your branch of the police,' I say. 'I don't know who is controlling Facilitator Johnson and I don't know why anyone would want to turn my life upside down, but I do know that I am a citizen of this country and the

Leadership will not allow this sort of violation of my rights. When I get to whatever hole you are taking me to, I will go straight to the top and even if I have to go to The Leader himself, you will be punished for this.'

'No need for all that,' says P.C. Wright, starting the car.

The back of P.C. Barnes doesn't move an inch.

As we're driving I realise that I have no idea where the local Academy is. Turns out it's on the outskirts of town, near the factory compound we were at yesterday. Right on the border with the Wilderness.

It's still dark when we arrive and I don't manage to see the building hidden behind the trees before we drive down a ramp and into an underground car park.

'I'm not going in,' I say. 'I refuse.'

'We could always just drop you off in the Wilderness,' P.C. Wright says. 'Would you prefer that?'

That shuts me up.

'You take him in,' P.C. Wright says to P.C. Barnes. 'I've got some paperwork to do.' He grins and opens the glove compartment, pulling out a paper bag. The smell of baked goods fills the car.

'Come on,' P.C. Barnes says to me, opening the car door.

We cross the car park and get into a lift. P.C. Barnes presses a button and the door closes.

'Listen, kid,' he says. 'Your name is Blake now, Blake Jones.'

'But—'

'Don't interrupt. I've seen this before. If you tell the Academy your real name, then you can be traced, they'll find you and kill you.'

'Who—?'

'You've got an opportunity here to slip through the net. This is probably the safest place for you. Change your name, keep your head down.'

The doors open.

'Understand?' he says. His eyes are burning into me.

'No,' I say, my mind reeling with the idea someone would want to kill me, but he's already striding towards a reception area.

It's very different to the reception at the Willows. Here there's just a desk sat on the kind of carpet that is so flat that it feels hard underfoot. A woman with wiry brown hair and pursed lips sits behind the desk.

'Is this him?' she asks P.C. Barnes.

I raise my chin.

'Yes, this is Blake Jones.'

I wonder if I should deny it. But I don't. I don't understand what is happening here, but I think P.C. Barnes does.

The woman gives him a quick nod and turns her back on him to pick up a pile of clothes from the desk. It looks like some kind of uniform.

'As I explained to the enforcer, the boy has no record on the Register so you'll need to set that up. He's a bit vague about his parents,' P.C. Barnes says. He emphasises the last words to give me a hint. I get it.

'Be good, Blake,' he says and turns away.

I want to grab his arm. I need him to explain. Who wants to kill me? Why would they want to kill me? I can't believe he's leaving me here. In an Academy.

'P.C. Barnes?' I call.

The lift doors open.

He half raises his hand in an almost-wave, then the doors close and he's gone.

The stony-faced receptionist wants me to change my clothes right in front of her. I sidle into the corner and turn my back. As I unbutton Wilson's jacket I notice something in the pocket. It's an old-format, paperback book, *Everyman's Book of Verse*. I wait till the woman is typing on her computer and then switch the book into my new jacket pocket. It belonged to Wilson and I'm not letting anyone else have it.

The uniform is stiff and scratchy and I'm obviously not the first person to wear it. I fold my jeans carefully. They had better put them somewhere safe; I paid a lot of money for them.

When I'm changed she scans my fingerprints and my iris. The computer bleeps as it comes up with the *No record found* banner again. I don't understand. I feel like a ghost. Why would anyone want to remove all trace of me?

A boy in his late teens wearing the same coarse, grey uniform as me, but with a large yellow badge pinned to his chest, appears at the desk.

'You are student number one-two-four-seven,' the receptionist says to me. She looks at the boy and jerks her head to indicate he should take me away. He starts to walk. I don't move.

'I think you should know I don't belong here,' I say to the receptionist.

She looks at the boy. He grips me by the elbow and pulls me away.

'Don't you want to record my academic scores?' I call over my shoulder.

'That won't be necessary,' she says without looking up from her screen.

The boy leads me down a corridor to a thick metal door. He opens it by punching in a pass code. I try to watch but he covers one hand with the other. I can't believe that they use such an outdated system. They ought to get biometric security.

Once through the doors I try to shrug off his grip. The smell of him is making my eyes water.

He twists my arm up behind my back. 'Don't do that. I'm an impeccable. You do what I say.' He gives me a shove to get me moving. 'All times you do what I say.'

Great. As well as smelling like a caveman he also talks like one. He pushes me down a scuffed and scratched narrow metal corridor. It smells of disinfectant and something musky. It's not cold, but my teeth start to chatter.

'What's an impeccable?' I say.

'We've finished Academy learning. Now we work here. We're big good.'

I twist back and look at his glassy eyes and his collar cutting into his fat neck. If he's one of the big good I can hardly wait to see the small bad.

Halfway down the corridor he stops at a door with another punch code machine. This time I pretend not to watch, but out of the corner of my eye I see him laboriously type in CLASSROOM. Unbelievable. If you're going to use an old-fashioned system like this you need a nice random selection of numbers, letters and symbols. All this security is making me nervous. I know Academy students are supposed to be rough, but do they really need locking up?

The boy opens the door and pushes me inside. I turn round to point out that the shoving is unnecessary. But he's gone and I'm facing a closed door. I turn back. I'm at the top of several steps looking down on a room which is divided up into sections by partitions of metal lattice. The sections are like tiny prisons. In each one there is a seat sunk into the floor with a boy or girl sat in it. There must be more than twenty teenagers crammed into this weird room and they're all looking at me.

I swallow. 'Hello, my name is J— ah, Blake, my AEP score is 98.5. There's been some sort of mistake . . . and I really need to speak to whoever is in charge.'

Silence.

'Do you have a group leader?'

41

They stare at me.

'Your facilitator?' I feel like I'm speaking a foreign language, I struggle for more basic vocabulary. 'Where's your teacher?' I ask.

Some of the kids swivel round in their seats; I follow the direction of their gaze to the front of the classroom.

They're looking at a cage.

There's someone in the cage.

It's the teacher.

'Good morning,' I say finally. 'I'm—'

'Quiet,' the teacher says.

She's tiny and wiry. Her jaw is prominent and clenched. She reminds me of a fierce little dog.

'I am Enforcer Tong. Do not speak unless you are spoken to by an enforcer.' She leans forward to stare at me. What the hell is she doing in that cage?

'Sit,' she says.

Because the seats are sunk into the floor I have a clear view of where there is a space in the grid. There's only one gap, on the far side of the room. I make my way carefully between the metal walls till I reach the vacant compartment. I struggle with the catch to open the tiny door and sit in the sunken seat. I look up at the teacher. Her cage is mounted to the wall and made of metal; the gaps between the bars are so narrow that I can only make her out in long thin sections.

I let out a slow breath. This is all too weird. I never thought I'd end up in an Academy.

Locked in a classroom.

With the teacher in a cage.

Wilson would love this. Poor Wilson. Suddenly a vision of his crumpled body flashes through my mind. What am I going to do about him? I still need to find someone who will listen to me. I put my arm in the air, but the walls of the compartment are so high that only my hand sticks out. The enforcer raises her head from her computer screen very slowly. She stares at me and then at my hand.

'I really need to see the head of this establishment,' I say.

Someone in a nearby compartment giggles.

'It's urgent,' I add.

The enforcer continues to stare. Her mouth twitches into a Halloween-mask smile. 'Perhaps it would be best for you to meet the head.' She snaps off the smile. 'At the end of the session. Now put on your EMDs.'

'What are EMDs?' I ask.

The class laughs and the enforcer tuts.

'On your chair,' hisses a voice from the other side of the partition.

I look down and notice a red light flashing on the right arm of my chair. There's a small tray set into the arm and in it is a sort of bracelet. I slide it on to my wrist; rubbery stuff on the inside ensures that it is a tight fit. A thick metal cord connects it back to the arm of my chair. There's another one on my left side. I put that on too. I feel like a tethered chicken. This is absurd. I'm starting to despair of getting things straightened out. What if the head teacher is as unhelpful as everyone else has been?

I close my eyes and breathe in through my nose. I tell myself that everything will be fine. This madness has to end. I can't see the other students because of the partition walls around me, but I can hear them tapping away at their computers. My neighbour to my left is so close that I can hear the quiet click-clicking of his stylus on his screen. I look at my own computer. The screen is showing a circuit board. The aim seems to be to drag components into the right position. I pick up my stylus to look as if I'm busy and start to rehearse in my head what I am going to say to convince the head teacher that I'm not crazy.

'What's your name?' comes a whisper so low I barely catch it. It's the boy in the compartment next to me.

I open my mouth and then hesitate. 'Blake,' I whisper. 'What's yours?'

'Ilex.'

'Ilex, what's an impeccable?'

'They work for the enforcers. They're big mean and—'

I don't get to hear what else he was going to say next because he lets out an almighty scream.

'*AHHHHHHH!*'

I try to jump out of my seat to help him, but it's so cramped in the compartment that I can't do it without opening the door and the door seems to be locked. 'What is it? What's wrong?' I say.

45

'Silence!' says Enforcer Tong. 'No talking, new boy. If you talk you will be punished too.'

Punished? King Hell, how on earth did she make him scream like that without even coming near him? What kind of sick place is this? It's like she zapped him. Surely he'd have to be wired up to some sort of electric device for that . . . Then I realise.

An electric device, like the one attached to my wrists.

Hours later a buzzer sounds. The compartment doors click open. Enforcer Tong must control the locks from her computer. The other students are already scrambling out of their seats. They swarm past my compartment, pushing and shoving. I look up at the enforcer. She's staring down at me.

'Wait here, the head of the Academy, Enforcer Rice, will speak to you.' She disappears through the door in the wall at the back of her cage. I pull off the silly bracelets and step out of my compartment to stretch my legs. My body aches from sitting in the cramped box and from yesterday's beating.

I thought everyone had gone, but a thickset boy with shaggy brown hair is stood looking at me. He gives me a half-smile.

'Hello,' I say.

'Hello.'

There's a long pause.

'I'm Ja— Blake,' I say. How long is it going to be before I trip up on that one?

'I know. I'm Ilex.'

'Oh, I see. Sorry that you got that shock. I didn't know we weren't allowed to talk. Doesn't exactly encourage free exchange of ideas does it? It's bad enough that they keep you squeezed up in these pens. Why do they do that?'

Ilex squints at me. His eyes follow the arm that I've gestured to the compartments with. 'This is the grid,' he says.

'Uh huh, but why are you in the grid?'

Ilex shrugs. 'So we can't get out.'

I can't believe he's so casual about it.

Before Ilex can say anything else, the door in the back of the cage at the front of the room opens and a muscular man with close-cut, grey hair appears. He looks annoyed. Ilex shoots another half-smile at me and then disappears out of the classroom door.

'I am Enforcer Rice. I run the Academy. And you are new,' the man says, as if I've done something particularly annoying. I don't like the way they talk to you here.

'I shouldn't be here at all,' I say. I'm about to launch into everything that has happened when I remember P.C. Barnes' words about slipping through the net. Maybe I shouldn't tell this man too much.

Enforcer Rice is staring at me. He's waiting.

'I was at a Learning Community,' I say. 'There's been some sort of mix up. My records have been wiped . . .'

'What's your name?' He's not looking at me, but at a point past my left ear.

Something in the way he asks makes up my mind. Even though he's a teacher, I don't trust him. Before I can think about it any more, I say, 'Blake Jones.'

'Well, *Blake Jones*.' He forms the name carefully like he knows it's false. 'Have you anything to add to this fascinating story?'

'I . . . I was beaten up. Only yesterday. Some men attacked me and my friend. They killed him and tried to do the same to me. I think that I've suffered some memory loss.'

He rolls his eyes.

'I know it sounds unlikely, but I'm sure that you can appreciate that I'm not best suited to an Academy environment,' I say.

He purses his lips. 'You sound more like a Learning Community brat than a Wilderness ape. I'll give you that.'

I open my eyes wide. No wonder Academy students are so rude if this is the way their teachers talk. 'If I sound like a Learning Community *pupil* then you've got to ask the question, how have I ended up here?'

There's a long pause. 'It's not my job to ask questions,' he says. 'In fact, I find the fewer questions you ask the more likely you are to succeed. I don't know why you are here, young man, and I do not care. I imagine that it is a punishment for whatever trouble you have caused.'

I open my mouth to protest that I have never caused any trouble, but he ploughs on.

'The only thing that I care about is that you do not cause trouble here. And that means I don't want to hear about your "Learning Community" past or anything else that you might imagine makes you different from the rest of the students here. Is that understood?'

This is like the police all over again. It's so unfair. 'I'm not going to just stay here!' I say. 'What about my education? What about—'

'If you can't accept your life in the Academy and follow Academy rules then you will be punished.' He eyes my bruised cheek.

'Are you threatening me?' I say. 'You can't treat me like this—'

'Yes I am and yes I can,' he interrupts in a low voice.

'This is unbelievable.'

The enforcer turns away. He grips the door handle and looks back over his shoulder. 'Just think about this: how many things have already happened to you in the last few days that you didn't believe were possible?' He steps out of the door and closes it behind him.

I sink to my knees. I just can't go on with this. It's like someone has whipped the rug out from under me. I lean over till my forehead rests on the ground. I lie there staring at a black smudge on the floor till I go cross-eyed.

I'm starting to realise that no one is going to help me. I sit up. No one but me cares about what happened to Wilson and I'm stuck in an Academy with the head teacher threatening me with violence. But I can deal with this. I'm smart, I can deal with anything. I can pretend to toe the line if that's what Enforcer Rice wants.

But I don't belong in this place and I'm only playing along until I work out how to get myself out of here.

I try to focus my mind. The first thing I need if I'm going to deal with all this is food. It must be lunchtime by now. I go out into the corridor; it's heaving. Hundreds of students all in the same grey uniform are crammed shoulder to shoulder. I try to walk in a civilised fashion, but I keep getting shoved sideways or jammed in the back. A giant of a boy, with thick arms and slicked-back, auburn hair, steps in front of me and slaps his palm on to my cheek. King Hell, can't they just leave me alone? Then he pushes me to the side of the corridor and turns away. Why would he do that? He doesn't even know who I am. I wipe off the feel of his hand from my face.

'Do you mind?' I say.

He stops dead. The boys walking behind him crash into him.

'Watch i—' one of them starts to say, then he raises his head and sees who he is speaking to. He shrinks backwards. 'I didn't see you, Rex.'

But Rex is not looking at him. He's looking at me.

'What the efwurd are you saying?' He says to me. 'Why are you talking to me, you filthy little no-ranker?' He looks at me – at *me*, with my AEP score of 98.5 – like I'm something that has dropped out of his nose. What is wrong with these idiots?

51

The corridor around us has frozen. They're all staring at me.

'Get an enforcer,' I say to the girl next to me in a low voice.

Everyone bursts out laughing.

They're gawping at me and howling. The girl beside me is bent double and Rex's shoulders are heaving.

'Get an enforcer!' he squeaks in a high-pitched voice. 'I'm too little to fight! I want an enforcer to fight for me!'

He's mocking me. The rest of the apes fall about laughing. How dare they? Everything I've heard about Academy kids is right. They're savages. I draw myself up.

'I can't imagine what's so funny,' I say.

That makes them laugh even harder. I walk away, weaving my way between their stinking bodies.

10

I follow the flow of students to the dining room. Except it isn't a room. It's more like a vast warehouse. Beneath the high ceiling are row upon row of yet more cubicle type things. These are like narrow metal boxes with open fronts. They're hardly big enough to stand in, but that's what the other students are doing. The students seem eager to get to their lunch. One boy is actually running; when he gets into a cubicle he taps his fingers in agitation on the metal mesh wall.

I follow the girl in front of me down a narrow aisle. She enters one of the compartments and I step into the one next to her. It's like standing in a locker. On three sides there are walls of metal lattice, to the left I can see the outline of the girl next to me. On the wall in front there are three metal nozzles. One of them has a brown crust. It doesn't look very hygienic.

'Hey!'

A hand grabs the back of my belt and I'm yanked out into the narrow alley.

'Get out of my pod!'

I twist round to see a boy with matted hair and raised fists.

'There's no need to be aggressive,' I say. 'I didn't know it was yours, I didn't know they belonged to people.'

But he's not even listening; he's already stepped into his 'pod' and forgotten me.

I look up and down the aisle. Everyone is hurrying into position. Where's my pod? I'm so hungry and I don't know where to go. I feel like a forgotten child.

The girl I followed is staring at me. She raises her eyebrows and says, 'What's your number?'

'My name's—'

'Not name, *number*,' she says.

'I'm not going to answer to a number. It's dehumanising and—'

'Where your number is. That is where you eat.' She turns away, shaking her head.

I do remember the number the receptionist gave me. 1247. I would have remembered it even if it had been three times as long. Clearly no one in here is going to be impressed by my feats of memory, but that doesn't mean I can't work this out. I'm smart. I don't need their help.

I look around. As far as I can tell, the pods aren't numbered. I retrace my steps down the aisle and back to the door; I have to duck between the students streaming in. They take no notice of me. They're moving with urgency, as if they're rushing to an important event. The atmosphere is strangely charged.

Presumably the first pod in the row closest to the door is pod number one. I slip halfway down the first row, I count fifty pods, that means my pod must be in row twenty-five. I walk along the bottom of the rows. Almost all the pods are full now and I feel foolish and late, but I'm not going to run. Actually, no one is looking at me; their attention is fixed on the back of their pods. Some of them are fidgeting, twitching fingers or tapping feet. Some of them are murmuring and moaning. One boy is banging his head against the metal partition. I lose count of the rows. What are they all so desperate for?

I get to what I hope is row twenty-five and there, just where it should be, is an empty pod. I step in and lean gratefully against the metal grille of the wall. My pod. I found it all by myself. I straighten up and take a closer look at the nozzles. It seems that I've made it just in time, because a buzzer sounds and a red light flashes on the top of one of the nozzles. Then a thick stream of brown gloop pours out and all over my shoes.

I try to turn the nozzle off, but I can't. The brown stuff is all over the floor. What should I do? I look round the pod, but there's nothing to catch the flow with. I don't know what I'm supposed to be doing. Is this slop my lunch? The brown muck just keeps coming and now there's a disgusting lumpy pool on the floor. I look through the grille on my left at the boy in the next pod; maybe I can see what he's doing.

'Where do you get a bowl from?' I whisper.

He doesn't answer. As my eyes make out his outline in the gloom I realise he can't.

His mouth is wrapped around a nozzle and he is sucking that brown stuff down.

My stomach heaves. It's not even that the gloop looks and smells disgusting; it's the undignified way he's gulping at that nozzle. Like an animal.

And that's when I realise that this massive warehouse is totally silent.

I turn round. In the pod opposite is a girl sucking at the metal teat in the same way. Her eyes are closed and as she gulps her rigid body begins to relax. Next to her a boy is slurping so hard that the brown liquid is running down his chin. All around me the students are sucking hard on the metal nozzles, their eyes closed in pleasure. I look away.

I won't do it. I won't eat like that. I'd rather starve. The brown stream stops. I hear a sigh of contentment from the pod on my left. The buzzer sounds again and the middle nozzle gushes with an orangey liquid. I can't bear to turn back to the suckling students, so I'm forced to watch it mixing with the brown stuff. Finally, the last tap produces what looks like water. I use my hands to take a tentative sip – it *is* water. I have a couple more mouthfuls and then I try to rinse my shoes under it. The water thins out the puddle on the floor and it starts to run through the grille into the pod on my right. The room must be on a slight slope.

I turn around slowly. The students are lounging against the walls of their pods. Their bodies are relaxed and their faces are smooth instead of pinched and angry. I can only think of one way that the food could have calmed them so much. Now I see why everyone was so desperate to get to their lunch.

The food is drugged.

I am not eating drugged food. What kind of a place is this? No wonder the students are so weird. I need to find someone with a brain to talk to.

I step carefully over the sticky mess on the floor and bang straight into a tall boy wearing the same yellow badge as the boy who pushed me about this morning. An impeccable. Finally, someone who might be able to help.

'Would it be possible to get something to eat?' I say.

He stares at me without blinking.

'I, um, missed lunch.'

He lowers his gaze to the vomit-like puddle on the floor. I swallow.

'Yes, ah, I think maybe the tap is faulty,' I say. 'I couldn't get it to turn off.'

'No mess in the feeding pods,' he says.

'I didn't mean to. I'm new—'

'No mess in the feeding pods,' he repeats in a monotone.

I look about for help. Why is it so hard to make anyone in here understand? The girl from the pod on my right is standing to the side and slightly behind the impeccable. She must have been watching the whole time. I open my mouth to ask her to help explain, but she starts to slink away. Without taking his eyes off me, the impeccable shoots out an arm to his side and grabs her, but the girl doesn't even gasp, just purses her lips.

'You messed your feeding pod,' he says, looking at the floor of her pod, which is also covered in muck where it has dribbled through the grille from my pod. 'It must be cleaned.' He walks away to join a pack of other yellow-badged impeccables.

I'm so hungry.

The girl wheels over a cleaning trolley. She isn't very pretty, but her hair is striking – so blonde it's almost white. She slams the trolley into my foot, picks up a sponge and starts cleaning her pod. She isn't glassy-eyed like the other students, who are drifting out of the dining room.

'I was late,' I say. 'I didn't know where my pod was.'

She gives me a hard stare.

'It would be better if they numbered them,' I say.

She wipes away a brown streak and gestures to the floor. 1248 is marked in large numbers on the base of her pod.

'Oh. Well, maybe they should think about something to catch the mess under the nozzles.'

She reaches up and yanks out a sliding drainage tray.

I tap at the wheel of the trolley with my toe. This is one of the first conversations I've had with a girl that isn't about school work. I don't think I'm impressing her. 'We don't have to do this, you know. We're not cleaners.' I say.

She doesn't reply.

'It's not like I did it on purpose. I'm sure if we explained—'

She springs to her feet, grabs me by the collar and slams the side of my face against the metal grille of the pod. It rubs against my swollen face like a cheese grater. She's tiny, but I can't twist out of her grip.

'Don't say *we*,' she spits. She shoves me away from her. 'You talk all big words, but no things you say are good. The only right thing you say is that *I* don't have to do this.' She throws the stinking sponge at my head. 'You do it.' And she walks off.

What a bad-tempered girl. I dab a bit at the gunge. I can't believe they expect me to do this. I'm not trained to. I see a shaggy figure at the end of my aisle.

'Ilex!'

He walks over.

'Do you realise that rancid muck coming out of the taps is drugged?'

Ilex screws up his face. 'I don't know your words,' he says.

'The food,' I say pointing to the nozzles behind me. 'It's . . .' I make my eyes go spacey and sway my head.

'Oh. We say softener. There's softener in this one.' He points to the first nozzle. 'It comes morning and lunchtime, not dinner.'

'Why just the morning and lunchtime?'

He shrugs. 'They want to make us not fighting in the grid.'

'Don't they mind if you're fighting after dinner?'

'After dinner fighting is okay. The enforcers are thinking when the Specials are fighting after dinner then they don't get fighting in the grid.'

So they're drugged to keep them quiet in lessons. I try to take it in. 'What's a Special?' I say.

Ilex breaks into a smile. 'All Academy kids are Specials.' He nods to a boy walking slowly down the aisle. 'He's a Special,' he says. 'I'm a Special and . . .' He points a finger at me. 'You're a Special.'

I look down at my slop-splattered grey uniform. I certainly look the part. But I'm not a Special.

I'm me.

Whoever that is.

Ilex helps me to clean up the pods. I think we should just leave it, but he says you've got to do what the enforcers and the impeccables say or you get punished. I tell him no one is going to be giving me an electric shock, but I finish cleaning up anyway. Then we go back to the classroom, or the grid, as Ilex keeps calling it. I want to say I won't go, but I realise that I don't have any choice.

The afternoon drags. We're all locked back into our little compartments and have to use our computers to simulate assembling a motor. I use the time to have a look around their computer system. There isn't much to see. A lot of programmes about parts-assembly and electronics. There's also a communications system, but it's flawed and outdated. I could have written a better one myself. And it's internal only. A sickening coldness creeps over me as I realise that I have no way of contacting the outside world and no one knows I'm here.

Finally the buzzer sounds again. My stomach contracts

painfully. I'm starving. I follow Ilex out of the grid. The boy on the other side of me seems to have a chunk torn out of his ear.

'What are you looking at?' the boy says.

'Your ear,' I say. 'I mean, more the part that's missing, so really I'm looking at nothing,' I babble.

He scowls. 'Don't look at me. You look at me, I hit you.'

Before I can reply he has walked away.

'Why is everyone so rude?' I say to Ilex. But he doesn't seem to understand 'How come no one is saying they're going to hit *you*?' I ask.

'You talk. I don't talk,' he says.

He leads me upstairs, asks me for my student number, and then shows me my dormitory. 'I have to go,' he says and then disappears into the throng of students. My heart sinks. I wish I was back in my own bedroom at the Willows.

I walk into the dormitory. The walls are swamp-green and, like all the other rooms I've seen today, it's huge. There must be fifty beds down either side. These are metal and they're bolted to the floor. At the end of every bed is a small box-shaped locker. That's it. There's nothing else in the room. No cupboards, no pictures, no windows, not even a carpet.

Something else is bothering me. Lounging on the beds and looking in the lockers are both boys and girls. This is a mixed dormitory. I feel my face grow warm. How on

63

earth will I get undressed? And what about the girls getting undressed? Whoa. I run my hand through my hair and realise that I'm staring at a girl sat on a bed. It's the blonde girl from the dining hall. She looks up and catches me gawping at her and I have no choice but to walk over.

I raise my hand and spread my fingers in the national Learning Communities gesture of friendship. She doesn't respond. She just stares at me.

'I'm Blake,' I say. 'AEP score 98.5. I was wondering . . . I mean, I'd appreciate it if you could explain a few things to me.'

She tilts her head on one side. 'I don't know your big words.'

Is she giving me the brush off? 'I want to talk,' I say.

She looks at me, but says nothing. Her lips are pressed together. Maybe I should have chosen a different girl to talk to. Maybe one that I didn't get into trouble with a pool of lumpy brown stuff.

'Sorry about everything earlier. I didn't really understand how the system works,' I say.

'I don't know your big words,' she says again.

'I'm just trying to talk to you.'

'I don't want to talk to you.' And she rolls over on her bed so she has her back to me. My eye catches the number printed above her on the wall: 1248. I turn round; the next berth is labelled 1247. My magic number. I sit on the edge of the bed. It sags under my weight. There's a stiff green blanket and a limp, stained pillow. This place is disgusting.

'Are there any single rooms?' I ask.

The girl turns back with a scrunched forehead, like Ilex. I can't believe they have such trouble understanding me.

'A small room. A bedroom with just one bed for me.' I point to myself.

She snorts. 'No. No dormitories with one bed.'

I suppose I already knew that. 'Is there anywhere I can get something to eat?'

'You eat in feeding pod,' she says slowly, as if I am the stupid one.

'Can't I eat now?'

She looks me up and down. 'What place do you come from?'

'I'm a Learning Community student. I've got an AEP—'

'Oh, you're a brainer.'

The way she talks makes me bristle. It seems like Academy students really have got a limited grasp of language.

'This place is so uncivilised,' I say.

'I feel sad-for-your-trouble,' she says but she doesn't look sad, she looks amused.

And what on earth is sad-for-my-trouble? She sounds like an old lady. 'What trouble?' I say.

'The trouble you're going to get because you don't know things,' she says.

Oh that's great. Now I've got an Academy girl feeling sorry for me.

'I *know* things. You don't need feel sad for . . . you don't need to feel sorry for me. I shouldn't even be in an Academy. I've got a big future ahead of me.'

She blinks at me. 'In here,' she says slowly, 'you are nothing. You've got no fight ranking. You're not a Red and I have the think that you've got no shrap either.'

I stare.

'I do feel sad-for-your-trouble because you don't know what I'm meaning, do you?'

I shrug my shoulders. How can I be expected to know what she's on about? Not only is she an Academy 'Special', she's also a girl. It's like trying to talk to a double alien.

'You think you know all things. Don't you?' she says.

'Maybe not quite all . . .' I say.

'But you don't know things in here.'

'Well no, I don't understand things in here, just like you lot don't understand proper spoken English. It's nice that you've made up your own language like little kids.' A smile escapes me. 'But you can't expect me—'

Smack. She punches me in the mouth.

'*Ow!* What the hell did you do that for?' The space where those men knocked out my tooth fills with blood.

'I understand what laughing means,' she says and walks off.

66

I've only been in the dormitory half an hour when another buzzer sounds. I follow the others down to the dining hall for dinner. I remember what Ilex said about dinner not being drugged so I use my hand as a scoop to eat what the nozzles produce. The first stream tastes like a bland vegetable soup and the second is some kind of mashed-up fruit.

After dinner, I find Ilex in an almost deserted dormitory across the hall from mine. He lets me sit on his bed.

'What's a Red?' I ask him.

He looks at me in surprise. 'Reds are leaders. They tell you what to do.'

'Like enforcers?'

He laughs. 'No Reds are Specials. But they're the big good Specials.'

'Good at what? Science? Public speaking?'

'Fighting.'

'Oh. So to be in the Red gang you have to be a good fighter?'

Ilex shakes his head. 'You are a Red when, y'know, when you are a baby. When you start.'

'When you're born?'

He nods.

'That's not a system that allows for upward mobility is it? What can you do if you're not born a Red?'

'All Specials fight here. If you get a good fight ranking you can be an Hon Red.'

'What do they call the Specials who aren't Reds or Hon Reds?'

'Bad names.'

'That'll be me then.'

'Me too.' He stares at his hands.

'So, you have these fights and if you win you get points?'

'If you have winned lots of fights then you get a good rank.'

'What rank are you?' I ask.

'This time I'm a three-fifteener.'

'That's . . . nice,' I say.

Ilex laughs. 'It means I fight fifteen fights and I win three.'

'I see.' That's one fight in five. I'm not sure I could manage that. Ilex is kind of slow, but he's pretty hefty.

Ilex eyes my long, skinny legs then his head jerks up. There's a lumpy-looking boy standing next to me. I turn to look at the boy and he grabs my arm.

'*You* come downstairs,' Lumpy says.

'I think I'll stay here,' I say.

The boy blinks at me. 'Come now.'

'Blake . . .' begins Ilex.

'No, really, Ilex, I think I'll stay here,' I say. I'm tired of being told what to do.

Lumpy's mouth drops into a shocked 'O' and he lumbers off.

'Blake, he works for the Reds. You have to do the thing they say.'

'I don't have to do any—'

I'm grabbed roughly from behind by my shoulders and forced on to my feet. There are two huge boys on either side of me.

'Hey!' I shout, but there's hardly anyone in the dormitory to take notice – except Ilex, who just shrugs and follows behind as they manhandle me towards the door.

'Downstairs,' says one of the oafs.

I'm half dragged down the stairs and along a corridor to a large, cylindrical room. There are tiers of seats around the sides, all full of Specials, who are cheering and hooting at two boys fighting in the centre of the room. I look around for an adult, but there are none. The Specials watching are jumping up and down, smashing their own fists into their palms and screeching at the fighters. The dark-haired fighter has blood pouring from his nose. He grabs the other boy by his blond hair. Blond Boy tries to twist away. Dark Boy kicks the back of his legs so that Blond Boy is knocked to his knees. Dark Boy drops down beside him then he lifts Blond Boy's head and smashes it against the ground. I feel sick. A broad-chested boy blows a whistle. The crowd start bellowing again. I turn towards the door, but one of the oafs blocks my way.

'Listen, I'm not really into spectator sports,' I say. 'I think I'd just like to get back to the splendour and comfort of the dormitory.' I try a smile.

'No, no going,' he says.

'Why ever not?' I ask.

His pudgy face moulds itself into a smile. 'Your turn now.'

I've got thin arms and legs. And a thin all the rest of me, come to that. I've never wanted big muscles, but now that I'm about to have the first fight of my life, I can't help wishing I was stronger. I look at first one oaf and then the other, trying to work out which one is the brains.

'What if I won't fight?' I say

'Then your fighter is going to have a good win,' says someone behind me.

I turn round. It's the boy from the corridor, Rex. He looks even bigger and more powerful than he did earlier.

He sucks his teeth. 'What's your name, boy?'

I don't think he even remembers me from before.

'Blake,' I say, squaring my shoulders. He can't be much older than me.

'You have to fight, *Blake*. All Specials fight. You fight, you get a fight ranking.'

'Oh, that's all right, I really don't mind about the

ranking – you can just put me at the bottom. You can leave me off the list altogether,' I say.

He squints at me. I feel like I'm talking Cantonese in this place. 'You talk good,' he says, like it's something horrible. 'Do you fight good?'

'I don't want to fight,' I say.

He shakes his head at me and walks away into the centre of the circular floor.

'Hey all,' he shouts. 'Hey Reds, Hon Reds and the crimson Dom . . .' A strawberry-blonde girl in the crowd stands up and blows kisses. Rex pauses to leer at her, then goes on. 'This fight is Deon Collins . . .' A squat boy, built like a bull, leaps out of the front row of seats. 'And first-fight boy Blake!'

The Specials scream and shout and Deon walks towards me. His walk turns into a charge. I jump to my right just as he reaches me, but even so he smacks into my left side with such force that it spins me round. I spread my arms, try to regain my balance and . . . *crack*! He punches me in an upwards movement under the chin. It feels like my head has snapped off my neck. I fall backwards and taste blood from where I've bitten my tongue.

Get up! I think. I don't know why I worried about my arms being too weak; at this rate I'm not even going to get to swing a punch. I struggle to my knees as Deon is gesturing to the crowd that he's going to grind me into the ground. He powers a punch into the side of my face. Just how mangled will I have to be before they call it off? My head is ringing.

I'm going to be beaten to a pulp. Again. *Think*. I can only remember one thing about fighting and that's a conversation between the girls at the Willows about self-defence. I'm swaying on my knees and Deon is towering above me, jeering and yelling out to the crowd while he's deciding how to finish me off.

So I take the only piece of combat advice I've ever been given and punch him in the balls.

Luckily for him he realises at the last moment what I am going to do. So he doesn't get the full force of my noodle arm. But he does crumple over and lie clutching his stomach. I get to my feet. Someone in the crowd is booing. Have I broken some rule? But someone else in the crowd catches my eye. He's miming for me to kick Deon. I look at my opponent. It seems unfair to kick him while he's down. Couldn't we just finish it here? I look about for Rex. He's talking to the pretty strawberry-blonde girl and has his back to me.

Umppff! Deon flings his arms around my ankles and yanks my legs out from underneath me. I crash down, crunching my shoulder against the ground so hard that I cry out. Deon doesn't stop to wonder whether it's ethical to kick a man when he's down, he just lays into me.

All of a sudden I'm back in the corridor with those men, thinking that I'm going to die. But I survived that and I'll survive this. I'm not going to die here. I'm not going to be forced into some dirty little brawl with a boy

73

I've never even spoken to. I scramble to my feet and try to run for the door.

But he won't let me go; he's caught hold of the back of my shirt. I thrash wildly, trying to pull away from him. We veer so close to the front row of the crowd that I see some of them drawing their feet up out of the way. Deon is still trying to pin my arms down or to land a punch on me, but I just keep moving. I put my head down and thrust an elbow backwards into his stomach. There's not enough power to really hurt him, but it makes him wobble backwards and trip over someone's extended foot. He falls, trying to take me with him, but my shirt tears out of his hand.

'Idiot,' he says as he goes down and, as soon as he hits the ground, I throw myself on him. I kneel on his chest and smack him around the head as hard as I can. Then I hear the sound of the whistle and Deon pushes me off and stalks away. I try to stand up without letting anyone see how much I am shaking.

Rex appears and lifts my arm. I've won. I think Rex missed most of the action while he was chatting up the girl called Dom, so I'm not sure he's best placed to make a decision, but still . . . I won. I feel almost pleased.

'Not bad,' says Rex. 'You look angry now. You fight gooder angry.'

Damn right I'm angry. Nobody calls me an idiot. Especially in here.

My pleasure drains away as soon as I walk off. I can hardly move, I hurt so much. I've never been in a fight before and in the past few days I've been attacked twice. I'm tired and I realise that I really need to work out what I am going to do to get out of here. I head for the door, but I spot Ilex sitting a few rows back. He waves me over. I clamber between Specials and squeeze into a space beside him.

'You're not good,' he says.

'I don't really care if I was good or not. It's ridiculous,' I say, 'forcing someone to fight. I object to being treated like a stupid bull. Look at all this.' I gesture to the room.

The next two competitors are up. Two girls. Surely they'll be less aggressive? The whistle blows and the taller girl screams, 'Take that, you tight-legger!' and kicks the other girl in the face.

This is horrible. The Specials' noise rises to a roar.

'It's bedlam,' I shout to Ilex. 'Where are the enforcers?'

'No enforcers at fights.'

'Well, I'm not doing it again.'

'You have to. It's gooder if you just let them win you in little time.'

'We shouldn't put up with this,' I say. 'Why don't people say no to the Reds?'

'You can't fight the Reds.'

I turn to look at him properly and I realise that there's a little girl of about seven or eight sat next to him. She's leaning her head on his shoulder.

'Who's this?' I say.

Ilex looks down at her and his face softens.

'This is my sister, Ali,' he says.

75

'Hello, Ali,' I say.

She stares up at me.

'Ali is no talking,' Ilex says.

'Do you mean she's shy in company or that she's a mute?'

Ilex shoulders tense and he repeats firmly, 'Ali is no talking.'

'Okay, okay. I was just asking why not?' I'm thinking that maybe those stories about the inbreeding between factory workers producing sub-normal children are true. But I notice Ali's bright eyes flicking between me and Ilex. She's paying attention.

Ilex struggles for words. 'I don't think she likes it here.'

I almost laugh. Does anyone like it here? 'Do the little kids have to fight too?'

'All Specials fight,' Ilex says.

I look at Ali. I can tell by her face she doesn't enjoy fighting either. She's got pathetically thin arms and her eyes are massive in her pale face. I don't think she's getting enough to eat.

'I'm not doing any more. I don't care about their ranking,' I say.

'You should think about ranking. If you're a good-ranker then it's more good.'

'What do you mean?'

'Some more foods. And the Reds don't hit you. You can be a Hon Red and go to their meetings.' He leans in close to me. 'They have food there too.'

'Delightful as that sounds, it seems unlikely that I'm ever going to be a high-ranker – so what's the point in me fighting?'

'They hit you if you don't.'

'I'm going to get hit if I do.'

Ilex spreads his palms. 'I fight to not be bottom-ranker. It's not good to be bottom-ranker. No Special likes you. And they make you do things.'

'What things?'

'Things that make trouble with the enforcers. And one time or two time I'm thinking that Specials the Reds don't like were sent out to the Wilderness.'

There are lots of stories about who gets sent to the Wilderness. Crazies and criminals and even terrorists who are plotting to overthrow the Leadership. There's probably some truth in those rumours, but I refuse to believe that a bunch of school kids have got the power to have other kids sent into the Wilderness. I'm too tired to even think about it at the moment.

I look around the room. The girl called Dom is on her feet, shouting to the fighters. She's one of those girls you can't help looking at.

Ilex follows my gaze. 'All the boys think she's crimson.'

She's got very long legs. Her hair is shiny and her breasts push up against her shirt, but there's something strange about her torso.

'I don't know, she's a bit of a funny shape. Her belly . . .'

'She's got a baby belly.'

'A what?' I look again at her rounded abdomen. 'You don't mean? She's not . . . she's not having a baby, is she?'

Ilex nods and turns back to the fighting. How can he be so casual about something like that? I stare at Dom. I've never seen a pregnant teenager before. I thought babies were always born to married parents. I don't even know anyone who's had sex. At the Learning Community having sex would have been completely impossible. Firstly, you'd never have found a girl willing to sacrifice everything to do it with you and secondly, as soon as you were found out, that would be your whole life ruined.

Ilex doesn't even seem to realise how serious this is. Or maybe it's not so serious here. They do say that Academy kids are wild and reckless. Or perhaps this is another Red thing? One thing is for sure, when the enforcers find out, Dom will be in big trouble.

I'm jolted by a blast on the whistle. The fighters are finished and Rex is holding up the arm of the tall girl with ginger hair and freckles.

'The winner is our Red, Shannon!' Rex says.

I look at Rex and the Red girl and then at Dom and I remember what Ilex said about being born a Red. My mouth drops open.

'Ilex,' I say, 'what did you mean when you said you're born a Red?'

'When you are a baby they know it. Reds have—'

'Red hair,' I finish.

This is crazy. The Academy hierarchy is based on hair colour. It doesn't matter how smart I am, I won't ever be successful here because I'm not ginger.

'That's stupid,' I say to Ilex. 'Being red-headed doesn't necessarily mean you're a good fighter.'

'Shh,' Ilex says and looks around to see if anyone is listening. 'Reds say that they're different. That they are made different, more gooder.'

'You don't think that, do you?'

'The thing isn't what I think. The thing is what the Reds think. They're in charge.'

'Let me tell you, when you leave the Academy and go out into the real world it won't be like that.'

'We don't go real worl'. We go to the factory.'

'Yes, of course, most of you—'

'No. All Specials go to the factory. All Specials same working.'

Of course I knew that Academies provide factory

79

workers, but I think I imagined that Academy Specials would be matched with a job in the same way that Learning Community students are. Ilex seems to disagree.

'You know that the Reds won't be in charge at the factory, don't you?' I ask.

Ilex looks me up and down as if he suspects I am winding him up. 'Where do you go when you are seventeen at your brainer place?'

'We don't leave school at seventeen like Specials. We leave when we're twenty-one. Then we get jobs in the Leadership.'

'Is it no Reds in charge there?'

'No.'

He shakes his head like he doesn't quite believe me.

I lean back in my seat. Suddenly the hall falls silent. Everyone's attention is focused on a dark-haired boy who has just walked in. I stare too. His face is purple and swollen. He looks even worse than I do. His eyes are slits in the swelling and his nose is puffed up like a balloon. Out of the silence comes a faint tapping sound. I swivel round, trying to locate its source. It gets louder. A chinking. Metal on metal. Then it's all over the hall. I look at my neighbours and see that they're tapping together little bits of metal. Everyone is doing it. Even Ilex and Ali.

The Red who has just won her fight walks over to the purple-faced boy and lifts his arm. The hall erupts in cheers. Then the boy is led to a seat and the next fight is introduced.

'What was that?' I say.

'What?' says Ilex, as if nothing unusual has just occurred.

'Who is that boy? Why did you make that noise?'

'He is Lanc. We do the . . .' He taps a metal washer against a nut that has been driven through his belt and fastened with a bolt. 'We do the thing to say we think he is not scared.'

'Not scared of what? Falling on his face?'

'Enforcer Tong hit his little brother.'

'From what I've seen of Enforcer Tong, I can well believe it.'

'Lanc hit her back,' he adds.

I suck in my breath. I've been here long enough to know that hitting an enforcer would mean big trouble. 'Did *Tong* do that to his face?'

Ilex shakes his head. 'The impeccables. Maybe Rice too.'

I think about being locked in a room with Rice and a brute squad.

'You mean he's brave,' I say.

'What?'

'When you did your tappy tappy, it's because he's brave. When someone is not scared to do something like that, it's called brave.'

'I'd like some brave,' he says.

I look down at Lanc in the front row. I gently touch my own sore eye. I wonder if getting your face kicked in hurts less when you're brave.

'I need to sleep,' I say.

Ilex nods.

I raise my hand to Ali. 'Bye, Ali,' I say and, to my surprise, she raises her hand in reply.

Back in the dormitory I curl up under my stinky blanket. I've been here a whole day, but I'm no closer to knowing how I'm going to get out of here. I need to think. It doesn't hurt to understand the Academy, I tell myself. It's important to know your enemy. I have to survive here while I work out what to do. I've got to get out, but I can't go back to the Willows. I'll have to go to my mother. I'll be careful. I'll find the right moment and then I'll break out and I'll head to Mother's flat.

Suddenly, P.C. Barnes' words come back to me. If it's true someone is out to get me, will I be safe if I leave the Academy? Will they track me down?

I shiver. How the hell did I end up making escape plans like some sort of criminal?

My thoughts are disturbed by the blonde girl jumping on her own bed and saying, 'You're not a good fighter.'

'And you're not terribly bright,' I reply. I've had enough of today.

She blinks.

'Oh, I'm sorry,' I say. 'I thought we were taking it in turns to state the blatantly obvious.'

Her expression doesn't change. She's got no idea what I've just said.

'You big-need to learn to fight,' she says.

'And you're offering to teach me?' I roll my eyes. She's built like a bird and around five-foot nothing. Her pale hair makes her look young, although I suppose she must be the same age as me since we're in the same class. Her arms are delicate and I can see that her legs are thin even through her trousers. I look at her little boots and realise that they seem oddly familiar. Last time I saw one of those boots, it was sending Deon sprawling. King Hell, how embarrassing; some scrap of an Academy girl is trying to look after me.

'I saw what you did in the fight,' I say.

She shrugs. 'I can think-back my first fight.'

I wait for her to say something more, but she doesn't. 'Well, it's nice that I'm bringing back tender memories for you, but I really don't need your help,' I say.

'What's "help"?' she says.

'What?'

'What's "help"?'

I'm annoyed. I'm annoyed that I had to have help from a girl in a fight and I'm annoyed that no one here understands basic English. 'Oh, my life,' I say. 'King Hell on a sunny day. You've got a really, really basic vocabulary haven't you?'

I'm pretty sure she still doesn't understand what I'm saying, but she obviously picks up on the tone because she sticks her chin out and stands up to leave.

'It's doing something for someone,' I say. I sound like

Facilitator Johnson when he thought we were being dim. 'Help is . . . aid?'

She shakes her head.

'Assistance?'

And again.

'Oh for efwurd's sake, you won that fight for me! *You did a thing for me.* You were being nice.'

She tilts her head. 'I didn't do a thing for you. I don't like Deon. I didn't want him to win,' she says.

'Listen, in future, just remember, I don't need your help.'

'You do need *help*,' she forms the final word carefully. 'But I won't *help* you.' She walks away and calls back over her shoulder, 'And I'm not nice.'

I try to stay awake, but I'm worn out and my whole body is aching from both my recent beatings. The last thing I remember is listening to the dormitory door slamming shut and wondering if they were locking us in for the night.

I end up sleeping through until a buzzer wakes me. All around me Specials clamber out of bed. I peer out from under the blanket to see how they manage getting dressed. Most of them seem to disappear to the bathroom and re-emerge fully clothed, but some of the boys don't seem to care. I could really do without starting the day with a view of some boy's hairy backside.

The blonde girl leans over my bed. 'Get up time,' she says.

'What if I don't want to get up?' I say. 'What if I just stay here? What can they do?'

'Okay. You stay and find out the thing they do.'

I suppose I'm not getting any closer to getting out of this place by just lying here. So I get up. I feel grubby from rolling around on the floor yesterday and sleeping in my clothes. I need a hot shower.

The showers are strangely empty, which probably explains why the Specials have their own interesting smell. I open up one of the cubicles. The shower head is crusty with rust. The drainage hole is clogged with hair and there are splatters of black mould up the tiles. I try the next one, it's no better. I turn on the squeaky tap and I'm blasted with icy-cold water. I shrink back against the door, hoping it will warm up, but it doesn't. I have a quick splash and then give up. I'm in such a hurry to get my clothes on before anyone else comes in that I end up with my trousers sticking to my damp legs.

I follow the stream of Specials down to the dining room. Breakfast is the same horrible nozzle-sucking business. I don't eat from the one with the sedative, or whatever it is, in it. The best part of the meal is a piece of bread which has been left in each pod on the drainage tray. After I've eaten I realise I probably should have saved the bread. If I'm going to break out of here I'll need supplies. Food, water and something to carry them in. I've got to take my time and get properly organised.

The day goes by in a blur, and the next few days pass in much the same way. I can't see how I'll ever be able to escape. During the day the enforcers keep us locked in the grid and the rest of the time there are patrols of impeccables watching our every move. I spend a lot of time observing. I keep quiet and try to blend in.

In the grid we mostly study electronics, I'm surprised by how advanced some of their work is, but it all has a practical basis, so I suppose they're preparing the students for work in an electronics factory. To my horror the other main lesson is Physical Education. Most afternoons we're taken to the drum-shaped room and are expected to run and jump and generally throw ourselves about. Enforcer Tong keeps telling us how we need strong, healthy bodies to make our contribution to society, but I've never felt more weak and exhausted in my life.

Secretly, I keep expecting someone to appear and take me away from this place, but it doesn't happen. No one wants to listen to me when I tell them I don't belong here. Ilex is the only person who talks to me, but he spends a lot of time with Ali in the kids' dormitory.

Mostly, I sit around thinking about food and watching the blonde girl. I notice at mealtimes that she doesn't drink from the first nozzle either. I wonder if she's getting food from somewhere else. Last night I woke up when she got up to go to the bathroom and she didn't come back for a really long time. She's definitely up to something. So tonight I'm keeping myself awake.

Just when my stomach cramps are fading and I'm starting to get warm and sleepy I hear the squeak of a bare foot on the tiled floor. I open my eyes. The girl is creeping down the dormitory. She swerves into the bathroom. I wait a moment and then I follow. The freezing bathroom is deserted and silent except for the echo of a dripping tap. The stalls are all empty. The girl has gone. In the corner there's a tiny strip of light around the edge of a door that must lead on to the corridor. I try the handle. It's locked. I can just about make out a keypad next to it. The girl must know the code. I remember the impeccable typing CLASSROOM into the grid door-pad, on the day I arrived. Maybe all the codes are ridiculously simple. I tap in CORRIDOR. But nothing happens. I try LANDING. There's a high-pitched beep and the door clicks open. Incredible. I can't believe Specials aren't pouring in and out all night long. I slip out of the door, squinting at the brightness, even though the lights are on a night setting. There's no sign of the girl. I decide that I may as well take advantage of my freedom and head for the kitchen.

I sneak down the stairs and round to the dining hall. I tiptoe between the shadowy rows of feeding pods. I keep expecting someone to emerge from one. I find the door that I've seen kitchen workers use and lift my hand to the punch-pad, but the door is wedged open with a chunk of wood. Someone else is already in the kitchen. I put my eye to the crack. It's too dark to see. Slowly, I open the door till there's enough room to creep in.

Inside, it's vast. Everything in the Academy is on such a big scale. Sometimes I feel like a marble rolling around in a box. There are no windows. The only light comes from a lamp on top of the largest fridge I have ever seen.

Knelt in front of it is the girl. The room is a mass of shadows; darkness pours out of the corners. I creep towards her. Down the centre of the room is an extremely long, seamless metal block which must serve as a preparation table. Opposite me, against the wall, are the same trough-like metal sinks we have in the dormitory bathroom. The fridge is at the far end of the room. I tread lightly up the length of the kitchen. The girl's hair looks white in this light.

As I get closer I can hear a wet chewing. I wince. She's cramming food into her mouth. My stomach contracts painfully. It's been a long time since I had a decent meal. I stop a few metres behind her, feeling awkward; should I clear my throat? Say good evening?

Suddenly she springs up, turns around and raises her fists, all in one move.

I take a step backwards and half raise my own fists.

'Oh,' she says. 'It's you.' And she turns back to the fridge.

My arms droop like wilting flowers.

'Did the impeccables see you?' she asks.

'What impeccables?'

'There's an impeccable patrol. Lots of nights.'

'Oh. No, I didn't see any impeccables.'

'It's bad you're here,' she says through a mouthful.

I draw in my breath to say something, but let it go again. There's no point getting cross. 'Why?' I ask.

'Specials can't go in the kitchen,' she says.

'Well, we *can* because here we are. I suppose you mean we're not allowed. What will happen if we get caught?'

'We get cor?' she repeats. 'If they see us we'll be put in the LER room.'

I don't know what that means, but the way that she freezes with a slice of ham halfway to her mouth and looks off into the shadows suggests to me that I really don't want to find out.

'Can I have some ham?' I say.

'No.'

'Oh.'

She carries on chewing.

I have to swallow because my mouth is watering so much. 'Listen, I'm starving. I think I've got as much right to be pilfering food as you have.' I move towards the fridge, but she catches hold of my arm.

'Not ham,' she says. 'I take one of all things. If we take all lots then they'll see.'

She's got a point and I'm actually pretty impressed that she's been smart enough to think of it. I help myself to a cold potato with one hand and a tomato with the other. My mouth folds around the potato. It's delicious; the middle is so soft and salty that my jaw aches with the unexpected pleasure. I ought to be putting things in my pocket for later, but I'm just so hungry.

'Who eats this stuff?' I say. The fridge is jam-packed with all kinds of tasty food that they'd never serve to a Special.

'The enforcers,' she says.

'Why don't all the Specials come down here?' I ask, cramming in a chunk of cheese.

'Not big lots,' she tells me, carefully repositioning the cheese dish to where it was. 'Not all people can . . .' She mimes punching in the code.

'Not everyone knows the code?' I say. I look at her hard. 'If you don't know the word "code" what happens in your head when you think about it?'

'What?' she says.

'When you were telling me, did you have a word in your head for "code" or did you just think of . . .' I copy her mime.

'I have my words for it,' she says, her face half hidden by a chunk of bread.

'What are they?' I ask.

She lifts her chin. 'I say "the get-food number". But now I say "code".' She shakes back her silvery hair. 'I'm not stupid.'

I look down at the fridge door and realise that it's got an electronic lock attached. Goodness knows how she got it open. She's right. She's not stupid.

When the girl isn't watching I put a small apple in my pocket. She turns to look at me with suspicious eyes, so I say the first thing that comes into my head.

'You're not a Red.'

'I know,' she says.

'Are you an Hon Red?' I frown. 'That's like a half-Red, isn't it?'

'I'm not an Hon. It's like Red, but no . . .' She tugs a strand of hair.

She frowns at the fruit bowl and repositions a banana to cover the gap left by the apple I took. 'I will be an Hon Red.' Her eyes light up. 'I'm going to be next Dom.' She says it in a low voice as if she's letting me in on a big secret.

I've gathered that the Dom girl is important. She and Rex are like the Specials' king and queen.

'That'll be nice,' I say. 'If you like hanging around with a bunch of violent bullies.'

She sucks in her breath. 'Dom is the best. I'm going to be the best.'

I consider asking her if her complete lack of both ginger hair and height might be an obstacle, but she's all starry-eyed and I don't want to annoy her, so I butter the tiny chunk of bread she's allowed me. That's when we hear voices coming from the dining hall. I freeze. The girl doesn't freeze, she whips two containers back in the fridge, screws on the lid of the massive bottle of milk, replaces it in exactly the right position, closes the door and starts reconnecting the electronic lock.

'I suppose you're expecting something to eat,' the voice from the hall says.

They're getting closer.

'Door,' says the girl, without looking up from the wires she's fiddling with.

'What?' I say. She can't mean we're going out through

the door; we'll run straight into them. I look about for a back door.

The girl tuts and drops the wires. She sprints silently across the kitchen and prods the wedge of wood out from the door and eases it shut. She runs back to me, rapidly twists in a final screw on the lock, flicks off the light, grabs me by the wrist and pulls me through complete darkness into a cupboard.

I hear the kitchen door open. A wave of fear washes over me and I feel like someone has sucked the bones out of my legs and they can no longer support me. I am too terrified to stand. I sway on my feet, but the girl grabs me by the back of the shirt and holds me up. I realise that I've still got the butter knife in my right hand. I concentrate on not dropping it.

There's the sound of a cupboard opening and the rustling of a packet. 'Here, you can have this. Now listen, I'll keep this short,' says the voice on the other side of the kitchen. 'I know you find it hard to follow lengthy instructions.'

It's Enforcer Tong's voice. I'm sure of it.

'Uh?' comes the reply.

That doesn't sound like an enforcer. It must be one of the Specials, or maybe an impeccable.

'I hear some Specials are planning trouble for the enforcers,' says Tong. 'I don't like trouble. It is your job to find them for me and it is my job to punish them. You find these bad Specials and you will get more food.'

93

'Uh-huh,' the impeccable grunts.

There are footsteps and the sound of the door closing. I relax and the sense of relieved tension is so strong that I almost wet myself. I have cramp from standing rigid and I start to roll my shoulders, but then I notice that the girl's hand is still on my back and I stop mid shoulder roll. I turn to look at her, even though it is too dark to see. She takes her hand away. I slowly drop my shoulders in what I hope is a casual fashion. Neither of us speaks.

The girl pushes past me out of the cupboard. She turns on the light again and I notice that there *is* a back door in the corner. Maybe I should get going. The girl checks that the lock on the fridge is secure then she sweeps up the crumbs we've made on the counter with her hands.

'What was all that about?' I say.

'Tong makes people do the things she wants. And stops them doing things she doesn't.'

'Control obsessive is she? I don't like the way they use older kids to keep an eye on—'

There's a noise behind us. I spin round. The door is opening. We're in big trouble. There's absolutely no escape now.

17

Before I can move, the girl turns off the light.

It's pitch black. The door clicks shut. They must know we're in here. They must have seen the light and now we're trapped.

There's a silence.

Nobody moves.

It can't be Tong; she'd be bellowing by now and she would have switched the lights straight back on. It must be the impeccable – why doesn't he turn on a light? Then I realise that maybe he doesn't want *us* to see *him* because he's ashamed of being in league with the enforcers. Which is fine. Dark is fine. We can escape under cover of darkness. All we've got to do is get to the back door.

I stretch out my left hand and grasp the girl's arm. I pull her firmly along in the direction of the door I saw in the far corner. I feel like a kid in a virtual haunted house booth. Any moment now I'm sure something is going to come rushing out at me.

There's a great clatter from the middle of the room. The impeccable has knocked a pan off the preparation block. That means he's coming closer. I graze my shin on something and suck in my breath involuntarily. I curse myself inwardly for giving him a clue to our whereabouts. We've reached where the door ought to be, but when I grope in front of me there's nothing. I take another step forward. And another. My hand hits the wall.

I pull the girl in close behind me and feel for the door frame. I've got it. I fumble for the door handle and push it down as gently as I can. Thank goodness there's no code punch on this one. I start to pull the girl through the door, but she's yanked backwards out of my grip.

I hear the noise of a struggle, but neither of them calls out. I lurch back, blindly sweeping my arms in front of me trying to find them. Moving towards the grunting and scuffling, I eventually scoop a handful of the girl's long hair – it's cool to the touch. I manage to get my hand under her shoulders and pull her away from the flailing arms of the impeccable. I aim a kick where I imagine his groin to be and I hear him hit the ground with a groan. But just as we reach the door, I feel the girl pulled back again.

I'm not going without her. I owe her for the first decent feed I've had in ages. I swing my arms out, but find only air. I crouch down and locate a hand gripping her ankle. I keep hold of his hand to help my aim and then I plunge the butter knife I'm still holding into the back of his wrist.

'Arggggghhh!'

The hand releases her ankle and the girl falls forward. I pull her up and together we push through the door, stumbling into a corridor of more blackness. We run blind. My face is pulled back, wincing, expecting to smash into something any moment. I keep my hands raised and soon they hit another door. I try the handle, but it's locked.

'We need code,' the girl whispers.

I grope about for the keypad. 'What is it?' I say.

'I don't know. I don't know this code.'

'Where does this door go?' I ask her.

'To feeding pods.'

I picture the position of the letters on the key pad outside our classroom and, using my sense of touch, I tap out DINING ROOM.

My hands are shaking. I'm not sure how many Os I've typed. I try the door, but it won't open. The door at the other end of the passageway crashes open and we hear the impeccable feeling his way towards us.

I try again. DINING ROOM. There's a click. The door opens. We tumble through and slam it behind us. We're back in the faintly lit hall of feeding pods again. This time at the far end. The girl widens her eyes at me and breaks into a smile. I smile back.

We speed back to the bathroom and then into our beds. I tell her in a whisper how the butter knife saved the day.

'What's your name?' I ask.

'Kay,' she says.

'Mine's Blake.'

'I know, you told me.'

'Oh,' I say.

'You eat big slow, Blake.' She yawns. 'But you stab good.'

'Why would anyone want to work for Tong?' I ask Kay the next morning while she's lacing her boots. It's unnerving to think that the impeccables are constantly spying on everyone.

'More big food, less big hitting, all the enforcers say, "No EMDs for you, good boy".'

'Well, I'd like all those things, but I wouldn't grass up the Specials,' I say.

'What's that?'

'I wouldn't talk to the enforcers and tell them what Specials were doing.'

Kay looks sceptical.

'I wouldn't! I might not be any good at fighting, but I'm not a traitor and you should remember that I was pretty good with the butter knife when you were in trouble.'

Kay laughs. 'You are knife-good, yes.'

'Anyway, shouldn't your Reds be doing something

about bad impeccables like that? What do they do to Specials who get Specials into trouble?'

'They kick their heads in,' she says.

'That's what they do to everyone.'

Kay scowls. I don't think she likes me criticising the Reds. I won't push it because this morning she has been just a shade less aggressive with me and it seems like a good time to get some answers. I think Kay is a little more aware than Ilex and there are some things I need to know.

'Can Specials send emails?' I ask.

'No,' she says.

'Do you know what an email is?' I say.

'No. That's how I know we can't do it,' she says.

'What about letters? Can Specials send letters?' I say.

'Letters?'

'Like a message,' I say. 'You write down what you want to say to someone then the . . . er . . . letter-man takes it to their house.' It's odd how weird a lot of things that you take for granted sound when you try to explain them.

'No. No talking to people not in the Academy. No communicator talk, no writing talk,' she says.

'Couldn't I bribe an enforcer to send a letter for me? Bribe is—'

'I know bribe,' she says.

'You don't know letter, but you know bribe? That's a sad reflection on your education, Kay.'

She can tell I'm taking the mickey and sticks out her

tongue at me. 'The enforcers are bad-and-more-bad. They like being bad to you. A bribe won't work,' she says.

'What about someone else? Couldn't I bribe a cleaner?' I say.

'What with?'

I take stock of my worldly goods. One book. Unless I can find a cleaner who really likes poetry I don't have anything to offer.

'You need shrap,' says Kay.

'What's shrap?'

Kay sits up straight. 'Shrap is what all Specials want.' She goes to the locker at the end of her bed and brings something to show me.

It's a bolt tied to a string necklace. She puts it round her neck and looks down admiringly. She's also got a nail on a string and a small section of copper pipe. Shrap appears to be junk metal. I remember the nut and bolt on Ilex's belt and all the Specials making that chinking noise to show their approval of Lanc.

'Apart from being able to make a rather annoying noise, what's the point of that?' I say. 'Why would anyone want that rubbish?'

Kay pulls back, cradling her shrap to her chest. 'It's shiny,' she says.

'But it's not worth anything,' I say.

'What's worth?'

'Things that have worth, you can . . . get things with them,' I say.

'You can get things with shrap. You can get a mate. You can get food. You can get Specials all looking at you and saying, "*Ooh shiny*".'

In the real world I have a bank account with over two thousand credits in. I have an AEP score of 98.5. I own valuable scientific equipment. Here, I am a pauper because I haven't broken off bits of metal from the building and strung them round my neck.

Fantastic.

On my thirteenth night at the Academy I decide to try to escape. The day before, I get Ilex to draw me a map of the Academy. He traces it out in the dust under his bed. There's the long corridor with grids coming off on either side. At the north end, stairs lead down to another floor of classrooms and up to two floors of dormitories. Before the stairs, on the left, is the door that I came in by. Ilex says this door leads to the older part of the Academy which isn't used any more. I also know that reception is down this corridor and, most importantly, an exit.

Past the main stairs the corridor curves into the dining hall and kitchen. There's another exit close to the dining hall and running away from there is another corridor that I've never been down. At the south end of the main passage and off to the left is the drum-shaped fight room. Also at that end of the corridor is a lift and the door to the enforcers' sleeping quarters. There are several other corridors with no exits on. Ilex says they're where the Making rooms and the LER rooms are. I still haven't visited them, but I don't think I need to bother about them.

Looking at the map, I realise how few exits there are. Imagine what would happen if there was a fire. The enforcers would run off without so much as opening a door and hundreds of Specials would die in either the flames or a stampede.

My plan is to try all possible exits. I have to get out of here. I have to get to my mother. She'll have tried to call me on my communicator by now and when she gets no answer she'll try the Learning Community. What will she do when they tell her that I don't exist? I don't want her to think that something terrible has happened to me.

I lie awake till the breathing of everyone around me is regular, including Kay in the next bed. She's told me she's not going to the kitchen tonight, so there's no chance of bumping into her. I slip out of bed and head for the bathroom, leaving the room the same way I did the night I snuck out to find Kay.

I try my first hope – the door at the bottom of the stairs which connects to the passage leading back to reception. I check down the corridor, there's no sign of an impeccable patrol or anyone else, so I type RECEPTION into the keypad by the door. There's the same high-pitched beep as on the bathroom door and I know I've got it right. A tiny screen on the keypad flashes: *Swipe ID card*. Damn. This is going to be more difficult than I imagined. I find a cancel button and press it, in the hope that no one is going to be alerted to the fact that I've tried to get through the door.

Why the ID card? We don't need one for the kitchen or the bathroom. Which I suppose is lucky really. I guess the difference is that this door isn't internal. It leads somewhere they really don't want the Specials to go – outside. I may as well test out my theory so I head for the door near the dining hall. This time I can't even get the code right. I try OUTSIDE, BACK DOOR, GARDEN, then I make myself stop because even if I get the code, I can see this one also has a reader for a card that I don't have.

I had told myself that it might not happen tonight, that I might have to make plans and try again, but secretly I was hoping that by now I'd be on my way home. Suddenly, I'm desperate to get out of this place. I've got one last chance tonight.

My final hope is the door to the enforcers' quarters. It's risky, but it's just possible that they have a separate exit to the outside world, so I have to give it a try. The door probably doesn't work without a swipe card either, but I've got to see for myself. I steal down the long corridor lined with classroom doors. The last door on the right leads to the enforcers' part of the Academy and, at the end of the corridor, the entrance to a lift juts out.

I'm about to try the door to the enforcers' section when there's a humming sound above me and I realise that someone is in the lift. I look up at the digital floor display. The lift is on the floor above me and it's coming down.

I'm in trouble. I look around desperately. The corridor is bare. There's nowhere to hide. The buzz of the machinery is getting louder. If I try to get into a classroom they'll hear the pneumatic door, but I haven't got time to run back up the corridor. The only place to hide is in the shadow between where the lift sticks out and the corridor wall. I hope whoever it is doesn't turn round.

I slip into the shadow and take a deep breath to try to steady my breathing. What will they do to me if they catch me? My heart is galloping.

The hum of the lift slows. There's a *ping* and the doors slide open. I press back into the shadow. An enforcer comes out of the lift and takes the few steps back along the corridor towards the enforcers' door. I can see only the back of his head, so I don't know who it is. He flicks his fingers over the keypad and the door clicks open. He pushes the door and steps inside and I am about to wilt with relief when I do something without thinking. I whip over to the door and catch it before it clicks back into place. I stand there, supporting the door with my flat hands so that it remains a few centimetres open. I wince, expecting the door to be yanked open again at any moment, or for an alarm to go off, but nothing happens.

I breathe in through my nose and slowly push the door open. I'm looking down a dimly lit passageway. Everything is quiet. The enforcer has already disappeared and no one else is about. I feel in my pockets, but there's nothing there. I can't let the door close behind me because I don't know the code to get back out, so I take off one of my socks and wedge the door with it.

On tiptoes I make my way down the corridor. I bet they don't make the enforcers sleep in dormitories. I'm sure they've got showers that work too. I peer into the first room. It's some sort of social area with comfortable chairs and a coffee machine. No exit in there. I turn to leave, but I catch sight of something that puts all thought of outside doors from my head.

It's a communicator.

Checking the corridor again, I creep into the room and softly close the door behind me. The communicator is in a booth, like they have in shopping centres. I step inside and click the privacy button. The door seals and now I'm in a soundproof bubble. I lift my hand to type in my access code. No. That's Jackson's unique code. If P.C. Barnes was right and someone is after me, maybe I shouldn't be activating my account. You can trace these things. Instead I type in the code of an unregistered account that I set up when Wilson and I were trying to purchase some A.I. components that nobody wanted to sell to teenagers.

The home screen pops up, showing three layers. At the top a message marked *Urgent* is flashing red. A still of my mother's face is next to it. I didn't know she knew about this account. I tap it with my forefinger. A projection of my mother appears in the centre of the booth.

'J—' she starts, then closes her mouth again. '*Sweetheart*,' she says, '*listen to me carefully. Everything is going to be okay. I found out where you are and I'm coming to get you. Don't tell anyone who you are. Just –'* she takes a deep breath *'– just don't move. This is really important. For now you should be safe where you are. Whatever happens, wait at, er, that place and I will come.'* She brings a hand up to her forehead and rubs her eyebrow. *'I should have told you . . .'* There's a knock on the door behind her. She drops her voice. *'Just wait there for me.'*

It cuts to static.

'Mum?' I say out loud. What the hell happened there?

I check the date on the message. Yesterday. I touch *Reply* on the screen and, as I do so, I realise that this is not my mother's official communication account, nor was she using a registered communicator. What the efwurd is going on? Why wouldn't my mother use her normal account? And why is she talking about 'safe' places? Does she know something about what's happened to me? The connection hums, but no one picks up. Usually accounts have a message service. It just buzzes on and on. I turn round so I can watch the door. I'm sweating. I wait and wait for an answer. Nothing.

I cut the connection and buzz her official communication account. There's an instant pick up. Thank goodness. A projection flicks into life. But something is wrong.

It's not my mother.

It's a recording. A tight-lipped woman wearing a uniform.

'*Do not retry this connection,*' she says.

A wave of cold washes through my body. She's staring right at me.

'*This account has been terminated.*'

My mind is spinning. They don't just cut off people's accounts.

Terminated.

I have a horrible feeling that something has happened to Mother. Like she's somehow tied up in all this craziness too. Suddenly I can't breathe. I'm sweating, but shivering at the same time. I fumble to get out of the booth and crouch down, panting for breath. A door slams out in the corridor. I spring up, looking for a place to hide. I duck behind a sofa. I peer over the top and strain my ears for sounds of movement. The door opens and I drop back.

Someone walks across the room. I lean to the side and see the legs of an enforcer. There's a sigh. It's a woman. The legs move towards me and bend at the knees. I'm dead. They must have seen me. I freeze. A hand stretches out and picks up an old-style paperback book not more than thirty centimetres from my head. The hand pulls back, the legs straighten. I don't breathe. The enforcer moves back across the room and the door clicks behind her. I *have* to get out of here.

I gently open the door, check both ways and run on bent knees. Thank goodness the door back to the main part of the Academy is still being held ajar by my sock. I scoop it up and ease the door shut behind me.

Then I run. I don't even think about the noise, I just run all the way back to the dormitory and bury myself under the covers. The word 'terminated' blows up like a mushroom cloud in my head.

'I told you not to go to the kitchen all lots,' Kay says quietly from the next bed.

I lower my covers and glare at her.

'Don't you have a thing to say?' she asks. 'When I say a thing, most times you like to say a thing back. You think it's a laughing thing but I—'

'I think my mother is dead,' I say.

She stops. The smile falls from her face and she looks right at me. 'That's bad,' she says. And I know she means it. 'How do you think it?' she asks.

I wonder how much I should tell her. I keep it simple. 'I called her on a communicator and her account has been terminated.'

The girl looks down in concentration. 'A communicator? Like on the Info and you're all talking to the person that is not here?'

'Yes,' I say. 'So don't you think—?'

'What's terminated?' she says.

'Finished. Ended.' My voice cracks.

'How does that give you the think that she's dead?'

I shake my head. 'You don't understand. Accounts aren't just terminated. Everyone has an account. Everyone.'

'I don't,' she says.

'What?'

'I don't have a 'count. No Specials do.'

She's got a point.

'She might not be dead. She might be locked up.'

I stare at the girl. She's right. The woman in the message was wearing a security uniform. My mother's not dead, she's just . . . caught up with the police somehow. Which doesn't make any sense either. I can't shake the feeling that this is all connected to what's happened to me. But she'll sort it out. My mother is really good at fixing stuff.

'You're right,' I say. 'She's not dead.'

The girl nods.

'And you know what? She's coming to get me out of here. All I've got to do is wait.'

'No mothers in the Academy,' she says, lying back down.

'Mine will come,' I say.

The next day I feel better. More positive. All I have to do is keep up my false identity, try to avoid getting into any more fights, and manage to eat enough to keep healthy until my mother comes to get me. Simple.

Kay asks me to meet her in the Specials' recreation room – the salon. Ilex shows me the way.

As we're going downstairs, a herd of Reds come pushing past us. One of them deliberately trips me up. Ilex helps me to my feet.

'Where are they going in such a hurry?' I ask.

'I think it's a more-food time,' he says.

'Food? I'd like some food.'

'It's not for us. It's for Reds and Hon Reds.'

I'm sick of all this Reds stuff. It's so unfair that they get extras.

'Where does the extra food for the Reds come from?' I say. The whole time I've been here we've only ever had three meals a day. If you can call the slop from the feeding pod a meal.

'It's Academy food. On sometimes the kitchen workers get all the food things that aren't big good and say "You can eat this" to the Reds.'

So the kitchen periodically has a clear out, but the Reds don't let everyone else have a fair share. It makes me so angry that this group of jumped-up gingers control everything.

'Why don't we just go too?' I say to Ilex.

He just looks at me, not wasting his breath to tell me what a stupid idea it is. He's right, it would be stupid. I'd get beaten up. But I can't just let it go.

At the bottom of the stairs I see an enforcer coming out of a classroom and heading down the corridor towards the teachers' quarters.

'Enforcer?' I call.

She jumps. 'What is it?' she says, but keeps moving down the corridor.

I jog after her. Ilex stays at the bottom of the stairs.

'Enforcer . . .'

She looks back over her shoulder as she walks.

'The kitchen is giving out leftover food,' I say. 'Everybody is hungry. We'd all like some food . . .'

She's reached the enforcers' door and taps in the code.

'Wait! Some of the students won't let the others eat.'

She pulls open the door. I can't believe she's just ignoring me.

113

'But it's not fair!' I say.

She looks me up and down. 'We don't interfere with the Reds,' she says and the door closes behind her.

Ilex was right.

You can't fight the Reds.

I slink back to Ilex, who laughs at me and shakes his head, but thankfully doesn't say anything. He takes me to the salon, which turns out to be down the extra corridor on his map. Surprise, surprise – it's a barn of a room. There are a lot of cheap padded chairs with the stuffing ripped out and a massive screen on one wall. As we walk in, there are a bunch of boys having a spitting competition.

I roll my eyes. This is the 'salon'?

Ilex goes back upstairs to see Ali and I find Kay in the furthest corner of the room.

'Well, Lady McKayington,' I say to her. 'I do hope the maid will bring the tea soon,' I say, putting on my poshest accent.

'What?' she says.

'The salon is so nice that I feel like The Leader. Soon they'll bring us piles of food and lovely drinks and maybe rub our feet.'

Kay shakes her head, but I can see that she's smiling too.

We sit in battered chairs. The Info is on the big screen with the sound turned down.

'I'm surprised they let you watch TV,' I say.

'What's "surprised"?' Kay says. 'What's TV?'

'This is "surprised" . . .' I widen my eyes and suck in my breath.

Kay nods. It's a lot easier to explain words to Kay than to Ilex. With Kay it's like she already knows the idea of the word and you're just labelling it for her. I think Ilex would rather I just used the words he knows.

'And that's TV.' I point at the screen.

'That's the Info,' she corrects me.

'Yes, but as well as the Info you get—'

Kay shakes her head.

'Just the Info?'

She nods. 'Just one little Info, all the days.'

Weird. I'm amazed that in a place like this, the one thing they let them watch is the news. And it's odd that the Specials haven't picked up more vocabulary from it. I look at the screen. There are images of The Leader visiting a factory. He shakes hands with the smiling workers. I move towards the screen and slide the volume icon up with my finger.

'. . . *factory workers are working hard,*' the voiceover says. '*The Leader is pleased. "We must all work hard," he says. The workers who do the most work meet The Leader. They are happy . . .*'

'What the hell is this?' I say. This isn't what the Info is usually like.

'The Info,' says Kay, looking confused.

I don't need her to tell me that this dumbed-down pap

is what they listen to every day. I feel ill. Maybe I shouldn't be so surprised that the Specials haven't developed speech properly when they've only got this junk and the barking of an enforcer to learn from. And then a second wave of revulsion undulates through me. These voiceovers must be specially prepared. I realise that I'd been holding on to a tiny hope that maybe this place was just a really bad example of an Academy. That it was because of Rice and his staff that the conditions are so poor and the Specials are treated so badly, and that maybe other Academies were a bit better. But if they're specially preparing these 'news' reports then I guess that they're shown in every Academy. Does that mean *all* Academies are like this one? My head is spinning. I know that Specials' education is designed to equip them for their lives in the factories, but I can't help thinking that surely they deserve to be taught to talk properly.

'What's bad?' Kay says, seeing the look on my face.

'You do know that that is not how people speak?' I say, jabbing towards the screen. 'You do realise that when the rest of the world watch the Info, the newsreader uses more than ten words – they talk like me, Kay. Most people talk like me.' My shoulders sag. 'I just don't understand why it has to be so nasty in here and I don't understand why they want to keep you down by taking away your language as well.'

Kay looks at me. She shakes her head sorrowfully. 'I don't know your words,' she says.

And it's all so horrible that I want to punch something.

'The Academies . . .' she says, and she looks at me to try to tell me something that she can't with words. She holds my gaze and her huge eyes are both sorry and angry. I think she does understand.

'I don't . . . I don't think Academies should be like this,' I say. Even as the words escape I'm looking around to make sure no one has heard me.

Kay touches my arm. 'When I am Dom, I will make things more good. I will help the little ones. I will make the Specials be . . .' She draws her hands together. She breaks into a smile. It's not something she does often, it's nice.

'Closer? Together?' I say, smiling back.

She looks at me. 'Are you laughing?' she asks.

'No! No, I just, I thought you wanted to be Dom so you could be adored and showered with bits of shrap.'

'Yes, and that.'

We sit down on some ripped-up chairs and I try to get my head straight while Kay talks about when she first started at the Academy and how every day she would ask a Red girl called Ama if she could make Kay's hair red.

'I had the think—'

'Thought,' I say.

'I had the thought that if I was big good she would make my hair red.' She smiles at her foolishness. Then she shows me her best trick fight move. I know that she is trying to distract me and I let her.

117

Later on, in the dormitory, I look at Kay sleeping and consider how she has completely changed the way she thinks since she was a little girl. I realise that I've been thinking the same things, in the same way, all my life. All because of what I was told. I just assumed that anyone who thought differently to me was wrong. And now I keep finding that things aren't exactly as I thought. It's not so easy to be certain that I know the right answers.

Sometimes I wonder if I even know the right questions.

The next day is Friday. In the afternoon we have P.E. At the front of the drum-shaped room Enforcer Tong has got an impeccable demonstrating some dreadful routine of punches, jumps and kicks. I manage to position myself near the back, next to Ilex. The two of us are not really built for sport.

'Why do we have to do this all the time?' I ask him in a pant.

Ilex's mop of hair has wilted and a drop of sweat is running down his nose. He bounces a little closer to me so he can whisper without Tong hearing. 'The Leader says, "Good bodies is good workers".'

I suppose at the Learning Community we were pushed to exercise our minds instead. Funny how no one there ever bothered about our physical fitness, though.

I catch sight of Kay's white-blonde ponytail whipping about near the front. When she kicks her leg she can touch her own ear.

'How was the salon with Kay?' Ilex asks me.

'It was . . . good. Do you know Kay well? I mean, do you know a lot about her?' I ask.

Ilex shrugs. 'Not big lots.'

'What's she like? She seems to be into all this Reds stuff.'

'Work harder!' Tong shouts. For several minutes we can't talk because all our breath is going into squat thrusts.

Eventually Ilex says. 'She wants to be an Hon Red but . . . she's not like Red girls. She doesn't do all that . . .' He breaks off from a star jump to an impression of a pouting girl flicking her hair and wiggling her hips.

I snort.

'No talking at the back,' Tong says.

'Do you mean she's nicer?'

'Not nicer. Harder.'

Tong relocates to just behind us and we can't talk any more, but on the way back to the grid Ilex says, 'Are you all liking for Kay?'

'No! No way. I just thought she could be helpful.'

Ilex smacks his lips together in a kissing noise and, for a moment, he reminds me of Wilson.

Actually, I have been thinking about asking Kay to come down to the salon again. Last night was the first time since I've been here that I've enjoyed a conversation. But for some reason I feel shy about suggesting it.

Finally, after dinner I follow Kay up to the dormitory.

As she walks through the door she spins round and says, 'Why are you all little-space to me?'

'I, ah, um, well . . .'

'What's eyearumwell?' she says.

King Hell. Why is conversation suddenly difficult?

'Do you want to come down to the salon?' I say in a rush.

'No,' she says.

That went well.

'It's Friday,' says Kay.

Is that supposed to soften the rejection?

'You know that Friday is Fight Night for big Specials,' she says.

'Not you then?' I say. Kay is a good eight inches shorter than me.

She grabs hold of my wrist and twists it up behind my back. 'Ha ha,' she says. 'Do you want to be my next win?'

'After my big win last time, I hope I won't have to fight again,' I say. I'm acutely aware of how close behind me she is.

Kay laughs. 'You didn't do fighting last time. You did running.' She drops my arm.

'I don't see why Specials should fight other Specials,' I say.

'You have to fight to get a ranking.'

I sniff. 'I don't need a ranking. What does some silly number prove?'

Kay looks at me sideways.

'What?' I say.

'Inyway—'

'It's anyway,' I correct her.

'*Any*way, you have got a ranking. You're a one-one-er.'

'Well that's a relief,' I say.

'It means you have fighted one fight and winned one fight.'

'That's a good ratio. What's your rank?'

'I'm a seventeen-seventeener.'

I blink. 'Like I said, doesn't mean a thing, does it?'

'It means things to Specials,' she says and walks off.

Looks like an evening in for me.

On Mondays and Wednesdays the little ones fight, but it's the Friday night seniors' fights that's best attended. Ilex says it's not compulsory to go to any of the fights, unless you're one of the fighters. But it seems that everyone else must enjoy watching Specials pulling each other to pieces because the dormitory is deserted. Everybody else is at the fight. Of course I could go down there myself, but I've had enough violence in the last couple of weeks to last me a lifetime. Anyway, I feel a bit slighted by Kay. Not that it matters. I flop on to my bed. I can feel myself sinking into a depression. It's all pointless. I'm trapped in this terrible place and even if I could get back to my old life . . . well, I'm not sure that things are the same any more.

I give myself a shake. What I need to do is take action. Do something. In fact, I have been waiting for some time alone because there's something I really want to look for. It's only a small thing, but having a goal for the evening is making me feel brighter already.

There aren't many places to look for things in the Academy. One of the most depressing things about this place is how bare it is. There are no *things*. I miss the clutter of studies and workrooms full of books and papers.

There's nowhere to look in the dormitory so I go into the bathroom. It's big. Everything here is big. Sometimes I wish there was a closed-off room somewhere for me to hide in.

There's a great long sink all the way down one wall. There are lots of metal cubicles; showers down the long side and toilets across the short wall. Spaced out down the length of the sink are two types of dispenser, one with soap and one with disposable teeth-cleaning kits. Sometimes they're full, although more often they're empty. But the refills have to come from somewhere. I scan the room. I notice one of the metal panels behind the door I've just come through isn't quite aligned with the others. It's a cupboard. I'm sure of it.

I feel around the edge of the panel and something clicks. The whole metal section swings open. Inside, there are stacks of cardboard boxes. I run my hand across the cardboard and start to open them systematically and carefully. It's probably best that no one knows I've been in here. In the first box are rolls of loo paper. In the second there's a plastic container with a foil seal. I tear it off.

Inside are replacement sachets of soap. I get rid of them by filling up the nearest dispenser. Then I take a look at the container. It's roundish and fairly sturdy. Just what I look for in a bowl. I feel a rush of triumph, which is ridiculous when I think about my position. That's okay. Even small victories are good ones. I just have to keep inching my way forward through this mess until I work it out. There's got to be some sort of solution.

Before I click the panel back into place I fetch Wilson's poetry book from where I've been hiding it under my mattress. I'm pretty sure that if an enforcer saw it they'd confiscate it. I stack two boxes together and climb on top of them. As I suspected, the lightweight tiles that form the ceiling of the cupboard can be pushed upwards out of place. I slide the book into the airspace above and drop the tile back down. I put the boxes straight and click the cupboard door closed. I've got a hiding place. That's another small victory.

22

For two days no one but Kay even notices my bowl. Then Rex and a couple of Reds appear outside my pod at dinner-time.

'What's that?' Rex says.

'If you're asking about the food, I've got no idea of its content or origins. If you're asking about the bowl, it's a bowl.'

He narrows his eyes at me. 'Why have you got a bow?'

'I've got a *bowl* because I don't like eating with my hands.'

Rex sniggers and the other two join in. 'You don't eat with hands, you eat with mouth, you no-ranker.'

I consider pointing out that technically I do have a rank, but I'm not sure where this little chat is going so I keep my mouth shut.

'This Special thinks he's big good, doesn't he?' Rex says.

'He doesn't like doing what Specials do,' one of the goons says.

I'd like to leave this conversation, but Rex has caught the attention of the Specials in the pods around us. They've finished eating and they're coming out to have a look at what's going on.

Rex loves a crowd. 'He doesn't want to eat like a Special or fight like a Special,' he says to the onlookers.

The gathering group make noises of agreement. Am I going to get thrashed by this whole gang? I look through the partition for Kay, but she's not there.

'He's got a *bowl*. Look at his *bowl*. He thinks he's more good than Rex, so he's got a *bowl*. Do you think you're the goodest, Blakey?'

More Specials have gathered around. They're waiting for something to happen. I look up and see Kay in the crowd. She's watching too. I don't know why, but I don't want the ginger ape making me look stupid in front of her.

'I don't think I'm better,' I say. 'I don't think I'm really good. I just think that I – that *we* – should have some things. They keep us in these pods like we're Wilderness or like we're animals. And they make us bend down and suck on unclean nozzles.' I plough on, trying to keep my language simple. 'I don't like the enforcers. I don't think they should tell us how to be and hurt us. I can't tell the enforcers they're wrong by hitting them. I'm not strong or brave like Lanc, but I can refuse to be treated like an animal. I don't have this bowl because I think I'm more good. I have it because I think we should all have one.'

There's a silence. Rex is thinking.

'I want one,' says someone. It's Ilex. 'I want a bowl to tell the enforcers they can't make me eat that animal way.'

'I want one too,' says one of the little ones.

And then they all start talking and calling out. Saying we should have bowls and that we're not animals and that we shouldn't do everything the enforcers want.

'SHUT UP!' bawls Rex. 'It's a right thing that we show the enforcers we don't do all things that they say.' He nods at them as if he is doing the convincing. 'I am Rex and I help the Specials. I'll get you bowls.'

The Specials erupt in cheering and a bevy of gushing girls surround Rex as he swaggers off.

Amazing. Not a word to me. No one seems to remember I'm here, let alone that this was my idea. I glance up and find myself looking right into Kay's eyes. I notice for the first time that they're very dark blue. I look down and step out of my pod. I don't mean to look at her again, but somehow I can't stop myself. She's smiling. I think she's laughing at me.

'That's a good bowl,' she says.

I unstick my eyes from hers and focus on her left shoulder. I can't think of anything to say, so I nod my head.

'Is it that they eat like that in the Wilderness?' she says.

'What?'

'You said nozzle eating is like Wilderness.'

'Well, I don't actually know how they eat. I think they just club things to death and eat them raw.'

She looks at me hard.

I shuffle my feet.

'*Do your duty, do your best or you'll be sent to the Wilderness,*' she sings.

My eyebrows shoot up. 'Do Specials say that too?'

She nods. It's incredible that the only thing in here that seems to have any connection with my old life is a creepy rhyme about the Wilderness.

'What do you know about the Wilderness?' I ask. For a daft moment I think that maybe she'll know more about those rumours of terrorists hiding in the Wilderness amongst the criminals and the crazies, but instead she says, 'They send the trouble Specials out to the Wilderness.'

I remember what Ilex said about the Reds getting people sent out to the Wilderness. Maybe there was some truth in it.

Kay is studying me. She puts her head on one side. 'Don't be trouble all the times,' she says and disappears into the thinning crowd.

Ilex comes over and slaps me on the back. 'What is Kay saying? Is she saying you're crimson and all?' He pulls a kissy face at me.

'No,' I say, pushing him off. 'I think she was warning me.'

128

23

After dinner on Wednesday, Ilex meets me outside my pod.

'Come to Fight Night with me?' he says.

I screw up my face. 'I don't want to watch little kids fight.'

'It's Ali,' Ilex says. He doesn't know the word 'please', but there's a 'please' all over his face. 'She's not a good hitter. And she can't talk the tough words. I'm all . . . I don't know the word. What's the word?'

'You're worried,' I say.

He nods his head.

'All right, okay, I'll come just to watch Ali.'

We walk down to the drum-shaped room. Ali is waiting for Ilex outside. She raises her hand in greeting to me. I smile at her. She's pale, but she doesn't look nearly as nervous as Ilex. Inside the drum room there are Specials shouting and laughing and shoving each other to find a seat in the rapidly filling tiers. I move towards an empty section in the middle centre. Ali grabs my arm.

'That's for Reds,' Ilex says.

Dom is sprawled along the bench, giggling with two younger, red-headed girls. She looks at me and whispers something to the girls, who burst out laughing. I let Ilex pull me away to squash on to a bench over to the right.

I find myself scanning the room, looking for a white-blonde head. I find Kay sat a few rows behind Dom, on the edge of the Reds crowd. I try to catch her eye, but she's busy talking to an Hon Red girl from our class, Flavia. Kay's doing strange things with her face. Moving it into different expressions. Smiling. Giggling. She doesn't look like herself.

Rex strolls into the room, accompanied by a pack of attentive girls. Some of them can't be more than thirteen. Kay's head snaps round to watch him. I don't know what she sees in him.

'How did Rex get to be in charge?' I ask Ilex.

He turns to look at me.

'I know about the hair,' I say. 'But Mark in our class has got red hair.'

'Rex fighted him.'

'What about Pete? He's sort of ginger and he's just as big and ugly as Rex.'

'Rex fighted him too.'

'So it's about brute force then?'

Ilex lifts his hands in question. He doesn't understand.

'I mean strength. The Red who wins the most fights?'

Ilex screws up his mouth. 'It's some about fighting.

But we all knowed Rex would be the boss. The old boss was all times talking to him and saying him things to do.'

'I see. They trained him up, did they? What about Dom? Did you know about her?'

'Nah. Rex chose Dom. The boss boy chooses the boss girl.'

'How old-fashioned. Why did he choose her?'

Ilex laughs and indicates with his eyes across the room to where Dom is lounging across her seat. Even with her neat baby bump, she is arresting. Unlike most of the girls she is wearing a skirt rather than the regulation trousers. I can't imagine where she got it or why the enforcers allow her to wear it. But then, as far as I can tell, she doesn't seem to have got into any trouble for being pregnant. It seems like the enforcers let Dom and Rex get away with anything.

It's hard not to stare at Dom's long slim legs. She moves to her feet and stretches up so that her breasts strain against her shirt and her glossy hair ripples down her back. I look away.

'She's not really very red-headed,' I say. It's true. She's practically blonde with just a hint of copper.

'Rex says she's a Red.'

I remember Kay's ambitions. 'Does Rex have to choose a Red to be Dom?'

'No. He just chooses. Dom goes to work at the factory soon. So Rex chooses a new Dom. There aren't big lots of big girl Reds so he chooses any girl he wants.'

I look around the room. He's right. Almost all of the red-headed girls are sat in the central seats. There aren't many of them and only a handful of those are senior girls. This whole Reds thing makes sense in a way. Ginger hair is rare and it's not like they've got much else to prize around here.

Rex peels himself away from his band of admirers and strides into the centre of the fight floor.

'Specials!' he shouts. 'Let's see some fighting. Come on little Specials, be big good!'

The audience cheers. What is wrong with this lot? Who wants to see children tearing strips off each other?

'First fighter is . . . Ali!'

I expect Ali to hang back or even to cling to Ilex, but she stands up and makes her way calmly down to the centre of the floor.

'Ali fights Urva!'

Ali's opponent springs out of her seat and skitters down the steps. Her hair is scraped back from her face in a ponytail so tight it looks painful. She's got a sharp nose and tiny eyes. She looks like a rat. She reaches the centre of the room and swipes out an arm at Ali's head. Ali ducks out of the way.

'Hey!' Ilex shouts. 'It's not fight start. You wait!'

Rex stands in between the two little girls, smirking. He can barely contain his amusement. He takes Urva's chin in his hand. She beams at him.

'Look at the teeth!' Rex says.

Urva snaps playfully at him.

I look at Ilex. His shoulders are tensed up and his hands are twisted together.

'Start fight!' Rex shouts.

Urva launches herself at Ali with her arms flailing. Ali stares at her with wide eyes. She puts out her hands, but she is knocked to the floor. Urva rolls on top of her and smacks her about the face. Ali manages to twist out from under her. She gets to feet and backs away. Urva scrambles across the floor and tries to grab Ali by the ankles. Ali stamps on her hand.

'Efwurder!' shrieks Urva. She yanks her hand away.

Ali's face remains smooth. She looks down at Urva thrashing and turns away.

Urva is furious. 'You think you're a brainer. You notalker!' She leaps at Ali's back. She wraps her arms around Ali's throat and brings her crashing to the ground.

Ilex half rises in his seat.

The girls roll over and over. Urva struggles into the on-top position. She pins Ali's arms down. All the time she snarls and spits insults at Ali. Ali stares back at her and then turns her face away as if she is nothing to do with this fight.

Then there's a tangle of limbs and a high-pitched shriek and I can't make out what's happening.

Out of the blur Ali manages to lift her head. She puts a hand to her face. She's got blood on her cheek.

Ilex stands up and pushes his way between Specials. 'Stop!' he shouts. 'Rex! Stop her.'

He's not the only one on their feet. The boy I fought, Deon, wades into the chaos of Urva's flying arms and pulls her out by the scruff of her neck. Ilex reaches the floor, but Rex rushes up behind him and pushes him out of the way. Rex blows his whistle. He takes Urva from Deon by lifting her by her belt. Her feet hang just above the floor, but she's still trying to fight. She bicycles her legs and stretches out clawed fingers in an attempt to get at Ali.

Ali stands just out of reach. Watching.

'What is it?' I ask the little boy sat next to me. 'Why have they stopped?' It can't be the blood. I've seen Specials come back to the dormitory covered in blood after these fights. No one seemed to mind.

The boy looks me up and down. I wonder if he's going to bother to answer me at all.

'No weapons,' he says.

No weapons? I look back at the fight floor. Rex is prising something out of Urva's hand. It catches the light. It looks like a jagged piece of shrap.

'Are weapons against the rules?' I ask.

The boy nods.

I'm surprised. I never imagined the Specials would have rules.

'Well, that's something,' I say. 'At least I won't be knifed in my bed.'

The boy stares. He snorts. 'No weapons in the fight room. If they want to bed-knife you, they can.'

He turns back to his friends.

Oh.

Ilex lumbers along our row and sits down beside me again.

'That Urva,' he says. 'She's . . . she's a . . .' he looks at me.

'A cheating little rat?'

'Yes. A cheatin' lilrat.'

Rex blows his whistle again to silence the raucous Specials.

'All Specials,' he says. 'No weapons in fights!'

Some of the Specials mutter in disapproval. King Hell, what would it be like if they *were* allowed knives on the fight floor?

Rex leans towards Urva, who is tight-lipped and scowling. 'You get weapons, little girl, then you get a lose.'

He lifts up Ali's arm and the crowd cheers.

Ali walks towards the seats.

'No talker!' shouts Urva.

Ali blinks, then turns back to the furious girl. She pushes a fist into her palm then points downwards with two fingers in a quick gesture. Some of the younger Specials burst out laughing.

'What does that mean?' I ask Ilex.

Ilex smiles. 'It means loser.'

I can tell by the expression of rage on Urva's face that she already knows that.

* * *

We don't stay to watch the rest of the fights. Ilex thinks Ali should rest, so we head back to the dormitories.

'Where did Urva get that shrap from anyway?' I ask out loud. 'She didn't have it at the start of the fight, did she?'

Ali taps her chest.

'It was yours?'

She nods.

'You wore a nice sharp bit of shrap dangling around your neck where Urva could grab it and use it on your face?'

She looks up at me. I realise from the look she gives me that it was no accident that she was wearing a dangerous piece of shrap. She wanted Urva to find it. Wow.

'Weren't you afraid she'd hurt you?' I say.

She gives me the kind of smile that teachers do when you've asked a question that shows you've completely misunderstood. She hugs Ilex good night and goes into her dormitory.

'I don't think you need to worry about Ali so much,' I say to Ilex.

Ilex crumples his forehead.

'I mean, don't think bad things will happen to Ali. She might not be able to punch or to talk, but she really knows how to fight.'

24

A few days later I'm lying on my bed looking at Kay sitting crosslegged on hers. I'm worn out. Today a group of Specials have really been winding me up. Once a Red starts making stupid comments then everyone joins in. I'm an easy target because I'm different. They call me 'brainer' and 'no-ranker' and then the pushing and shoving starts. I would never have thought that imbecilic remarks from morons would upset me, but it's really starting to get to me. I'm at the bottom of the pile here and I don't like it.

When I first arrived I thought that the only advantage of being a Red was extra food. I can see now that it means a lot more to the Specials. If you're a Red it affects everything. People listen to you and respect you. When you walk down the corridors people move out of the way. At Fight Nights you can choose any seat you want and, once you're sat down, everyone vies for your attention. The older Reds have the opposite sex fighting for their favour.

Even the enforcers treat the Reds better. I'm starting to understand why Kay wants to climb the Red ladder, but I'm not prepared to suck up to them. It seems that I'm the only one who thinks like that though. The other Specials don't resent the Reds at all. In fact, the Reds are treated like celebrities. In their spare time Specials gossip about the Reds' relationships and the power structure. People are already betting on who Rex will choose to replace Dom when she turns seventeen in a couple of months and goes to the factory.

The six o'clock Saturday buzzer sounded a little while ago and everyone else cleared out of the dormitory. I'm grateful to have a bit of time away from people. The buzzer signals the start of something they call the Making Hour. I think it's a bit like the Creativity group at the Learning Community. It's not compulsory and I'm not really into making things out of raffia so I've never been, but I'm glad it's so popular because it means that Kay and I are the only Specials left in the dormitory. We're in the dark; the light from the landing sends a shaft into the room, but it only reaches the first bed in a long line. I can hear the hum of a generator below me.

Kay is shadowy except for her pale, shining hair. I wonder what it would be like to stroke it. Probably soft and silky. Kay turns to look at me and blood rushes to my face. I don't know why I'm having thoughts like this about Kay. But increasingly I find myself thinking about her. I imagine her resting a small cool hand on my cheek.

Looking up at me with her dark blue eyes, then sliding her hand down my neck and over my chest and . . .

'Blake?'

Whoa. I roll quickly on to my front and press my burning cheek against the pillow. 'Hmm?' I say as casually as I can manage.

'What's your think?'

'I . . .' A vision of Kay wrapped in a white towel flashes into my mind. Oh no. I am *not* thinking about that. 'I was thinking about . . . our learning sessions.' Nothing sexy about Enforcer Tong.

'What about them?' She draws her knees up to her chest.

I bite my thumb. 'Well, ah, it's not exactly a varied curriculum is it?'

'You're talking big words again,' she tuts.

'I'm just saying I think we should be learning more.'

'Why are you all times talking about learning? I told you they don't want us to do brainer-learning they want us to be quiet-learn.'

'Well I wasn't suggesting that we study Boolean algebra.'

Kay scowls. 'Boo yourself.'

'All we ever do is assembly of parts and electronics. Maybe we could speak to someone about broadening the subject range,' I say.

Kay rolls her eyes.

'I mean maybe we could ask them to teach us some other things.'

139

'You're funny.' Kay shakes her head at me. 'It's . . .' She pauses and looks to the ceiling, 'It's . . . nice, like a little kid who thinks all people are good when you say, "we could ask them". Little-kid-nice, but stupid. You'll say we could ask them for burgers and chips in the feeding pods.'

'How do you know about burgers and chips?' I ask.

'On the Info I saw a factory where Academy kids go. In the salon they had a burger thing. The good workers get burgers.'

Given what I've seen of the Info that is broadcast in here I wonder if this is true or just another special newsreel created for Academies.

'I'd like a burger,' Kay says.

'If you've never had a burger how do you know you'd like one?'

'I know it. It looks good eating. Have you had a burger?'

We used to have burgers every Wednesday at the Learning Community.

'Yes, I've eaten a burger,' I say.

Kay's eyes light up. 'Was it good?'

I think about my table in the cafeteria at the Willows; the sun coming in the window, the sound of cutlery chinking on real china plates, and so much food. Anything you wanted: curry, pie, pasta, sandwiches, fruit, pizza, salad. Stacks of it, for you to just help yourself. Now I've seen Academy slop I realise why people think kids at the Learning Community are so privileged. At the time we

140

were all so busy talking about our latest projects that often I hardly noticed what I was eating. I remember Mel Ross, a girl in my Science group, was worried about putting on weight, so she'd leave most of her food. I think of her plate with a juicy burger and golden chips. Specials would kill to have food like that and we all just took it for granted.

'Was it good eating?' Kay asks me again.

'It was good. It was really good.'

Kay sighs and flops back on her bed with her hands behind her head. She's rolled her sleeves right up and I find myself looking at the pale skin on the inside of her upper arms.

'I tell you what, Kay. One day I am going to take you for a burger,' I say suddenly.

She laughs. 'That's a can't-won't. I'm going to stop hearing you; you put bad thinks . . . I mean, bad thoughts in my head. But you make me laugh.'

I puff out my breath. I know that the Leadership wants us to equip ourselves to fulfil our potential, but what does that really mean? Would it matter if Kay learned Algebra? And why shouldn't she have a burger?

'It just doesn't seem fair that they only teach you things that are useful for the electronics factory. Why can't you have some choice in your job?'

'What work do the Learning Community brainers do?'

'They're employed in the Leadership.'

'All the brainers are working for the Leadership?'

'Well, yes, but you could do lots of different things. Be an adviser, run a department, be a local leader, head an industry—'

'I don't know those things. Is it all for the Leadership?'

'Yes.'

'So no choice-ing for the brainers too.'

I feel a rush of annoyance. 'It's not the same thing. And anyway I'm trying to ask you about the Academy curriculum; do you ever do any text-based work?'

Kay stiffens. 'You keep doing it! You make me feel like nozzle crust. I don't know your big words.'

I screw up my face. 'Sorry. Sometimes I just open my mouth and . . . I just wanted to know, do you ever do any reading or writing?' I say.

Kay lifts her hands then slaps them down on her blanket. 'King Hell, Blake! You don't get it. They don't want reader-writer-brainers, they want factory workers. You can't have little-kid-nice thoughts all the time. Reading is trouble. Readers get . . .' She raises her hands again and moves them as if she's shaking me. 'They get . . .' She curls her fists. '*Urrr*! I don't know your big words!' She slams a fist backwards into the headboard. 'That's what readers get!' Then she throws herself on to her front and yanks her blanket over her head. 'Take me for a burger! Stupid!' she says.

And that's when I first realise: she can't read.

None of them can.

25

'I could teach you to read,' I say.

The lump under the blanket doesn't reply.

'No need to thank me. I don't mind giving up my time to help you,' I say.

'I don't need a help from you,' she says from under the covers.

'I didn't need any help from you in that fight.'

Kay flings off her covers. 'You did need a help. He was killing you.'

'Speaking of near-death experiences, what about that night in the kitchen? You let me help you then.'

Kay sticks out her chin. 'You can give me helps when it's a danger thing—'

'That's very gracious of you.'

'But reading is trouble. I don't want trouble.'

'Why is it trouble?'

'You know the things they do to Specials who do the things that the Academy don't want them to do.'

I do know. I've seen Lanc's face. I've smelled the singed hair of Specials when they receive electric shocks and I've heard the screams coming from the LER room. And what about being sent to the Wilderness? Would they really do that to someone just because they tried to learn how to read? I'm starting to think that they would. It makes me wonder about all the other people who get sent to the Wilderness. Do they deserve it?

'What is it?' Kay asks.

'I'm trying to understand why they wouldn't like it. Why it is that they don't teach you to read?' I say.

'We don't need to read to be a factory worker.'

'Everybody needs to learn to read.'

Kay pulls a face.

'Okay, what you're saying is that being a factory worker is the only job where you don't have to be able to read. So, if they don't let you learn to read then you can't become anything else other than a factory worker,' I say.

'What's "else"?'

'I mean you can only be a factory worker. If you can't read then you can't choose what you want to be.'

'We talked this before. I'm a Special. I don't get a *choose*. It's not a thing if I can read or if I can't read.'

'I guess that's what they want you to think, but I don't understand it. I mean if it doesn't matter, why would they try so hard to make sure you *don't* learn?'

She shrugs.

I think about all that stuff to do with potential again. I

don't see how anyone here gets to fulfil their potential, because the people running Academies have put a limit on what Specials can achieve. It's stupid.

'I think it's because they're afraid,' I say. 'You know – scared. If Specials learn to read you can learn more things, find stuff out, read about other people – different ways of living. Realise that you should not be treated the way that you are. Maybe they don't want you to learn to read because it would give you power.'

'You can get *power* from reading?'

'Yes. Yes, you really can.'

She pauses to consider this.

'Can you teach me all quiet and no telling?' she says finally.

'Yes, I can teach you in secret.'

She nods quickly.

I'm not really sure how to start, but then I think of Wilson's poetry book. I've never taught anyone to read, but I imagine the alphabet is the best place to start.

I go and get the book from my hiding place and bring it back to Kay. I open the book to the first page and point to the letter A.

'That's one,' Kay says.

'Yes, it's the first letter of the alphabet.'

'No, that goes with number one.'

She can see I don't understand.

'And this . . .' she finds a B and points to it. 'This is the two.'

'Second letter, yes. How do you know that? Do you know the third?'

She points to a C.

'Where—?'

'On the door code thing.'

Of course. All of the doors have keypads with both letters and numbers on. A is on the same key as 1.

Kay carries on pointing out letters in order and I tell her their names and sounds. She goes right through the alphabet.

'How did you do that?' I say.

'I just think-back the things, the letters, and how they go.' She draws a line from left to right in the air.

'You remembered what order they came in?'

'Yes.'

'Just from looking at the door-code keypads? Even though you didn't know the letter names?'

'Yes.'

'Even though they must have looked like random symbols to you, some of them with only minor differences to differentiate them and even though there are twenty-six of them and you were mostly only close enough to see them in the night, when it's dark?'

She laughs. 'I don't know what you're saying.' She smiles at me and my stomach flips over. 'What is it you think?' she says.

'I'm thinking you won't need too many lessons before you can read.'

I'm right. Kay is very quick and she's soon sounding out words. When Ilex hears about the lessons he wants to learn too. So he and Ali join us for every session. We have to find quiet corners to hide in so that no one finds out. Ilex is plodding and methodical, but he's getting there. It's difficult with Ali as she still doesn't talk. I have to ask her a lot of yes/no questions to gauge whether she has understood. I feel sure that she could speak. I try to get her just to make some noises to start with, but it doesn't work. She gets frustrated and tearful.

'It's okay, Ali,' Ilex says. 'The thing you want to say is, "Ilex is the goodest".'

'You mean "best",' I say.

'Yes,' he says. 'Ali wants to say, "Ilex is the best brother." You don't need saying it. I know it.'

This makes Ali laugh and smack her fist against her hand and then point two fingers downwards. It's the 'loser' sign that she did to Urva. It gives me an idea.

'Hey Ali, do you know any more signs?'

Ali's eyes flick sideways to Ilex. She shakes her head.

'I do. Shall I teach you some?'

When I was a baby my mother used to sign to me to encourage me to communicate before I could talk. It worked. She's always going on about how I could ask for 'more food' in sign language before the other kids my age had said their first word. We kept it up even after I learned to talk; we've used it less and less as I've got older, but I still remember a lot and when I don't know the correct sign to show Ali I just make one up. At first Ali is shy, but soon she's joining in with our conversations.

'You know what would really help us?' I ask one night when we're having a lesson crammed in a toilet cubicle just to be on the safe side.

More books? signs Ali.

'Burgers and chips?' Kay says.

I look at her. She gets this look like a naughty elf when she's taking the mickey. I pretend to scowl.

'What?' Ilex says.

'What?' I say absently, still looking at Kay.

'What would help?' Ilex says.

'Oh. A pen. Or a pencil.'

What's that? signs Ali.

Turns out that none of them have ever seen, or even heard of, a pen or a pencil. Although I shouldn't be surprised, they wouldn't be much use here. It's so strange what the Academies don't have; things I'd taken for

148

granted just don't exist to Specials. At the Learning Community, pens were left lying around on desks. At home we had a fat clay pot stuffed with them. Sometimes my mother would stick one in her hair, to hold up her messy bun.

I do my best to describe what a pen looks like to the others, 'We should all keep our eyes open for one. Then you could practise writing as well as reading.'

Ali nods.

'Yes,' Ilex says.

Kay looks at me solemnly.

I feel proud of my little class.

After Ilex drops Ali off at her dormitory he comes to sit on my bed. Kay is off chatting to Red girls who have just come back from one of their Red meetings.

'Ali likes reading,' Ilex says.

'Yep, and she's doing really well . . .' I pause. It's sweet the way Ilex cares for Ali – in the Learning Community no one took much notice of their siblings. But there's something that has been bothering me about Ali. She's a lot younger than Ilex; when he started at the Academy, at five, she wouldn't have even been born. And it's not like the Academy kids are ever let home for visits. 'Ilex? How do you know that Ali is your sister?'

'She is. I know it. She is my sister.' His whole body has gone tense.

'Okay, okay. I believe you, I do. I just wondered because, you know, when you left your parents she

149

wouldn't have been born – she wouldn't have been a baby. Do you understand what I mean?'

He stares at me and I'm not sure whether he hasn't understood what I'm asking or if he doesn't want to answer. He looks around when a couple of boys walk past, as if he's hoping for an interruption.

'Don't worry,' I say. 'It's none of my business, it doesn't mat—'

'It's the name,' he blurts out. 'Ali has my name. Not the Ilex name but the Dalton name. Ilex Dalton and Ali Dalton. I know she's my sister.'

That doesn't really answer my question, but he looks so uncomfortable that I want to let it go. Ilex and Ali both have someone to care about them. That's not the case for most Specials. 'Of course she's your sister,' I say.

The next day in the grid something is different. Usually when we come in, Enforcer Tong shouts at us for pushing, then tells us to start our first task on the computer while she becomes absorbed in her own screen. But today she's stood up in her cage waiting for us to settle. She's going to say something.

'Quiet,' she says.

No one was talking anyway, but now no one moves.

'Specials, I have a good thing to say.'

The thing I hate most about Tong is this simple way she talks to us. It's like she thinks Specials are so low that she won't even share her vocabulary with them.

150

'Lots of people are happy with Academies. They like the good factory workers that we make at Academies. They say that our factory workers are the best. So twelve more Academies are being made. Soon they will be opened and there will be a . . .'

She searches for basic words. 'A good time with food for you.'

There's a murmur of excitement.

'Quiet. The Leader is happy about the new Academies. On the good time day he wants to come to an Academy and talk to some of the Specials and put it on the Info.' She pauses and flicks her eyes around the room like a searchlight to ensure that she has everyone's attention. 'It's good because The Leader is coming to this Academy!'

Enforcer Tong looks at us expectantly. I don't know what she's expecting. If she wanted a round of applause she probably shouldn't have taught us that the slightest noise earns an electric shock. I keep my face smooth, but inside I feel a surge of hope. If The Leader is coming here I can speak to him. Tell him what's happened to me. He could sort it out. He can do anything.

'Well, you should all think about how lucky you are,' says Tong. She sits down and turns to her computer. 'Now start your work.'

The room is quiet again.

'MORE EFWURDING ACADEMIES?' someone shouts.

I turn round in my seat. It came from the back.

'Who said . . . ?' Tong springs to her feet. She reaches for the shock controls.

There's the sound of scraping metal as a compartment door is wrenched open. Tong must have forgotten to lock the doors.

'We don't want more Academies. We don't want more efwurding enforcers . . .'

'LANC! Sit down now!' Tong is frantically stabbing the shock button, but Lanc must have taken off his EMDs because it doesn't stop him talking.

'Stupid, no ranker enforcers who hit kids . . .'

I can see Lanc's head and shoulders above the walls of the grid now. He's striding towards Tong's cage. She shrinks back into the corner and hits the alarm.

Lanc reaches the front. Behind him someone else is out of their seat. It's Ilex. He puts a hand on Lanc's shoulder to stop him, but Lanc shrugs him off. Then Kay is there too, tying to talk to him. I scramble out of my compartment to help and some of the other Specials follow. Then everything happens very quickly.

I see Tong's face stretched in fear. Lanc turns sideways and slides something out of his sleeve. A stick. With something shining on the end. He thrusts it through one of the gaps in the cage and Tong screams. She's got blood on her hands. The door slams open. The classroom fills with impeccables and a bellowing Rice. Most of the class have climbed out of their seats. I try to pull an impeccable wielding a truncheon off of Ilex. I take a hit on the shoulder and fall backwards into the narrow aisle. Someone crashes down on top of me. Rice. I put out my hands to push his chest away from me. He scrambles to his feet, pulls me up by my collar and hands me to an impeccable, who hauls me out of the class. At the door I twist back and see that there are only a handful of Specials left fighting. In the centre, balanced on top of the grid wall is Lanc. He swings his weapon at the two impeccables trying to bring him down.

'NO MORE ACADEMIES!' he screams. His eyes are blazing. I think he's lost his mind.

I'm dragged down the corridors and taken through a door next to the LER room. It leads to a long narrow passage with what look like animal cages branching off on either side. I'm thrown in one of these cages. There's barely room to sit down. I can't see any of my classmates, but I can hear them shouting and swearing.

The absurdity of my situation suddenly strikes me like a blow between the eyes. What is happening to me? I'm a Learning Community student with an AEP score of 98.5 being trained to be part of the Leadership. What the efwurd am I doing in a cage? I've been in this awful place for weeks. This mess should have been sorted out by now. What's happened to my mother? Isn't she ever coming to get me? I'm so angry that I do what the other Specials around me are doing and kick the door of the cage over and over again.

When my rage is finally spent I'm horribly tired. The Specials have quietened down too. While I'm slumped there, waiting to find out what Rice will do to us, I make a decision: I'll hang on for one more week for my mother and then I simply have to think of my own escape plan.

Hours later, two impeccables return and start taking us out of the cages one by one. When it's my turn, they push and shove me through the Academy until we reach Rice's office. He keeps his back turned while the impeccables sit me in a chair facing his desk and stuff my hands through EMD bracelets. I can feel sweat forming under my arms. He's going to hurt me.

'Specials must not leave the grid during a lesson,' Rice says. He's not even looking at me. He taps the control pad. It's like being hit by a truck. A thousand needles of pain fizz through me. When it stops, my teeth are ringing.

'Specials must not fight.' He hits the button.

I'm smacked back in my chair again. I think I'm going to be sick.

He puts down the pad and starts to turn away, but stops and looks at me full on for the first time. He picks up the pad.

'And I told you to keep out of trouble.' He hits the button.

And then he hits it again.

* * *

I stagger up to the dormitory. I feel like my wrists have been in a vice. Kay is lying motionless on top of her blanket. She's even paler than usual. How could anyone shock Kay?

'Are you all right?' I ask, sitting down on her bed. It's a stupid question.

She doesn't answer.

'You know Rice landed on top of me during that fight? He weighs a ton. Really sharp elbows. And his jacket pocket was right in my face and . . .' I'm rambling. 'Well, look. I got this for you.' I hold out the biro that I grabbed from Rice's pocket during our grapple.

Kay takes it and turns it over in her hands.

'It's nice,' she says, but she doesn't look at me.

'What is it, Kay?'

'Lanc's not back.'

'I guess his punishment will be lasting a bit longer,' I say.

'No. Rice told Ilex that Lanc won't come back.'

I struggle to imagine what exactly this means. Will he be sent to another Academy? Or to the Wilderness?

Kay puts a hand on mine. 'Give me a lesson,' she says.

'You want a reading lesson now?'

'I need one.'

Kay is right. We don't see Lanc again. And nobody tells us where he's gone. I sink into a depression after the whole incident dies down. I'd been kidding myself that somehow everything would get sorted out. But now I feel like everything is wrong. Why doesn't my mother come? I'm starting to doubt that she'll be able to help. I don't even know if The Leader can help.

One good thing is that we don't see Tong again either. I wonder if she quit or if she was pushed out. Instead of Tong we have Rice covering our sessions. We barely dare breathe.

Kay doesn't get depressed like me. Instead she gets angry. She's furious with Rice and all the enforcers about what happened to Lanc. It makes her fiercely determined to learn to read, if only to spite them. She starts recruiting others to learn. I want to give up on the whole thing, but Kay won't hear of it. She reminds me of every argument that I made to her when we started. I let her talk me into it.

Five days after the Lanc episode, we're kept waiting outside the grid longer than usual. Finally the door opens. As we enter there's a ripple through the classroom and for a second I think that Tong must be back, but then I look up at the teacher's enclosure and I realise why there is a stir in the class.

We've got a new enforcer.

It's my mother.

27

She's here. She's finally here. I knew she'd come, but I still can't believe it. I stop, staring at the side of her face. Someone behind bumps into me.

'Move it, Blake!'

I stumble towards my compartment unable to take my eyes off her. I want to shout *Mum!* but I can't make a sound.

Then she sees me.

She rises from her seat and reaches out an arm towards me before she knows what she's doing. In that second I realise that we're both in danger. We can't let anyone know that we know each other.

So without showing any emotion I say, 'Yes, enforcer?'

She sinks back into her seat. My mother isn't stupid so she says, 'You should be seated by now.'

And I know we understand each other.

The other Specials are whispering. A new enforcer is a big deal.

'Silence,' Mother says. 'I am Enforcer Williams and this morning I will show you how to transfer information from storage to processor and then you will complete transfer exercises yourself. Before we start, make sure your EMDs are on,' she says.

She says it just right. Firmly and matter of factly, like she expects it to happen. But she's lifting her jaw a little higher than normal. I can tell that she's afraid.

Mother takes us through an example of information transfer. I barely hear her. Part of me is happy that she is so close. I want to rush up to her and hug her, but the rest of me knows that this is a dangerous situation. Enforcers only survive if they are cold and hard and hate the Specials. My mother is way too kind to be here. They'll tear her apart.

I try to concentrate on the numbers on my screen, but my eyes keep drifting up to look at her. She turns and catches my eye. She widens her eyes slightly, but I don't know what she means. She brings her palms together under her chin. It's not a gesture I remember her using. He eyes have gone back to her screen, but she separates then draws her palms together again.

I get it. She's signing to me. Palms drawn together means meet. She wants to meet me. Still focusing on her screen she shifts so that her chin is leaning on the back of one of her hands. After a moment she extends her forefinger so it is pointing downwards. Here. Meet here. Her eyes flick to me to check she still has my attention and she

158

moves her hand so it's supporting her cheek. But only two fingers are raised. Two o'clock. In the morning, I suppose.

My insides surge upwards. I want to be able to talk to her so much. I want to ask her what I should do. I know that it's risky. For both of us. But I have to see her, so the next time she darts a look in my direction I give the tiniest nod.

When we're dismissed for lunch I pull Kay right into the middle of the surging scrum of Specials and whisper in her ear, 'She's my mother. Our new enforcer is my mother.'

Kay's eyes bulge. 'Don't say it more times. Don't say to any Special,' she says.

'I won't,' I say.

'And don't do a wrong thing. Don't get into trouble.'

'I'll be careful,' I say.

Kay squeezes my hand and for a moment I feel nothing but happy.

I work hard not to look at Mother for the rest of the day. I'm tired out by the time we go to the dining hall for dinner, but once I'm in my pod I let out a long breath and try to relax a little. We rarely see the enforcers in the evening so hopefully Mother is safe from any difficult situations for the time being. I'm secretly hoping that she has a really good plan that will mean she and I and Kay, Ilex and Ali will soon be leaving this place, but I doubt that things are going to be that straight forward.

I spend the evening with Ilex and Ali. Ali looks pale. Ilex shows me where a chunk of her hair is missing. He's afraid that someone is picking on her, but Ali refuses to communicate about it. I look at their miserable faces. They need cheering up. I decide to tell them about my mother and how we'll all be able to escape soon.

Blake's mum is enforcer? signs Ali. Her eyes are wide with horror.

160

'She's not a bad enforcer. She's an okay enforcer like Enforcer Baxter,' Ilex says.

Enforcer Baxter is Ali's class enforcer. She's not as vicious as some of the others. She rarely uses the EMDs. I'm glad that Ilex can see that my mum isn't a monster. She's having to act tough, but you can still see that she's fair. Not like Tong.

'I didn't know your mum does enforcer work,' Ilex says.

'She doesn't,' I say.

'Why is she enforcering here, then?'

'She's come to get me,' I whisper, even though we're alone. 'She's come to rescue me. And you two and Kay.'

Ali looks questioningly at Ilex.

Ilex looks back at her. 'That's what mums do. They want you to be in the goodest place, I mean, the best place. What they think is the best place, that's where they try to make you be.'

I'm not entirely sure what he's going on about, but Ali seems to understand because eventually she nods her head.

'Bed for Ali,' Ilex stands up. 'It's a good for you to have your mum,' he says to me and leads Ali out of the dormitory.

That's not exactly the response I was hoping for when I told them that we're going to escape.

I get into bed at nine-thirty when the senior Specials' buzzer goes. Five minutes later the dormitory door is closed and locked. I've got no idea how I'm going to stay awake till two.

'Kay?' I say.

'Mmm?'

'What was your mum like?'

There's a long pause. 'I don't know. I can think-back her hair, it was like my hair. But I can't think-back more times with my mum.'

'Oh. I'm sorry. Do you remember anything about before you took the Potential Test and came to the Academy?'

Kay gives a sleepy groan. 'I don't know your words, Blake. What's Potential Test?'

'You know, the exam, when you're five years old they test you and—'

'No.' She yawns. 'I didn't do testing.'

'But everybody does the test. And then you get your score and they place you in the school where you can best fulfil your potential. Or, at least, that's what they say.' I haven't seen any encouraging of potential since I arrived here. 'Don't you remember?'

She doesn't reply. She's asleep. She must have forgotten. She said herself that she doesn't remember when she was little. Probably lots of people don't recall the actual test. That doesn't mean that they didn't take it. Otherwise, how would they know where to send you to school? That's why everybody takes the Potential Test.

Don't they?

After a while the whispered conversations in the dormitory die down. I try to keep my mind working. I run through the periodic table and then all the speeches I can remember from Hamlet. Kay's breathing is deep and regular. I imagine her pale hair spreading across the pillow and I think about pushing down her blanket and revealing her bare shoulders and . . . That is not a helpful line of thought to take. Although, I'm certainly not feeling sleepy now.

I wait a little longer and decide I may as well be in the classroom, where at least I will be able to see the time.

I ease myself out of bed. It's impossible to know whether everyone in the room is asleep, but have to assume that if they notice me they'll think I'm going to pee.

The floor of the bathroom is icy on my bare feet. I should have kept my socks on. I check that the cubicles are empty before keying the code into the door and slipping out on to the landing.

163

Downstairs, I hesitate in front of the door to our grid. I'm always a little worried that, somewhere on a computer, door openings are recorded. I could wait till my mother arrives, but really the classroom is a much better place to hide than standing vulnerable in an empty corridor where an impeccable patrol might come round the corner at any moment. I type CLASSROOM and the door releases. I'm shocked by the volume of the clicking and hissing. I've never noticed it during the day when Specials are clamouring to get in or out of the room, but now I twist around, afraid that the noise will bring someone. I step quickly inside and close the door behind me, wincing at the sound again.

When the wall clock finally shows two o'clock, my eyes are trained on the classroom door, but a sound from the front of the grid makes me spin round. The door in the back of the cage is opening.

My first thought is Rice. But before I have time to duck out of sight, the door opens and there is my mother. Of course. There's no reason why she should have to use the classroom door.

'John,' she says.

It's strange to hear my real name. Even before, no one called me that. I struggle to get my chilled limbs out of my seat. 'Mum.'

'I'm so happy to see you.' Her voice cracks and she presses a hand to her mouth.

I climb up on the platform, but the bars are too tightly

spaced to be able to comfort her. I can only jam a hand in up to the wrist. 'Why did you come this way?' I ask.

'It's closer to my room and it's a safer route than walking down the main corridor.' She takes hold of my hand. 'It's such a relief to find that you're all right. You are okay, aren't you? They haven't hurt you, have they? Do you get enough to eat?'

I remember when I used to speak to her on the communicator at the Learning Community. I'd complain if we were given the same dinner twice in one week or if I thought our study was too dusty. Now I just say, 'I'm fine. I'm really fine.'

She looks me up and down. I know I've lost weight and there's a bruise on my cheek from where Deon slammed me into a feeding pod the other day.

Tears well up in her eyes again. She takes a deep breath. 'I can't stay too long. I share a room with another enforcer – she's incredibly nosy and I can't risk her noticing that I'm gone. Sometimes I feel like she's watching me. The other enforcers are so suspicious of volunteer enforcers.'

'Why?'

'Well, it must seem rather odd; anyone wanting to do this. It's a terrible job.'

'Is it?' I'd never really thought about it. I suppose it seems like the enforcers are the lucky ones compared to the Specials.

'It's all right for Rice and his type.'

'What do you mean, "his type"?' I ask.

'Rice used to have a low-ranking job in the Leadership. They say that he was caught stealing funds and that's how he ended up running an Academy.'

Which explains a lot about the way Rice is.

'But they don't all treat you like Rice does, do they?' she asks. 'Some of them seem like decent people.'

I wouldn't describe any of the enforcers as decent. Some of them like Rice and Tong seem to enjoy hurting Specials. Some of them don't seem to care about anything and the best of them try to be fair and to avoid using the EMDs.

'How many of the enforcers are here as a punishment?' I ask. I'm struck again by the rough deal that Specials get. How can they learn when they're given dishonest rejects for teachers?

'Quite a lot. There are a few volunteers, but I get the impression that volunteers are usually here because they want to escape something on the outside. And occasionally they use ex-Academy students.'

'They take ex-Specials?'

'I met one today. Enforcer Baxter. She had an exemplary record as a Special and she was glad to be taken on here. It meant she didn't have to go to a factory.'

I'm reeling. The idea that anyone would be grateful to be taken on as an enforcer is pretty grim. Even more worryingly, it suggests that Enforcer Baxter knows something about factories that most Specials don't. I've heard Dom talking about leaving to go to the factory and the way she describes it you'd think she'd been invited to a party. If Enforcer Baxter would rather be here, it means there's something pretty awful in store for the Specials when they leave the Academy.

'How did you know where I was?' I ask.

'I didn't know what to do when I couldn't get in touch with you at the Learning Community, but eventually I managed to track down a policeman who remembered taking a boy to this Academy the day after you disappeared. He took a lot of persuading to talk to me.'

Barnes, I think – he seemed to know something wasn't right the day he left me here. I'm so glad that my mum managed to find him. The relief at knowing she's OK and that I have a chance to get out of here is overwhelming.

My mother glances at the clock. 'I need to go soon. Listen carefully. Firstly, I know that you've already realised that we mustn't acknowledge each other, but I want you to remember to be very careful about it. Don't be afraid to blank me or to be rude about me or to behave however you behave towards other enforcers. People mustn't notice anything different about us.'

I nod my head.

'The next thing is to stay out of trouble while I make plans to get out of here. I'm on probation at the moment. I won't get full security clearance until I've been here for a month. That's when I'll be able to access the exits.' She's talking so fast that it's making her breathless. 'Is that okay? Can you hang on till then?'

'Yes, of course. But . . . when we go, we have to take my friends with us; Ilex and Ali and Kay.'

She creases up her face and rubs the spot between her eyebrows. For a moment I think that she's going to say no, but then she says, 'We'll see. I'll have to think about it.' She squeezes my hand and lets it go. 'I love you sweetheart. Everything will be all right. We just have to wait until we can get out quietly. We can't meet often, so—' Her eyes dart to the main door. Someone is moving about in the corridor outside.

'Go,' I whisper.

'But you—'

'I'll hide.' I stretch my eyes wide to emphasise the danger we're in. She must realise that it won't help for both us to be caught.

There are voices out in the corridor.

She gives my hand one last squeeze and slips out of the door.

I scan the room. There's nowhere in here that can't be seen from the doorway. Unless . . . I speed across the room, climb the four steps to the exit and position myself behind the door. The voices are closer. It must be the impeccable patrol. They won't come in, I tell myself. There's no reason for them to think that anyone would be in a classroom at night.

There's the click of a catch. The door hisses open.

I press myself against the wall. If they push the door all the way open, they'll feel me behind it.

'It was noise,' one of the impeccables says. 'It was a talking noise.'

'I'm the top. I say how we do this patrol. There's no people here.'

They start arguing. *Make them leave, oh please, make them leave.* One of them swings a torch around the room.

'See? No thing and no people. You nozzle crust.'

'Don't bad word me. I tell Rex on you.'

'Shut up.'

There's the sound of scuffling feet and the smack of fist on face. They must barge into the door because it swings back even further, crushing me against the wall. I can't help but expel air in a puff when it hits my chest.

'What was that?' They stop fighting.

My heart freezes.

'Down there. An enforcer coming. Look good, you no-ranker.'

I hear footsteps approaching. The enforcer is going to find me. I try to think of an excuse for being in the grid in the middle of the night.

'Enforcer, there was talking in this grid—'

'There's no Specials – Enforcer, he says there are noises all the times.'

The footsteps stop outside the door. 'Quiet, boys.'

Oh my efwurding hell, it's my mother. She must have run all the way through the enforcers' quarters and come out of the entrance by the lift.

'There's trouble in one of the dormitories. You must go upstairs and check each one now,' my mum says.

'But the grid—'

The door opens a little. 'No one in there,' she says. 'Come with me.'

The door closes and their muffled voices soon fade to nothing.

I steady myself on the door handle. She shouldn't have done that. What will happen if those impeccables speak to Rice about this so called 'trouble'? What if she's caught going back to bed? There's no sense in my waiting. I open the door and creep out. At the top of the stairs I wait until I hear the impeccables talking on the floor above. I sprint along the landing. I only hope they don't hear the door.

Back in my bed, I ease the knot of worry in my stomach by listening to Kay's gentle breathing until I fall asleep.

The next day my mother is in the grid and we continue with our sessions as usual so I assume that she isn't in trouble about last night. At least, not yet. In the days that follow I try not to think about when I'll get to meet her again. It's hard work remembering not to stare at her and trying to act naturally in the grid, so I make myself focus on other things.

Our reading groups continue to increase in size. Kay is an excellent recruiter. She knows who will be interested in going against the enforcers and she's persuasive too. Keeping busy takes my mind off worrying that my mother will be discovered and, amazingly, teaching reading improves my life in the Academy. I'd just about resigned myself to the fact that my low-ranker status meant that I was always going to be ridiculed or ignored, but now that I've made friends with a lot of Specials at the reading classes I find that instead of getting pushed around on the corridor I have people saying hello to me. I'd forgotten what it's like to feel popular. It doesn't change the way that Rex feels about me though. He continues to treat me with contempt and, once he notices that some of the other Specials seem to like me, I get the impression that he's just waiting for an opportunity to remind me that he's the boss.

After a reading session the following Saturday, Kay is sitting on her bed singing the alphabet under her breath. She's pulled her hair into a ponytail and I keep finding myself staring at the nape of her neck. I don't know how or when it happened, but I can't stop thinking about her. I close my eyes. We're alone again in the dormitory while the others are downstairs for Making Hour.

'What do they do in Making Hour?' I ask Kay without opening my eyes.

'Why are you all the time asking things?' she says.

'Asking questions is the way to learn things.'

'Or it gets you a fight,' she says.

'Maybe you're right.' I open my eyes.

Kay frowns and turns to look at me. 'Maybe?'

'Maybe means perhaps, or possibly, or . . .'

Kay is still frowning.

I screw up my mouth. I can't believe how hard it is to explain even simple words. You can't explain words without words. 'I could say, *maybe* we will go downstairs later or *maybe* we will stay here,' I say.

Kay nods.

I sit up. 'And I could say, maybe you should answer my question. What do they do in Making Hour?'

'Make things,' she says.

'Make what?'

'Babies.'

Babies? She can't mean what I think she means. I drop my eyes to the floor; I feel blood rushing to my cheeks. Kay has got to be winding me up. I risk looking up at her through my hair. She's watching me with a straight face.

'No Making Hour at the Learning Community?' she says.

'No!'

A smile spreads across Kay's face.

In our spare time at the Learning Community we were rebuilding an antique computer. I mean, obviously I did think about sex. Quite a lot, actually, and Wilson and I talked about it a lot too, but it was only talk. We were taught that sex is for after you finish your education, establish your career and get married. If they'd caught anyone at the Learning Community having sex, they would have been kicked out. I never heard of anyone getting pregnant. If that had happened I imagine you'd have been sent straight to the Wilderness. I mean, it's wrong, isn't it? I rub my eyebrow. 'Do the enforcers know?'

She shrugs. 'Yes.'

'But don't they . . . ?' I splutter to a halt. I knew that Dom was pregnant. I thought that maybe some of the other Reds were having sex too, but I assumed that it was a big secret and that Dom had been allowed to get away with being pregnant because the enforcers always seem to let the Reds get off lightly. I can't believe that all the senior Specials are at it. Every Saturday night.

Kay is looking at me.

'Do you mean the enforcers just let them do it?' I say. 'But they're not married! They're not even grown up.'

She tips her head on one side. 'I'm thinking sex is not the same in your Learning Community.'

'There wasn't any sex in the Learning Community.' I press my hand to my cheek. My face is hot. 'But what do they do?' I say. I study the last button on my shirt.

Kay leans towards me across the gap between our beds. I can smell her hair. It's like warm grass. Her knees are almost touching mine. I keep looking at my button.

'Don't you know how they do sex?' she asks.

Without meaning to I find myself jumping to my feet and moving to the end of the bed. There's nothing there but my locker so I open it and pretend to be looking for something. 'Yes,' I say too loudly. 'Yes, obviously.' I'm nodding my head. I keep nodding my head. I'm nodding too much so I stop and fold my arms.

Kay lets out a peal of laughter. 'You're all red-face-looking-down!'

I stop looking at the floor and shake my head. I unfold my arms, but my hands seem to be dangling about so I put them in my pockets, but then my arms are stuck out like a chicken so I fold them again.

'No I'm not,' I say.

Kay giggles. 'All those big nice words you know and you're too red-face to talk about s-e-x.'

I look away towards the bathroom.

'Blake's a tight-legger.'

I've heard the boys calling girls that name, but it's only now that I realise what it means. 'Don't call me that. Anyway, that doesn't even make sense. It's a derogatory term for a girl.'

'It's what?'

'A bad name for a girl, not a boy.'

'That's stupid. Why are all bad names for girls?' She breaks into a smile again. 'There needs be a word for you. You're all little boy-y about shagging . . .'

Kay falls back on the bed laughing and kicks her legs in the air in delight. In a terrible rush of blood and heat I imagine throwing myself over her and pressing myself against her body.

'Humping and . . .'

'Stop it!' I say. I walk off to the bathroom.

In a cubicle I press my hot head against the cold tiles. I count the cracks in the grout so that I don't think about Kay lying on the bed again. This is crazy. I can't get her out of my head. I think about the Making Hour. It's mind-blowing that the Specials are allowed to have sex. I shouldn't be so shocked, Kay obviously thinks I'm over-reacting, but she doesn't realise that Learning Communities are not like Academies. Specials are not treated like brainers. I used to think that that was a good thing. Now I wonder how they could insist that what they taught us at the Learning Community was right when they teach Specials something completely different.

When I've decided that now probably isn't the best time for me to re-evaluate my attitude towards sex and I've stopped feeling like a pulsing ball of heat, I walk back into the dormitory.

Kay keeps her lips pressed together, but her eyes are sparkling.

'What's the word you said to me for when you've done a bad thing?' she says.

'Sorry.'

'I sorry you.'

'For a girl with a limited vocabulary you know a lot of words for sexual intercourse.'

Kay smiles. 'Words for sex? All Specials know words for sex. And fighting. But I want to know more words for all other things. Tell me "maybe" again.'

I try not to look at Kay's mouth. 'Maybe I'll win my next fight,' I say.

Kay snorts.

'Okay, maybe you'll win your fight on Friday,' I say.

'That's not a "maybe" that's a "yesbe".'

I smile. 'You mean a "definite". You will "definitely" win the fight.'

'Do you want me to have a win?'

I nod my head out of politeness, but then I realise it's true. I do want her to win. I want her to have anything she wants.

176

Even though I usually try to avoid the Fight Nights, on Friday I arrive early with Ilex and Ali to get a front row seat to watch Kay.

'Do you think she'll win?' I ask Ilex.

He looks at me in surprise. 'Kay doesn't lose.'

I suppose I already knew that was true. Even so, there's a knot of tension in my chest and I realise that I'm nervous for her.

The drum room fills up with jabbering Specials. On Fight Nights the atmosphere is always charged. There's a lot of high-spirited banter and jostling and shoving. It feels like we're balanced on a knife edge. Everybody is having a good time now, but I think it would only take a few wrong words and the whole place would erupt in a free-for-all.

Kay catches my eye as she bounces through the door. She weaves swiftly between the crowds to come and speak to us.

'Shout for me,' she teases Ali.

Some scuffling between a group of Red boys breaks out on the floor. The knot in my chest has tightened. 'I still don't understand why the enforcers allow this,' I say to Ilex. 'I know you said that they'd rather Specials fight Specials than have them getting aggressive with the enforcers, but it's so dangerous.'

Ilex looks to Kay for an answer.

'Specials like it,' Kay says.

I don't imagine that the enforcers are particularly interested in Specials enjoying themselves. Maybe the enforcers have other motives in allowing so much violence. 'Maybe they want the Specials to be good fighters,' I suggest. 'Maybe they're afraid of another war.'

'What's war?' Kay asks.

My jaw drops open. 'You know – war, like the Long War?' I can see by her face that she doesn't know what I'm talking about. 'Has no one ever told you about the Long War?'

'No,' Kay says.

Ali shrugs.

'No war talk in the academy,' Ilex says.

Unbelievable. It really is like being on a different planet in here. The enforcers control the Specials' entire world. Why on earth would they hide the war from them?

'What's war?' Kay asks again.

'A war is a fight. A really big fight between countries or even different, um, types of people. The Long War was

178

between our country and the Greater Power. The Greater Power invaded – that means attacked – our neighbours, that's the country next to us, and started using their people as slave labour.'

'What's that?' Kay asks.

'When they make you work and don't pay you.'

'Oh.'

'So . . . then we got involved, but the Greater Power started bombing us – that's how the Wilderness was made. The Wilderness is the area that got the worst of the bombing. Didn't you even know that?'

Ilex looks at his feet.

'I thought the Wilderness was there all the times,' Kay says.

'No. Only after the war. So . . . the Greater Power cut off our supply routes. There were food shortages. People were getting really angry and then the old government was overthrown by the Leadership. They took control and made a peace deal and started sorting everything out.'

All three of them are just staring at me.

'Why are you telling this?' Kay asks.

'Because you should know! Everyone should understand what's happened in their past and what it means for them. It's because of the war that The Leader decided that we needed to train more factory workers to make our country great again.'

Kay narrows her eyes. 'So that war thing means I'm in the Academy learning to be a factory worker?'

'Well, yes, but that's not all that the war—'

'I knew that.' She flicks her ponytail over her shoulder and heads for the centre of the floor.

I sigh. Why is it so hard to explain things in here? It's like the whole structure of sense has been torn down. I turn to Ilex and Ali. 'You'd never heard about the war and how important it was either?'

Ilex's eyes slide to Ali. She shakes her head firmly.

Ilex points to the centre of the room. 'It's starting,' he says.

Rex struts on to the cleared fight floor. The Specials start shouting at the top of their voices. I wonder if Rex would be able to gain control if a riot broke out. He'd probably just join in.

'Do you want fights?' he shouts.

The audience roars back. Ali shrinks closer to Ilex.

'Let's have good fights. Now it's tough girl . . . Kay!'

I shout this time, I can't help myself. And I'm not alone; Kay might not have reached the inner circle of Reds and their friends yet, but people know who she is and they know what a good fighter she is.

Kay bounces lightly into the middle of the room. She looks full of energy.

'And Kay fights our Red . . . Lou Emerly!'

I spin round to watch Lou get up from her seat in the centre of the Reds crowd. She smoothes her dark auburn hair behind her ears and makes her way towards the fight floor. As she passes Dom, Dom whispers something in

Lou's ear and gives her a high-five. When she reaches Rex I can see that she's pretty skinny and not much taller than Kay. I don't think the fight will last long.

Rex blows his whistle and the Specials start screaming.

Kay raises her hands, but before she can get a punch in Lou slams her fist into Kay's cheek. She stumbles backwards. While Kay is off-balance Lou swings her skinny leg up and aims for Kay's stomach. I expect Kay to twist out of the way, but instead Lou's foot connects and Kay is knocked to the ground. *Get up*, I urge but Kay stays down. Lou stamps a foot into Kay's middle again. Finally, Kay rolls over out of the way. She gets to her feet, but slowly.

'What the hell is the matter with her?' I ask Ilex.

'She won't win it,' he says.

'Why on earth not . . . ?' Then I realise. Lou is a Red and also Dom's best friend. Kay doesn't want to upset them. 'That's stupid. I thought Kay wanted to be the best fighter. Is she going to lose just because Lou is a Red?'

But Ilex isn't listening to me; he's watching Ali, who is staring at Lou with an expression of horror.

'What is it?' he asks.

Ali shakes her head.

Ilex looks back at Lou, who is trying to get her hands around Kay's throat. 'It was that one, wasn't it? Lou is the one that got your hair out.'

Ali gives the smallest of nods.

Ilex gets to his feet.

'No, wait,' I say, pulling him down.

The fighters are locked in a hold. Kay is clearly holding back.

'Kay!' I yell above the sound of the shrieking Specials.

She turns her head so she's looking at me.

'Lou is the one who pulled Ali's hair out.'

Kay's eyes scrunch. I don't know if she can hear me.

'Lou hurt Ali!' I shout as loud as I can.

Kay breaks out of the hold and looks up at Lou. Lou is saying something to her. Some taunt.

Kay's whole body changes. She pulls up. It's like I can see the power running through her. In a blur she lifts Lou's arm up high, spins under it so she has her back to Lou and yanks on the hand to flip Lou over her shoulder. Lou lands hard on her back. While she struggles to get up, like an upturned beetle, Kay lays in with the kicks and punches.

The Specials love this change of fortune. They're on their feet screaming Kay's name. It's like the charge in the air has suddenly ignited.

'What is it?' I ask Ilex.

'Reds *don't* lose,' he says.

He means that Reds are always allowed to win. I didn't know. I've tried not to watch many fights. I should have expected it. I should have known that even in a fist fight Reds get the unfair advantage. My stomach contracts. What will happen to Kay if she beats a Red?

Lou is back on her feet. Kay storms in with a double jab to the stomach followed by a high spinning kick which catches Lou under the chin.

'Come on, Kay!' I shout. 'Give it to her. Take her out. Show her—' Halfway through my scream I notice a dark figure in the doorway. An enforcer. I look up. It's my mother. She's staring right at me. My words die on my lips. She doesn't look impressed to find me ranting at the fighters. But she doesn't know what Lou did to Ali. She doesn't know how much every non-Red kid in here wants to see a fair fight for once. And I can't tell her. I hold up my hands in a helpless expression. My mother looks back to the fight. Kay has Lou in a headlock with one arm. She jams her other elbow down on her. Mum's mouth is open in horror.

Lou breaks away, but Kay hounds her with a series of punches to the head followed by a powerful kick that sends Lou crashing to the floor. Kay swoops down on her, pinning her arms behind her back and pressing her face into the floor. Rex blows his whistle. The audience go crazy. She's done it. She's won.

My eyes swing back to my mother. She shakes her head in disgust and slips back out of the door.

Marvellous.

This isn't exactly the way I pictured my mother meeting the girl I like.

For days, all anyone can talk about is Kay's victory. Lou is furious. The morning afterwards, she and Dom push past Kay in the corridor and the rest of the Red girls follow their lead; none of them will speak to Kay.

'Don't worry about those Red girls,' I say to Kay, while we're chatting in the salon. 'Who cares what they think?'

'King Hell!' she growls in annoyance. 'You don't get it, do you Blake? *I* care. I want to be Dom!'

She's right. I don't get it. She won that fight fair and square and she did it for Ali. She should be proud of that. Why does she care so much about being Dom and what the bitchy Red girls think? I want to tell her that she doesn't need them, that she's better than them.

'Listen, Kay—' I start, but I'm interrupted by Rex walking into the salon with Dom and his usual train of followers.

'Hey . . .' he says, stopping by our chairs. 'It's our no-ranker brainer boy.'

I flinch backwards as he reaches out to slap me on the back. His entourage laugh. Rex smirks. He doesn't seem to mind me so much when he's making fun of me.

He turns his grin on Kay. 'And our top-ranker, Kay.' He turns to Dom, who is hanging on his arm. 'Kay's a big good fighter, isn't she?'

Dom narrows her eyes at Kay. 'Yes,' she sneers. 'Kay likes the win.'

Rex winks at Kay and he and his pack move on to the other end of the salon.

I shake my head in disgust, but Kay is beaming. 'Maybe you're right,' she says. 'Maybe I don't care what the Red *girls* think.'

I don't get the opportunity to explain to my mother about why I was cheering Kay on in her fight, because the last time I saw her we didn't have time to arrange our next meeting before we got interrupted by the impeccables. I have to wait for her to sign me a message in class. Finally, eighteen long days after our first late-night meeting, my mother signs to me that we should meet tonight.

When she arrives through the back of the cage at two in the morning she starts talking straight away. 'I'm sorry it's taken so long for me to meet you, but I'm worried. Every time I turn around Rice is watching me. He knows I saw that fight.'

It wasn't a smart move. Enforcers never go to Fight

Nights so it was bound to draw attention to Mum. 'Why did you come?' I ask.

Her face falls. 'I didn't realise how infrequently enforcers leave their quarters after lessons are over. I just wanted to see how you were getting on. I know it was silly. And anyway, you were . . . busy.'

I remember the look of disappointment on her face when she saw me cheering Kay on, but I don't think we have time for me to try to explain that now. 'What did you say to Rice about being at a fight?'

'I told him that I was interested to observe the students in their leisure time. He said that wasn't the way we do things here. In fact, what he said was, "We're not here to be interested. We're here to enforce." Ever since, I've had the feeling that he's checking up on where I am and what I'm doing. I think he's asked my roommate to watch me. She even follows me to the bathroom sometimes.'

'Do you think it was safe to come tonight?'

'This will be the last time before we get out of here. I have an appraisal scheduled for two weeks on Friday, after that I'll get my security clearance and ID card, which means access to the exits. We'll leave on the Saturday night. Meet me here at two a.m. Wear both your uniforms, it'll be cold out.'

I nod. 'I'll tell Ilex, Ali and Kay.'

'I don't know about that,' she says slowly.

'What do you mean?'

She bites her lip. 'I hear from Enforcer Baxter that Ali

is a sweet little girl and I know that Ilex has been a friend to you, but I just don't know if we can help them. It's going to be hard enough to look after ourselves.'

'What about Kay?'

She sighs. 'I can see that you're . . . fond of Kay, but we've got to be careful. The more people who know about us leaving, the more likely we are to be found out.'

I can't believe she's saying this. 'You don't trust her, do you?'

'I'm not judging her; I know that her life has been hard and that she's grown up with different values. I understand—'

'No you don't,' I snap.

'I can imagine—'

'No you can't.' I'm raising my voice. I try to get control of myself and bring it back down to a whisper. 'I've been living here for months now and there were times when I thought you weren't ever going to come for me. There were times when I thought that I was going to end up in a factory and that I would spend the rest of my life as a Special. But even I can't, for one minute, claim to understand what it's like to be Kay. I know that you're a good person and that you want to be able to empathise and that you try to understand her motives, but until you have lived the life of a Special, a life that's devoid of hope or joy or comfort, you will never know what it feels like.'

My mother is quiet. There are tears in her eyes. 'I'm sorry,' she says.

'You have to go,' I say. 'I don't want to fight with you.'

'I just want to get you out of here,' she says.

'I know.'

'Promise you'll be here on the night after my appraisal?' She pauses and looks at me, before adding, 'You *and* Ilex and Ali and Kay.'

I smile at her.

She does her best to hug me through the bars and then she's gone.

A few nights later it's Saturday again and Kay and I sneak into 'Rex's Room' – namely, the toilets next to the salon – for some privacy. Only Reds are allowed in here but they'll all be heading for Making Hour in a minute. Kay is writing words using pieces of string to shape the letters, this way if anyone comes in we just bunch up the string and there's no evidence. She shapes 'Academies suck' and looks at me with a smile. This would be a good time to talk to her about the escape plan, but I've found myself putting that off. Even before I had a definite date, every time I tried to talk about leaving Kay kept changing the subject. It's like she doesn't believe it's going to happen.

The six o'clock buzzer sounds, which makes me think of something else I've been meaning to say. 'I wanted to ask you about Making Hour again.' The words tumble out of my mouth.

Kay raises her eyebrows. 'Do you want to Make with me?'

'No! I mean, it's not that I . . . I just wanted to know

what it's all about.' King Hell. Why can't I have a conversation with Kay about this without turning into a babbling idiot?

'Blake, I told you they—'

'I know what they do, I wanted to know why . . . I mean, I know *why*, but why is the Academy encouraging them?' Once again my face is purple.

'Come with me,' she says and leads me out of the toilets. 'The Leadership says we need factory workers. To make the workers they need Academy Specials.'

I nod. Everybody knows that the factory workers are vital to our economy.

'They need lots of Specials. So they get Specials Making more Specials in the Making Hour. They say, "Do it for your country" and all like that.'

That bit, I didn't know. Even if factory workers are important, I can't believe that they encourage teenage girls to get pregnant. At the Learning Community they taught us that sex and relationships must wait until we'd completed our education. At the Academy they're telling them they can serve their country by having sex. It seems like another way that everyone is being pushed into believing something without questioning it. 'Are you sure you've got this right? Are you sure that the Leadership even knows about Making Hour?' I ask her.

Kay shrugs.

'Does the Making Hour happen in all Academies?' I ask when we get on to the main corridor.

Kay frowns. 'I don't get you, Blake. You're a brainer, yes?'

'Don't call me that. I'm smart, okay?' But actually I'm not even sure about that any more. 'Well, at some things anyway.'

'So why don't you know all-things? You know about old things like Long War, didn't they teach you about things that are . . . now?'

We did learn Topical Issues at the Learning Community. It's only now that I realise that what we covered was pretty narrow and, again, we were never taught to question what we were told. It's hard to explain to Kay that no one at the Learning Community has any interest in what happens at Academies or factories. We're completely focused on our future roles.

At the bottom of the stairs, instead of walking straight down the corridor where the second lot of grids are, she turns left down a smaller corridor.

'You're missing the point of a Learning Community,' I say. 'It's about ideas and theories.'

'What's "missing the point"?'

'It's when you don't understand, you don't get the most important thing. "Important" means the biggest thing, the special thing.'

'People are the most 'portant thing. People are the point,' she says.

I open my mouth to answer her, but I can't explain. Kay is staring at me. Why did I never ask myself the questions that Kay asks?

I stop and shake my head. 'I know I don't know lots of things,' I say. 'But I do want to know. Has the Making Hour . . . er . . . worked well here?'

'Yeah,' she sighs. 'Lots of babies to put in Academies and then into the factories.'

'Babies?' I sound like an idiot, but it's out of my mouth before I can stop myself. 'I haven't seen any babies.'

'When they're borned they go to a place. There have been lots. That Lou I beat had one a bit before you came here. Dom is having one. And Carma in our dormitory, she doesn't all times fat-walk like that you know.'

'Have you ever . . . ?'

Kay laughs. 'You know lots of words, but sometimes . . .' She nods at me to show she has remembered this word from when I explained it to her a couple of days ago. 'Sometimes you can't talk the right words, can you?' She tugs at my arm to make me walk down the corridor. 'No, I've not-one-time had a baby,' she says. 'Carma's had two before this.'

'Two?'

'She had two same-time babies.'

'You mean twins?'

She nods. 'Same-time babies.'

'So how old do they . . . er . . . start?'

Kay looks amused. 'Making is only for the biggest Specials. You can Make when you're fifteen. Carma says baby-ing is crimson, but you can't fight with a baby-belly. It's hard for Carma because she likes to be fighting with her long nails all the times.'

192

'Why does she do it then?' I say.

'Baby-belly girls get more food and more rest and the enforcers are all no-hitting, no-shouting. Carma says the more babies you have the littler you work at the factory.' She rolls her eyes.

'Don't you believe that?' I ask.

'Believe?'

'Do you think it's true? Not a lie?'

'I don't know. It's nice to have some believes.'

We've reached a different corridor; this one is white. Leading off it are white doors with *Vacant/Engaged* signs on them.

'Is this where they . . . ?' I look at the door nearest us. The sign says *Engaged*.

'Yes, Blake, there is where they have sex.' She crosses to the nearest vacant room and pushes the door open, then she turns back and looks over her shoulder at me. My stomach turns over. Does she want me to go in there? With her? I try to walk towards her, but I seem unable to control my legs; my feet feel massive. I'm surprised I manage to get through the door. The room is tiny. Kay is sat on a white bed. Should I close the door? I try not to think about Kay. Other than the bed, which I am not looking at, there's only a wash basin in the corner. Under the sink are two great big rolls of tissue. I feel myself blushing.

Kay is leaning back on the pillow. My hands are sweaty.

'Close the door,' she says.

I wonder if I should kiss her. I don't think I know how

to kiss, let alone how to do anything else. I tell my brain to move my legs towards the bed.

'One day I'll be here Making with Rex,' Kay says to me.

I tell my brain not to move my legs, but the message is all confused and I stumble and crash down on to the bed.

Smooth.

I hate Rex.

'So,' I say. 'Do you come here a lot?' I hate myself.

'Sometimes I come to have a nice quiet lying down on a not-dirty bed.' She cuddles a pillow to her and draws up her knees.

Oh. I edge as far away from her as possible. I've got to stop thinking about kissing Kay. She's not interested. She thinks I'm an idiot. I look around the room again. She's right, it's much cleaner than the dorm.

Kay stops talking and after a while her eyelids start to droop. Soon she's asleep. I'm mesmerised by her breathing. She turns her head, exposing her collar bone. I want to kiss her there. Imagine if I did and she woke up and gave that breathy sigh like she does sometimes and then kissed me, put her tongue in my mouth and took my hand and—

The buzzer sounds.

Kay opens her eyes and stretches. I cross my legs.

On the way back upstairs I say, 'Why Rex? You don't even like him.'

'I think you're missing the point of sex,' Kay says.

When I finally get up the nerve to talk to Kay about escaping she reacts with almost the same words as my mother.

'I don't know,' she says.

'What do you mean, you don't know? We can get out of here. We'll be free. No more enforcers. No more EMDs.'

She looks at me for a long time and finally her lips curve into a half-smile. 'Okay, Blake. I'll come when you go to meet your mother.'

I wish that she would just use the word 'escape', but I don't want to push my luck so I leave it at that. When I tell Ilex and Ali the plan they agree solemnly to wait for me to come and pick them up from their dormitories. I think it's best not to have too many people roaming about in the night until we know that my mother has sorted everything.

Even though we're leaving soon, Kay's enthusiasm about the reading lessons remains undiminished and I find myself looking forward to them. For some reason this small defiance against the enforcers makes me feel better. And I'm not the only one. About a quarter of all the Specials are learning to read now. We have to work in small groups because I'm afraid that a big congregation of kids will draw attention. Kay teaches the little ones. I feel ridiculously proud of her.

I go to meet her after a lesson in one of the junior bathrooms. I'm trying to decide if she looks pleased to see me when a little boy called Marn stumbles up to us. He stands with his hands behind his back and looks at the floor.

'You did good reading, Marn,' Kay says.

He looks up at her. 'I want to say a good thing for learning me reading. Can you tell me a good thing word?'

Kay smiles at him. 'When you are happy that someone did a thing for you and you want to tell them, you say, "thank you".'

'Fank you, Kay, fank you, Blake,' he says. He wriggles on the spot. 'I want to give you a thing.' He holds out his hand. In the middle of his palm is something small and black like a button. It's his shrap. The little ones rarely manage to get hold of metal, so they make do with bits of plastic.

Kay pats his shoulder. I take another look at the button.

'Thank you, Marn,' Kay says. 'But we like to show you reading. You can have your shrap. We don't—'

I reach over and pick up the button that isn't a button. 'Actually, Kay, I'd really like this.'

'Blake! Don't take his—'

I hold the piece of plastic up to the light. 'Kay, do you know what this is?'

'It's a little boy's shrap,' she says, trying to snatch it off me.

'No. It's a rec. A bit old-fashioned, but definitely a rec.'

'A what?'

'Do you like it?' Marn says. He grins from ear to ear.

'I do like it,' I say. 'And if we're lucky, it's going to be very useful for the reading lessons. Come with me.'

I lead Kay and Marn down to the salon, which fortunately is empty. I head over to the Info screen. I press the rec to the corner of the screen and it holds in place as I knew it would. The screen flicks to an image of the Peace Day parade.

Marn widens his eyes. He's never seen anything on screen without the Info logo plastered across it.

Kay looks at me. 'I'll shut the door,' she says.

We manage to get our hands on five recs. Marn says there used to be more in a box at the back of the cupboard in the salon, but the little ones fought over them for their shrap collections. We ask all the kids, but I'm sure some of them keep them hidden away because they can't bear to part with them.

Four of the recs are of The Leader. It seems that some time back they thought that the students at the Academy needed to hear what The Leader had to say, even if he does use a broad vocabulary. I wonder when they changed their minds about that. The fifth rec is an 'instructive' film about leaving the Academy and going to work in a factory.

Ilex is disappointed when we show him a bit of one of The Leader's speeches.

'It's like the Info,' he says. 'All The Leader smiling and moving his hands. I've seen it lots.'

'You might have seen it.' I say. 'But you haven't heard it. Listen.'

Ilex tilts his head and screws up his face in concentration.

'*A leadership must arise in which every citizen can have confidence.*'

'He talks the talk like you,' Ilex says.

For a moment I'm flattered by the idea that I sound like The Leader, then I remember we've got to stay focused and careful. I take the rec off the screen. 'Most people talk like that,' I say. 'You'll talk like that soon. And these recs will help us because you can watch them to learn the words.'

'Let's watch more,' Kay says.

'Wait a minute,' I say. 'We need to make sure that no one who might get us into trouble sees us.'

Kay pouts. 'I hate all this careful-ing. I want to do it now.'

'I know but—'

'No people ever said no watching The Leader,' she

says. 'We didn't steal them. They were here in the salon. It's not a wrong thing.'

Somehow I don't think that's how Rice would see it.

In the end we decide to watch the recs early in the morning before breakfast. Most Specials stay in bed as long as possible, which means the salon is usually deserted at that time. Even so, we position a look-out on the door and another halfway down the corridor to let us know when someone is coming.

For the first early-morning viewing there are twenty of us in the salon. I wanted fewer because I was afraid that we might be missed from the dormitories. But Kay insisted. The reading groups are the largest they've ever been and a lot of Specials want to see the recs.

'I think we should watch a bit and then you can ask me about any words you don't understand,' I say to everyone before we start.

'And me,' Kay adds. 'You can ask me too. I know lots of words now.'

I put the first rec on the corner of the screen. Music plays and the camera pans across a vast crowd of excited people waving Leadership flags, to The Leader on stage. Under his suit he's wearing a shirt with a big, old-fashioned collar.

'I've seen this one,' I say. 'It's when he first became Leader.'

'*Fellow citizens, I am here today to give you a message of hope. I know that the conflict has brought hardships to us all, but now it is necessary to put behind us the hostilities of the past and to focus on the challenges of the present.'*

I pause it. 'Hope is believing – ah, thinking – that things can get better.'

'What's "conflict"?' Ilex says.

'He means the war. This is not long after the Long War finished.'

'Why doesn't he say "war"? Then people know,' he says.

'I expect he thinks "conflict" sounds better, or, at least, less awful,' I say.

'People still died,' Kay says. She taps the play icon.

'The people have spoken and we have listened.' He points into the crowd. *'You have shown us that you desire to rely on a moral framework. Without it we have not got a society at all, we have chaos. You have asked for discipline and direction under leadership. And we will give it to you.'*

I pause again. Marn is scowling. 'Why does he say "you"?' he says. 'Is he you-ing to me? How does he know I'm here?'

'He's talking to everybody, all people.' I say.

'Not me.' Marn shakes his head. 'He doesn't know me.'

I laugh. 'When he talks about "discipline"—'

'That's hitting and shocks,' a boy from my dormitory says.

'Not always,' I say. 'It means being firm, keeping rules, making sure that people do the right thing.'

'I want to listen,' Kay says. 'You can tell us words later.' She presses play.

'The problems of our country stem from individuals. Individuals who refuse to give of their time and talents to help rebuild our society. They have lost sight of the fact that it is only through hard work that we find dignity and self-respect. I ask you to stop thinking only of yourselves and of individual gain and instead to stand together. Alone we are nothing, as part of a prosperous society we are everything.

'The time for shirking is over. It is essential that we set about ensuring that every citizen is fully employed. No longer will the common man avoid hard labour; no longer will our young people drop out of education. Instead they will learn the rewards of a job well done. I urge you all to invest in our country, knowing that the success of our nation will ensure the success of every citizen.

'Our path is clear; it is of paramount importance that we all recognise our duties, duties that I know you will shoulder gladly to help rebuild our proud nation. Our task is to bring about full employment. Our task is to provide all our children with an appropriate level of education. Our task is to repair our society. In your hands, more than in mine, lies the power to bring us to new heights. I ask you to put your hands, your hearts

and your minds to our task. Together I know we will succeed.'

There's a roar of applause from the crowd. I pluck the rec off the screen and pocket it for safe keeping.

'What does "necessary" mean?' Kay asks. She's used the pen I gave her to write words on her palm.

'You'd better remember to wash that off,' I say to her. There would be all kinds of trouble if an enforcer spotted writing on her hand. '"Necessary" means something that has to be done.'

'What about "essential"?'

'It's the same thing.'

Marn wriggles in front of Kay. 'And "para . . . paramount 'portance"?'

'That's kind of the same too.'

Why does he keep saying the same thing? signs Ali.

'He's trying to emphasise the point – that means he wants it to be really clear,' I say. 'He wants people to listen to him.'

'By going on and on?' Ilex says.

I shake my head. I don't think they've enjoyed their first political speech.

'All of that section, that bit, is to tell people that they must contribute – that means they must give something, to society,' I say.

They stare at me. It's really hard to take some of The Leader's fine ideas and reduce them down to something simple. Once you take the descriptive words away they seem to mean less. I screw my mouth up. 'What he means is . . . What he's really saying is that everyone should give something to help.'

'That's nice,' Marn says. 'What do you give?'

I want to say: you give what you can, or what you're best at, but Kay's face frowning in concentration catches my eye and I realise that she's not going to be allowed to give of her talents. She's not even allowed to have talents.

'I suppose you give what they tell you to give,' I say eventually.

Kay looks up. 'The Leader's saying: do what I say.'

Sounds like an enforcer, signs Ali.

I pick out a few more words from the speech and write them using string to shape the letters. We talk about what they mean and practise using them in sentences. When the group breaks up I feel strangely deflated.

Is it better to say things all different ways? signs Ali when most of the other Specials have gone to the feeding pods for breakfast.

'The Leader is trying to get his point across by saying it lots of ways,' I tell her.

'I like it,' Marn says. 'I like all those words.'

Kay tugs at a strand of her hair. 'It's good if you want to sound like you know all things.'

Ali taps me on the arm. *But is it better than saying one thing? I think he should say the one thing he means,* she signs.

'Don't be a no-ranker, Ali,' Ilex says. 'That would

sound big bad. That would be like . . .' He walks across the room pretending to be The Leader, grinning like an idiot and grabbing our hands to shake. He climbs on a chair. 'Oh my feller cit'zuns,' he says.

Kay bursts out laughing.

'I have a big thing to say. Not lots of things. One thing.' He smiles broadly and widens his eyes. 'DO WHAT I SAY!'

The others are clutching their sides.

But maybe Ilex is right. And if he is, it's really not that funny.

35

As I head from the salon to the dining hall for breakfast, a crowd of girls from one of our reading groups catches up with me. They want to bring some friends to their next class.

'That's great,' I say. 'The more people the better.'

Ahead of us, just outside the hall, I spot Rex staring at us and frowning.

'Let's talk about it later,' I whisper. Then I say in a louder voice, 'I hope they've prepared something nutritious for breakfast. You lot will need your strength if you've got to look at Rice's ugly face all morning.'

The girls laugh.

Rex steps forward and blocks my way.

'Go,' he says to the rest of the group. They dart off to their pods. One of them gives me a sympathetic look.

Rex stares down at me. 'The girls are liking all that brainer talk,' he says.

I know it's a bad idea to get into a conversation with Rex, but I can't help myself. 'It's nice to think that some of the Specials appreciate intellect,' I say. 'Don't worry, Rex, the girls who get tired out by thinking still prefer you.'

He glowers at me. He clearly doesn't understand what I've said. I'm expecting him to blow up and lash out, but instead he snorts.

'You think you know all,' he says. 'But you don't. A brainer will never be bigger than Rex. You need to learn it.'

He gives me a sharp jab in the ribs and I double over. He laughs. 'You're going to learn it, brainer-boy.' He nods to himself as if he's decisively gained the upper hand. 'You're going to learn it,' he repeats.

He swaggers off and I'm left with a sinking feeling that he's got a plan to teach me a lesson.

It doesn't come as a surprise when, later on, Deon grabs me in the corridor and tells me that I'm on the list to fight on Friday. I've managed to get away without fighting since my first night here, so this is obviously Rex's way of showing me that he's in charge. He's so childish.

'I don't see why I have to go,' I say to Kay and Ilex. 'We're leaving soon. What can the Reds do to me?'

Kay raises her eyebrows.

Ilex's mouth is agape. 'Blake, there's big lots of things that they can do. Big lots of things that hurt.'

I suppose it wouldn't take long for the Reds to do some serious damage to me. Even so, I can't help whining. I should have kept my big mouth shut when Rex was getting jealous.

'You need to do it,' Ilex insists. 'If you want to be escaping, you can't be getting Rex and the Reds all angry and watching you.'

'I know. I just hate Fight Night.'

'Don't be scared,' Kay says. 'I can help you. I'll teach you some good fighting. You can be a good-fighting Special.'

'I'm not a Special and I'm not going to be here much longer. Learning Community students don't need to fight.'

Kay fixes her eyes on me and I realise that last time we had a conversation like this, I was the one trying to persuade her to learn something new. She smiles. 'Everybody needs to learn to fight.'

From the moment I wake up on Friday, my stomach is a gurgling whirl of nerves. I was lucky last time I had to fight. Kay helped by tripping up Deon and Rex stopped the fight before I got completely pounded. Both Kay and Ilex have tried to teach me some fighting skills in the last few days, but Ilex has told me about Fight Nights where Specials have ended up with broken arms and bitten-off fingers. We're getting so close to leaving and I'd really like to take all my body parts with me.

By the time evening comes, I'm a wreck. Kay, Ilex and Ali bombard me with last-minute advice as we walk to the drum-shaped room.

'Let them hit you then it will end more fast,' Ilex says.

Kay scowls at him. 'No! You have to fight. Do the things I showed you.'

I nod absently at both of them. I just want it to be over.

Ali tugs gently on my shirt. *Don't show you're frightened. Pretend you don't care,* she signs.

I smile at her. 'I'll try.' It's funny how Ali's vocabulary is so much better than most of the other Specials, including Ilex. When I taught her the sign for 'pretend' the other day she seemed to already know what the word meant. Maybe it's because she's spent so much time not talking that she's really listened to every word that she's ever heard.

The drum room is packed. The seats are crammed with shouting and laughing Specials. I wish I was looking forward to this as much as they clearly are. We squeeze into a space on the second row. I try to focus on next Saturday when we'll finally get out of this place.

I'm distracted by the door slamming open. Suddenly the Specials fall silent. In stalks Dom. She's done something to her hair. It's divided into tiny plaits that are twisted in loops standing away from head like a halo. She's also dripping with shrap. One of the little Specials next to us gasps in delight. Dom slinks across the floor, lapping up the attention. Close behind her are Lou and a number of the other Red girls, all with their hair styled in a similar fashion. The Specials break into applause and Dom's pout opens into a gracious smile. I look at Kay.

She can't take her eyes off Dom's head and when Lou's laser eyes swivel around to give Kay a triumphant look, I notice that Kay's hands start clapping. Obviously she hasn't entirely given up on what the Red girls think of her.

The Red girls are followed by Deon, Pete and a bunch of thick-armed Hon Reds. I wonder if it's one of them that Rex has chosen to teach me a lesson.

When everyone has taken their seats Rex runs through the door like a game-show host.

'Let's have fighting!' he shouts.

The Specials howl with approval.

I feel sick.

I have to sit through two other fights before Rex calls my name. I make my way on unsteady legs to the centre of the floor. I walk around a smear of blood left from the last fight. Rex is standing on one of the first-row seats. He gives me a wolverine grin. 'It's the boy that thinks brainers are best.'

The watching Specials laugh and jeer.

'Let's see his fighting. Blakey-boy fights . . .'

I resist the urge to squeeze my eyes shut. I need to see my opponent coming.

'. . . Ilex Dalton!' Rex gives me a self-satisfied smirk. He's done this on purpose.

My eyes find Ilex in the crowd. He clambers through the Specials on to the floor and lurches his way towards me, his eyes wide. He didn't know this was going to happen. No one told him he was fighting tonight. Rex has set this up because he thinks it will be a laugh to see me fight my friend, but Rex is the fool; does he really think that Ilex and I will hurt each other for the sake of the stupid ranking system? This isn't going to be the ordeal I thought it was.

Ilex joins me in the centre of the floor. I give him a conspiratorial look. He just shrugs in response.

'It's a big one, this fight, Specials,' Rex goes on.

'We'll have a bit of a scuffle and then we'll pretend you've got me pinned down,' I whisper to Ilex.

Before Ilex can reply Rex breaks in, 'Blake, Ilex, you are luckers . . .'

I realise that the audience are hanging on his words. What's he playing at?

'. . . big luckers because tonight it's a three-er!' Rex beams at us.

The Specials gasp in surprise and then revert to cheering. What the hell is a three-er?

Rex shakes a fist in the air. 'Yes Specials! A three-er! It's brainer Blake and slow-boy Ilex.' He turns to flash his teeth at me again. 'And they fight . . . me!'

'That's ridiculous,' I say. 'We can't possibly have three of us in a fight.'

Ilex shakes his head. 'Rex fights two Specials lots of times.'

Oh.

The Specials are on their feet, yelling and stamping already. It seems they're keen on a three-way fight.

Dom slinks her way across the hall to Rex and smothers him in a good-luck embrace.

I don't know why I'm so filled with dread. After all, this is better than me going one-on-one with a Red, which is what I was expecting. I step closer to Ilex. 'This is good,' I whisper to him. 'There are two of us; we can take him on.'

'Specials don't win Rex,' he whispers back.

Rex breaks away from Dom and hands Deon his whistle. Deon gives it a blast and suddenly Rex is striding towards us.

'We just need to work together,' I say, but Ilex is mesmerised by Rex's progress. 'Come on, Ilex! What move do you want to try?'

'Blake, look out—'

Rex smacks me across the side of the head and sends me sprawling into Ilex. I crash down on top of him, getting his elbow jammed into my neck.

Good grief. Two against one and we're on the floor already.

Rex reaches down and hauls Ilex up by his collar. Ilex has enough time to kick out at Rex's knees. I scramble up and throw myself on Rex's broad back.

'Hit him, Ilex!' I shout. Rex is bucking about, trying to throw me off. I tighten my grip around his neck. 'Hit him!'

Ilex reluctantly raises a fist, but Rex is quicker and punches him under the chin. Ilex spins away. Rex drops down to the ground and rolls heavily on me. He's crushing my lungs. I think one of my ribs is cracked. Ilex drags him off me and Rex starts laying into Ilex with a volley of kicks and chops. Ilex sidesteps the first one, but then takes a blow to the head, followed by one to the chest, then the stomach. As he backs away Rex drops into a low spin and uses an extended leg to take Ilex's legs out from under him. Just as Ilex goes down and Rex is getting up I try throwing myself on to Rex's back again. This time he's caught off-balance and tips forward to his knees, then over on to poor Ilex, bringing me with him, so we're piled in a stack, with me on top. Before I can get up, a mass of I-don't-know-whose limbs are scrabbling over me. Then we're all rolling about like animals in the dirt.

The Specials in the audience laugh. We must look ridiculous flailing about on top of one another like this. I try to push myself up, but someone's leg is across my neck. My hand connects with Rex's greasy hair and I dig my nails into his scalp. Suddenly Ilex's face is in mine. His nose is bloodied. 'Go down,' he says. 'Go down and let him win faster.' Then we roll again and somehow the two of us end up on top of Rex. I clench my fist and hit him in the nose and then as he twists away, I get him again in the temple. Something rushes through me. This is it. This is what he deserves. I smack him in the mouth. The impact ricochets up my arm but I don't care. I punch him with my other hand. *That's for being such a bastard*, I think. I want to pound him again and again, but he's twisting out of my reach. 'Hold him,' I say to Ilex, but Rex manages to half sit up and send a fist into Ilex's face. Ilex falls backwards and Rex yanks one of his legs out from under him and throws me off the other one. I'm staggering to my feet yet again when Rex punches Ilex full in the face. Ilex falls and I know that he'll be taking his own advice and that he won't be getting up again. Which leaves me and Rex. I won't give up. I want to land another satisfying smack on his smug face. Anger courses through me, powering me forward to deliver the best punch of my life.

Which is when Rex launches a spinning kick that sends his accelerating foot into the side of my head and knocks me out.

When I come round, Kay is leaning over me. 'Blake? Are you okay?' She bites her soft bottom lip and frowns in concern. My head is buzzing and there's an ache in my kidneys, but seeing her sweet face worrying about me helps me to push my battered face into a smile.

'I'm fine,' I say. I know I should just be grateful that it's over, but I wish Kay hadn't seen me get such a pummelling. 'We didn't do very well,' I say.

'You did a good punch.'

'I did four! Four good punches.'

'That's good.' She nods her head encouragingly like I'm a small child.

'You missed them, didn't you?' I say.

'Sorry, Blake, but Rex is so big and so fast that I couldn't see goodly what you did.'

I can't help but wince. '*Rex is so big and so fast,*' I imitate.

Kay scowls.

Ilex comes over to us. He's mopping at his bloody nose. 'Are you hurting?' he asks.

'Of course I'm hurting – or didn't you see the part where a boy the size of a rhino was crushing the air out of me?'

Ilex raises his hands in defence.

'Sorry,' I say to him. 'It's just . . .' I grimace as I ease myself into a sitting position and scan the room. Rex is at the centre of the Reds' seating area. There are girls all over him. 'I just feel a bit cross.'

'You wanted to win it!' Kay says. 'Were you really going for the win, Blake?'

'You can't win Rex,' Ilex says, rubbing his elbow. 'It's goodest to go down fast.' He grins. 'Like me.'

'Blake isn't like you,' Kay says to Ilex. 'He wants to be winning.'

She's right; it's ridiculous, but I would have liked to have beaten Rex. I used to think that all this fighting stuff was primitive and pointless. I thought that my intellect would win over every time. But look at Rex. He's got exactly what he wanted; he's shown me up by taking both me and my friend out in a matter of minutes and the girls love him for it. I thought the outside world was so removed from this place, but now I'm not so sure that it's only in an Academy where people like Rex are in control. After all, when you think about the Long War, the Greater Power was basically a bully and they were the ones calling the shots.

Kay helps me to my feet.

'Hey, Blake-boy!' Rex bellows across the hall.

I turn to face him.

'Good fight. The Specials loved it.' He beams at the two girls hanging on his left arm and then winks at me. It doesn't make me feel any better. Rex only seems to get

215

aggressive towards me when he sees me as a threat. Clearly all this magnanimity shows that he thinks he's reduced me to a nobody again. I acknowledge his beneficence with a nod and turn to leave the room.

But Rex hasn't finished being kind to the conquered. 'You got a good punch! You got me one good punch!'

The girls around him giggle at such generosity on the champion's part.

I stiffen. 'It was *four* punches,' I say under my breath.

Kay tugs on my arm to keep me moving towards the door.

'I think you're right,' I say to her in a low voice. 'I think everyone needs to learn to fight.'

'You are learning it,' she says. 'You've learned to want the win. That's the biggest lesson.'

Which gives me the strength to send Rex and his adoring crowd a cheery wave.

Because maybe he has taught me something worth knowing after all.

37

The next morning in the grid we study circuit board diagrams and then we're given a box of parts so we can practise component assembly. I empty out a jumble of wires and small parts.

'If you have finished, Kay, do some more,' my mother says.

Kay has finished. I haven't even identified all my components. I imagine Kay's dextrous fingers pushing pieces into place and I almost groan. Somehow it's become impossible to think about Kay without getting excited. I spend my time caught between extreme arousal and deep embarrassment. I sort my capacitors into a pile and try to think neutral thoughts.

Sometime later, an impeccable appears in the doorway. 'Blake to go with me to Enforcer Rice,' he says.

My mother shoots a worried look at me before she can stop herself. She's been fidgety since she saw my bruised face. She composes herself and says, 'Blake, go with the impeccable,' in a neutral tone.

My stomach plummets. Does Rice know about my mother? I avoid looking at her in case the impeccable has been told to watch us. I climb out of my seat and head for the door. Kay gives me a look that is both worried and encouraging as I pass. I feel a warmth in my chest and, armed with that, I make my way down the corridor behind the impeccable. Maybe this isn't about my mother – maybe Rice has found out about the reading lessons, or the recs.

The impeccable takes me to Rice's office and pushes me through the door.

His room is tiny and almost bare, but he's sitting like a king on his throne. I wish I had a private room like this.

When Rice sees my battered face he smirks to himself. I think about what my mother said about the enforcers. It's true that occasionally you see one of them looking uncomfortable, wincing when they use the EMDs or averting their eyes when one of the little ones cries. Not Rice. He always looks like he's having a great time. He continues to stare at me without blinking. I fight down the urge to speak; instead I look at him. He's not much taller than I am, but he still manages to look down his nose at me.

He screws up his mouth. 'You haven't had the advantage of growing up in an Academy, Blake,' he says. 'But I have already explained that you need to learn and to learn quickly that the way to get on is to obey.'

It's funny how Rice doesn't speak to me in monosyllables like he does the rest of the Specials. I'm sure he

218

knows that I really am from a Learning Community. But that doesn't make me any less nervous about where all this is leading.

'It seems to me that since the departure of Enforcer Tong there has been some slipping of standards in your grid.'

He's talking about my mother. He knows.

'But just because one enforcer is, as yet, unaccustomed to the requisite standards of discipline let me assure you that you will not get away with insubordination.'

Maybe he doesn't know. I bite my lip.

'I will remind you one final time that in this institution you *cannot* seek to express your own opinions,' he says. He's working his mouth so hard that he's spitting, but his face remains cold. 'You should not even have your own opinions, let alone seek to draw others into trouble by sharing your ideas about etiquette at meal times.'

This is about the bowls. I almost sag with relief. I can't believe it. Does this mean he doesn't know anything about my mum? But the bowl thing was ages ago; why is he bringing it up now?

'I will say this one more time. I don't want you sharing your ideas about crockery, about fairness, about education . . .'

Does he know about the reading lessons?

'. . . about anything at all. Now, as you have conducted yourself inappropriately you must be punished.'

He's smiling. The sick bastard. What's he going to do? Give me a shock? Cut my food? It doesn't matter.

Nothing matters as long as he doesn't find out about my mother before our escape. I look him in the eye.

'You are excluded, Blake.'

'Excluded? What does that mean?'

He stands up and walks out the door. He crooks a finger to show I should follow him. It's like he's pretending to be some sinister villain. Pathetic. He leads me back to the main corridor.

'Does this mean I'm not allowed to attend lessons?' I ask.

Rice just keeps striding along and doesn't reply. His face is pulled up like he's trying not to smell something nasty.

We walk past the empty dining hall. He stops at the back door. What the efwurd is this all about? Blocking my view with his body, he types in the door code. I hear the catch click and he pushes open the door.

The light hurts my eyes. I squint at a scrubby expanse of grass. Cold air splashes me in the face like water. I take a great gulp and suddenly I can feel the difference between the cold clean air in front of me and the thick warm stink behind me. I can't believe that I haven't had any fresh air for two months.

'You are excluded for forty-eight hours,' says Rice. The corners of his mouth twitch.

'I don't understand.'

He is looking at me so intently I feel like his eyes are leaving a mark on my skin.

'You are *excluded* from the Academy. You may not return for forty-eight hours.'

'But where do I go?'

'Out, Blake. You go out.'

He can't mean what I think he means. 'Out where?' My voice is shaking.

His lips curl into a self-satisfied smile.

'Out into the Wilderness.'

Rice grips my arm and steers me out of the door. I remember weeks ago when I tried to escape through this exit. I
didn't realise that it led to the Wilderness. The cold makes
me suck in my breath. He marches me down a path. Ahead,
I recognise a stretch of Wilderness fence. Rice unlocks a
gate in it, pushes me through and locks it behind me.

'I'll see you in two days,' he says. 'Or not.'

I won't allow myself to plead with him. I keep my
mouth closed and my face blank. He stalks back into the
Academy and slams the door behind him. I notice there's
no handle on this side.

Complete silence descends. I turn around to survey the
Wilderness. It's frosty. Scrubby, white-tipped grass
stretches away from me. In the distance to the right I can
see the remains of a building. To the left there are some
woods.

I take a deep breath of icy air and walk down the rough
path trampled into the grass. I'm obviously not the first to

be excluded. The icy grass squeaks as I swivel round to get my first real look at the Academy from the outside.

Unbelievable.

The building looks like something out of a fairy tale.

I'd imagined it as a hulk of steel and concrete, but it's made of red brick and has a tiled roof. There are patterns in the bricks and ivy climbing the walls. Over to the right is a funny little clock tower. The whole place is sparkling with frost. I would never have guessed it looked like this from the stinking interior. They must have knocked down walls and dug into the ground to make all the echoing metal spaces inside. I feel nauseous thinking about what lies underneath this rosy surface. It's like looking at a ripe apple, but knowing that just beneath the skin the whole thing is rotten right through.

The wind starts to pick up and a violent shiver goes through me. I'm only wearing the regulation shirt, jacket and trousers. I tuck my elbows into my sides and cup my hands over my mouth so I can blow on them. My head is spinning from what has happened in the last few minutes. I'm in the Wilderness. Kay told me that they sent Specials out here if they broke the rules, but I don't think I ever quite believed it.

I try to push down my fear. I wonder how far the temperature drops at night. Rice is either going to find my body beaten to a pulp or frozen to death. I stamp my feet and pull myself together, but not before a little voice in my head whispers: *I bet you wouldn't be the first.*

My first thought is that maybe I can sneak back into the Academy somehow. I follow the fence along to the left. Soon I can see the corner of the Academy. On the wall running away from me is a rusting fire escape descending from the top of the building to the bottom. I can't see how you would get to it from the inside of the Academy. This whole place is badly designed. Anyway, it's no use to me because I'm cut off by the fence which stretches as far as I can see, away to the left.

I plod back towards the gate where Rice threw me out and on past to see what's there. This time the fence doesn't stretch into the distance, it makes a corner. On the other side of the fence is a steep grassy bank. At the bottom I can see a metro line and beyond that, in the distance I can make out what I think is the business sector. I try to orientate myself. The accommodation block Wilson and I went to must be over to the right somewhere. If only I could get through this fence I could escape. I step a little closer. I can hear the hum of electricity coming off it. Unless I work out a way to get under or over the fence there's no way I can get out.

A little further away from the Academy the ground dips and there's a rubbish dump with a clump of bushes on the far side. Even in the cold air the rubbish stinks, so I give it a wide berth. Part of me wants to stay close to the Academy, but if I'm going to last two nights I've got to find some water. I decide to try the woods in the distance first, since they'll provide me with some shelter from the wind too.

I hope that walking will warm me up, but even with my hands jammed under my armpits, I can't feel my fingers, and my toes are even worse.

After a while, I look back at the Academy. It's glowing in the sunlight. I turn away again and something catches my eye. Something dark and low in the grass. I jog towards it, my breath streaming out in great smoky plumes. It looks like a box. I hope that it's made of something strong enough to shelter me from the wind. I haven't eaten since breakfast and I'd like to rest. When I reach the box there's something oddly familiar about its shape. It's made of metal and it looks like a knocked-over locker. I walk round it to find an open side at the front.

It's a feeding pod. What on earth would a feeding pod be doing out here? I crawl inside. It's a relief to be out of the wind. Someone has covered the bottom of the pod with shreds of dried grass. I pick up a piece, but my fingers are so numb it slips between them. The grass is paper thin. It must have taken for ever to make a pile. I stretch out my aching legs and my boots touch something soft. I reach down and find a blanket. My insides drop. A shelter with a blanket in it must belong to someone. I'm too cold to care. I'll have to borrow the blanket and rest for at least a while. But as I struggle to pull the blanket around me, I can't help wondering what sort of person would live in a place like this?

And what will they do if they find me wrapped in their blanket?

I'm back in the factory block. I'm leaning over the balcony, looking down on Wilson's twisted body. Suddenly he turns his head. I hear his neck cracking. He stares up at me, his eyes glowing. 'What have you done to me?' he says.

I wake up with a gasp and smack my head on the pod as I try to sit up. My face aches with cold. I must have been asleep for a while as night has fallen outside the pod. I rub away the ice on my eyelashes with the blanket. Wilson's contorted face is swimming in my mind. *Wilson's dead*, I think. *There's nothing you can do now*. I lie back and curl myself up as tightly as I can. I wish I wasn't alone. I wish Kay was here.

I freeze.

There's someone out there. I hold my breath to listen. Someone or something is moving nearby. I lean forward and stare hard into the darkness. The frosty grass is lit up by moonlight, but I can't see anything except the dark smudge of the woods in the distance. I lie completely still and strain my ears. I can hear my heart. Maybe it was an animal. I scan the open space in front of me again. I hold my body rigid. Nothing happens. I wait and listen; still nothing happens. I exhale slowly and start to relax my aching muscles.

Ting!

Something hits the back of the pod. There's something behind me. *Get out into the open*, I think, *run for it*. But I don't seem to be able to make myself move.

Ting!

Someone is throwing stones at the back of the pod. I struggle to release an arm; it feels numb and heavy as if it belongs to someone else. I pull clumsily at the blanket.

Ting!

I'm yanking at the material and pedalling my feet, but the blanket clings like seaweed.

Dumpf!

Something heavier hits the back of the pod. Something like a boot. My insides turn liquid. A wave of terror runs through me and for a second I close my eyes. *Come on*. I open my eyes.

Inches from my nose is a twisted and deformed face.

I scream.

It's Wilson.

For a split second I think that he has no eyes. Then I realise that his head is upside down because he's leaning over the pod from behind, looking in at me. My scream

227

startles him and the head disappears. How can this be happening? He's dead. I was sure he was dead. Am I still dreaming?

I clamber out of my shelter and to my feet. He's there, on the other side of the pod. One eye is closed and droops at the corner. His nose is crooked. We stand in the cold looking at each other; except he doesn't look at my face, he stares into the middle of my chest.

'Wilson,' I say, 'you're alive!'

'Wilson, Philip, AEP score 92,' he says without raising his eyes from my chest.

There's something wrong. Not just the bashed-up face and the mangled arm. His voice. His eyes.

'Wilson, what happened? How did you get here?' I say.

He doesn't answer.

'Are you all right?' I ask.

Silence.

'It's cold,' I say stupidly. I'm not sure what to do.

'In cold conditions the body attempts thermoregulation, for example the hypothalamus sends messages to the muscles to cause shivering. If the body is unable to maintain normal temperature then hypothermia can set in.'

I open my mouth then close it again. 'Yes,' I say eventually. His mind has gone completely.

He seems oddly pleased. He nods his head.

'Is this your . . . ?' I look down at the pod. 'Is this yours?'

He doesn't move. I wonder if this is shock or if he's got brain damage. 'Did you set this up? It's good . . .' I say.

Wilson's terrible mouth stretches into a smile. Half his teeth are missing.

I have to choke back from gagging. 'Did you put the grass in?' I ask.

'Thermal insulation reduces the rate of heat transfer,' he says.

'Yes, we need insulation out here.'

He nods again.

I can't believe I'm talking about the weather. 'Wilson?'

'Wilson, Philip, AEP score 92,' he repeats.

'That's right,' I say, like he's a little boy. 'Do you remember me? Do you know who I am?'

Wilson lifts his eyes to my face for the first time. He winces.

'Do you know who I am?' I ask again.

His lips quiver. 'AEP 98.5,' he says.

I close my eyes. 'Oh, Wilson, none of that matters any more.' I make myself look at his twisted face. 'I'm so sorry. I tried to get help, really I did. They wouldn't listen to me . . . I'm so, so sorry.'

He shakes his head in frustration. '98.5,' he says more insistently.

'Yes,' I agree. 'That's right, you're right. Well remembered.'

Wilson smiles at me and I have to dig my nails into the palm of my hand to force myself to smile back.

In the end we both cram into the pod. Wilson has another blanket wrapped around his shoulders and we share them both. He goes on about how our proximity will help conserve body heat, but I'm just grateful to be near another human being. I lie with my back against Wilson's and listen to the wind.

I thought he was dead. I thought it was my fault too. I thought that I should have stopped those men going after him, or found someone to help or something. And now he's not dead, but he's clearly sick. And I don't know what to do. A few months ago it would have been simple. I would have taken him to an adult and I would have known that they'd take him to a doctor and that they'd look after him. But that's what I knew then. It's different to what I know now. If anyone is going to help Wilson, it's got to be me.

When I wake up in the morning, my limbs are stiff. Moving my legs feels like cracking icicles. I blow on my hands and Wilson wakes up. He wriggles out of the pod and starts rubbing his arms and legs. When he sees me, he stops and blinks. He seems surprised to see me.

'Wilson, what happened after those men attacked us? I saw you lying on the balcony. I thought you were dead,' I say.

He shrugs.

'Did someone help you?' I say. Someone must have. Otherwise there's no way that he could have survived his injuries.

He frowns.

'When I came back you were gone. Where did you go?' I persist, I have to know what happened.

'To remediate mould growth in a dwelling, reduction of moisture levels is key,' he says.

Mould. In a dwelling. Maybe he's talking about that old lady from the accommodation block's room. She had mould growing on the walls. And we're not far from the block here. She must have taken him in after I went to fetch the police. 'Was it an old lady? Did she help you? How long were you there?' I ask him.

'It takes a number of weeks for bones to heal.'

'So you were there a long time? Have you just got . . . here?' I wonder if Wilson realises exactly where he is.

He breaks into a laugh. For a moment he looks and sounds just like the old Wilson. 'She thought I was Wilderness!' he says, slapping me on the arm.

But I can't laugh with him and the smile rapidly vanishes from his face.

So the old lady helped to fix him up and then sent him straight out into the Wilderness. How did she get him through the fence? Maybe the police did it. I've heard stories about people with mental problems being sent to the Wilderness. How could anybody be so cruel? It's amazing that he's still in one piece. I look at Wilson. His hair looks clean and his nails are short. I don't think he's been here more than a few days. I can only hope that we can avoid running into any Wilderness inhabitants for another couple of days.

'Have you seen anyone out here, Wilson?'

He looks away and prods his twisted arm with his good hand. 'When a bone breaks and is incorrectly or inadequately set, the bone can heal at the wrong angle. A malunion.'

'It should've been treated by a doctor, shouldn't it?' I say. He doesn't seem to mind. I hate the way he's so calm and accepting. He's not like the old Wilson at all.

'The ability to rotate is affected by a broken radius bone,' he says.

'The ability to rotate? Wilson, you can't use your whole efwurding arm.'

'If the ulna bone and the radius bone are different lengths it causes bowing of the arm,' he says.

His arm is hanging like a lump of meat and he sounds like a medical student talking about someone else's mangled body.

'Stop talking. Just stop talking like that,' I say. My voice is rising, but I can't help it.

Wilson drops his chin on to his chest and looks up at me with confusion in his eyes.

'I'm sorry,' I say.

Wilson sticks out his lower lip. I want to shake him. He doesn't have a clue that everything is wrong. That our whole lives were a sham. I take a deep breath. 'Listen, what are we going to do now?' I say.

'In adverse weather conditions fuel is particularly important to the body,' he mumbles.

Fuel. 'Do you know somewhere we can find food?' I ask.

Wilson grins.

'You do?' I just hope it doesn't involve any kind of dead animal. 'Show me the way.'

He smiles again and we set off back in the direction of the Academy.

We walk. It didn't seem far yesterday, but even the short walk back to the Academy is much harder after a night outside. My legs feel weak and the icy grass swirls in front of my eyes. I didn't get much sleep last night. I try to imagine what Kay is doing now, but all I can think about is water. I haven't had a drink since yesterday and my tongue is thick and heavy. I keep trying to move it to a more comfortable position in my mouth, which is making me even drier. There's a dull thumping on one side of my head. I'm dehydrated. There must be rules about sending students out for exclusion. I must be entitled to water. I snort out loud so that Wilson turns to look at me. Who am I kidding? As if Rice pays any attention to the rules.

Wilson is trotting along in a businesslike fashion. He doesn't seem to notice the cold. That's good.

'I wish we had some water,' I say.

Wilson looks round at me in surprise. He stops and reaches into the deep pockets of his army-style trousers. He pulls out a plastic bottle of water and hands it to me.

'How did you . . . ?' but I don't finish the question because I'm busy drinking. It's three-quarters full and I'm not sure how easily Wilson can get hold of more. I should be restrained, but before I know it I've drunk most of it. I screw the cap on and hand it back to Wilson; he doesn't seem worried by the amount I've used up.

'Where did you get water from?' I ask.

'Water is a requisite for all life,' he says.

I give him a smile. He's still pretty smart.

'Hey, Wilson, do you remember when we were going to go to an entertainment centre to meet girls?'

Wilson blinks at me. It's impossible to talk to him. I can't believe the boy in front of me is the same Wilson who's been my best friend since I was five. We carry on in silence.

When we're almost at the boundary gate next to the Academy Wilson veers off towards where I saw the rubbish tip yesterday. I find myself looking down into a hollow filled with junk. There are metal chunks of broken learning grids, torn-up chairs like the ones in the salon but with even less upholstery, broken circuit boards, dirty sheets and scraps of material. It's a dump for the Academy.

Wilson is wriggling his shoulders in excitement. He's really pleased to show this to me. I feel horribly tired all of a sudden. I sit down on the lip of the hollow, but Wilson grabs my hand and pulls.

'Get off!' I snatch my hand away.

Wilson draws back like a whipped puppy.

'Sorry! I'm sorry. Show me where the food is.' I've already got a horrible suspicion that I know exactly where the food is.

He rubs his hands in anticipation.

This is what he's like now. Swinging emotions like a little kid. Or like a really old man. What am I going to do? I've got to come up with a plan to get him into the Academy.

Wilson shows me an area of the dump where the black plastic bags are cleanest and newest. This is where we'll be looking for our breakfast.

I work methodically through the bags, but Wilson is easily distracted and when I look up half an hour later he's making a low note by blowing across the top of a glass bottle filled with scummy water.

'Frequency of the note is related to the length of the column!' he calls.

Whatever plan I come up with to help Wilson, it's going to take a long time to explain it to him.

Under some of the black bags I come across another bashed-up feeding pod, with the nozzles torn off. How did it get into such state? I guess all the stuff in here was broken by Specials. On the back of the pod there is a strut at each corner with the securing nut still screwed on. I can't believe they waste all this stuff. You'd think they'd recycle at least some of it.

Suddenly I realise what I'm looking at. This tip is filled with nuts and bolts and slivers of shiny shrap. I'm standing in a Specials' jewellery shop. I remember Kay cradling her necklace to her chest. I start unscrewing bolts and filling my pockets. I think about Kay's eyes lighting up when she sees all this shiny junk.

And then I just think about Kay.

Later I get back to the black bags; some are full of manky packaging and used paper towels, one of them oozes something green and stinking, but Wilson was right that some also contain scraps of food. I collect: one stale bread roll, some quite clean chunks of carrot, a half-eaten ham sandwich and an almost-full packet of Corn Crispies. Wilson and I double wrap ourselves in the blankets again and share the food. I feel much better and even slightly warmer when we've finished.

'We need to think about shelter for the night,' I say.

I debate whether we should move away from the Academy and maybe explore the broken-down building I can see in the distance, but I have the feeling that the further into the Wilderness we go the more likely we are to find some of its inhabitants. In the end I decide that we have the materials right here to make a shelter so we may as well use them.

In the thicket of trees and bushes next to the dump we spend the afternoon leaning together pieces of corrugated metal and sections of broken grid. We cover the whole thing with a sheet of plastic. It's not great, but it will help keep the worst of the wind out.

In the evening I divide up the rags and bits of clothing

we've come across and we huddle together in the shack. Waves of tiredness are washing over me, but I want to ask Wilson more about what happened to us that day.

'Wilson, why do you think those men at the factory block wanted to hurt us?'

He looks at me with his full attention, but he doesn't say anything.

'I mean, that was when all the weirdness started. It was almost as if they were waiting for us.'

'Waiting for the red jacket,' Wilson says.

'What do you mean?'

'They chased me and said, "This is the one, in the red jacket." You need accurate identification of the victim. A red jacket is not an adequate indicator.'

I look at Wilson with my mouth wide open. He returns my gaze without blinking. He doesn't realise the impact of what he is telling me. He is so badly broken that I don't think he fully understands what swapping jackets with me that day has done to him. *I* was the owner of that red jacket. It was *me* they wanted. It should be me with the useless arm and the shattered mind.

Within minutes Wilson is asleep, but I lie with my eyes closed, asking over and over again why someone wanted to kill me that day.

And if they still want to.

42

I wake up. Outside, something is howling. Fear spreads across my chest. I sit up. It's an animal. A dog. And there are voices. It's the Wilderness people coming. They sound angry and close. It's freezing and my heart is thumping. I turn to look at Wilson. His eyes are wide open and staring into the darkness above him.

'Wilson?'

He doesn't answer. He's completely still, not even blinking.

I eye the sides of our shelter; it's trembling in the wind. We're not safe.

'Wilson, it's the Wilderness people.'

He still won't answer. I shake his good arm. He whimpers and shrinks away from me. The dog is barking now. They're getting closer. I stand up, keeping my blanket wrapped around me, but the cold night air seeps in anyway. I push aside a flap of plastic and look out into the night. Everything is frost-tinged in the moonlight. The voices and the barking have stopped. My jaw aches from my teeth chattering. A breeze scythes through my hair. I listen hard. There's nothing but the wind making the shelter rustle and creak. They don't know we're here. Maybe they'll just go away again.

'In the bushes,' rings out a deep voice.

My legs go weak. I can see a group of them silhouetted, coming towards the shelter. They're getting closer. I twist round and lunge back into the shelter. I grab Wilson by the wrist and yank him to his feet.

'Wilson! We've got to run.'

I fight my way out of the back of the shelter, dragging Wilson behind me. My blanket falls to the ground and the cold rushes to cover me like icy water. I drop Wilson's hand to push through the thicket. 'Quickly,' I say and we sprint across the grass.

'There they are,' shouts one of the voices from behind.

I hear them running.

I head for the Academy. Wilson is just behind me. There's nowhere to hide. Soon we'll reach the fence next to the Academy walls and we'll be trapped. An image from the Info flashes into my mind: a boy slit open from chin to waist by Wilderness men. They're getting closer. My legs feel weak and useless. My left foot lands at an angle. I stumble forwards. My hands hit the ground and I have to scramble upright again. Wilson pulls in front of me. They're right behind us. I try to move faster, but I can hardly breathe. We've almost reached the fence, maybe someone from the Academy will see—

Smack! One of them grabs my legs from behind and I slam down on the hard earth. He clambers on to my back, jamming his knees into me, making it even harder to gasp for breath.

'You're dead,' hisses the deep voice in my ear.

My mouth is full of dirt. The ground is freezing. My hands are stinging. I try to lift my head, but my attacker slams it back down. I hear the dog barking on my left. It must have gone after Wilson. I hope Wilson found somewhere to hide. A pair of feet walk into my eyeline.

'Use this,' say the feet to Deep Voice.

My arms are yanked behind me and they tie my wrists together with some sort of smooth cord. They haul me to my feet.

When I get my first look at them I stare in amazement.

They're boys.

They're only boys. One of them is shorter than me. His hair is straggly and he has a scar down the side of his face. He looks me up and down and sniffs. He points to my legs and Deep Voice ties them together, but with enough free cord between my two feet so that I can shuffle along. Shuffle, but not run.

'Walk,' says Scarface.

I don't move. I want to stay close to the Academy. If I make enough noise someone might come out and intervene.

241

'Help!' I shout. Before I can draw breath to continue, Scarface kicks my legs out from underneath me. I land awkwardly on my elbow. He grabs me by the hair and ties a gag over my mouth.

'Do the things I say or your friend gets big hurt,' he says.

He jams a hand under my arm and I struggle to my feet.

I look up at the Academy, but there's not a single light on.

They walk me all the way to the woods. I strain to work my hands free, but I can't. I try to work out what they want with me. I've got nothing of value. I don't understand why they haven't killed me already. Eventually they stop in a clearing and tie me to one of the trees. Scarface pulls off my gag.

'You can shout all you want out here,' he says.

There's no sign of Wilson. I hope he got away. Maybe these Wilderness boys won't keep looking for him now that they've got me.

Scarface tells Deep Voice to build a fire. That's good, I tell myself. A fire is good. I'm shaking all over. My bones ache with cold.

When the fire is lit another boy with a face like a monkey comes crashing through the trees into the clearing.

'Efwurding Special got away and the mutt,' says Monkey-boy. He stops when he catches sight of me. 'Nice,' he says, slapping Scarface on the back.

I struggle against the cords that are wrapped around my upper body and arms, binding me to the tree. They hold fast. 'Whatever it is you want from me,' I say, 'couldn't we talk about it? I'm not dangerous . . .'

'Hah!' barks Scarface and all the Wilderness boys burst out laughing. '*Oooh hoo hoo hoo!* He says he's not danger.'

Monkey-boy sneers at me. I drop my gaze down. I can see how filthy and tattered his trousers are in the firelight. And his jacket.

His Academy jacket.

I can't believe it. I squint into the darkness at each of them in turn. They're all wearing Academy uniforms. They're not Wilderness. They're Specials.

'Did you get excluded too?' I say. 'I was excluded. I mean, we're on the same side really, aren't we?'

Scarface stares at me.

'How long for?' I ask. 'Haven't they let you back in yet?' I don't recognise them, but there are hundreds of Specials at the Academy.

Scarface wraps his hand around the cool end of one of the branches in the fire.

'They've got to let you back in sometime haven't they?' I say.

Scarface pulls out the burning stick and takes a step towards me. Deep Voice settles on his haunches, watching. I swallow.

'You've done well,' I say stupidly. 'Not many people could survive in the Wilderness.'

Scarface stops in front of me. He raises the burning branch in front of my face. My eyes sting with the smoke. I press back against the tree. He steps forwards.

'They ought to let you back . . .' My face is frying. I can feel my eyelashes singeing.

'Permanent,' he says.

'Sorry?' A spark flies off the branch and burns my cheek. I suck in my breath.

'*Permanent* exclusion,' he says.

Horrible visions of what you would have to do to be excluded permanently flash into my mind. I turn my face to the left as far from the heat as I can and find myself staring into Scarface's flame-lit eyes. He bares his teeth in a humourless smile. Now I understand why they've brought me all this way just to tie me to a tree.

They're enjoying themselves.

'Couldn't I help you?' I ask.

'Help? What's help?' says Scarface. It makes me think of Kay and suddenly I want to cry because I'm starting to think that I won't see her again.

'We don't need your stupid brainer word,' says Scarface pushing the branch even closer to my cheek.

'Stupid brainer words,' repeats the Monkey-boy and he spits on the ground. Deep Voice rises to his feet and comes to stand next to Scarface. I've got to offer them something so they won't hurt me.

'I can get back into the Academy,' I say. 'I could get

245

you supplies, things you need. If you'll just give me a bit of time . . .'

'Now,' says Monkey-boy.

'But I've got nothing,' I try straining against the cord again. 'I haven't got anything to give you. No water, no clothes. I've got no food . . .'

'You're wrong, you no-ranker,' says Scarface, passing the burning branch to Deep Voice and wrapping a hand around my throat. 'You are the food.'

My mind is whirling. This is what happens to Specials who get excluded? They get thrown out into the Wilderness and they get eaten. By other Specials. I think of Lanc. Is this what happened to him?

The Academy is evil. It's sick. My stomach heaves, I'm going to throw up.

'Ahh rah rah rah rah!' There's a volley of barking behind the boys.

Scarface drops the hand at my throat and turns round. 'Stupid dog. Go and see,' he says to Deep Voice. Deep Voice makes his way through the trees. I'm afraid that the dog has got Wilson. The barking stops and we listen to Deep Voice ploughing through the trees. 'It's efwurding dark,' he calls back.

Scarface raises his hands in annoyance. He turns to me. I watch him pull a knife from his pocket. I try to swallow. His eyes zoom in on me like lasers. I thought he'd wait. I feel cheated. He raises the knife and holds the point to my neck. It's like someone has turned up the volume inside me. I can hear my heart thud and my blood rush and my lungs pump. I can feel every nerve ending tingling and every strand of hair standing on end. And the point of his knife dragging on my skin. Even though I'm about to die, I feel very alive. Scarface's eyes widen and—

'*Aiiiiiiiiiiiiiieeeeeee!*' someone behind him screams.

'What the efwurd?' Scarface lowers the knife and spins round.

I slump with relief. Only the cords are holding me up.

'*Ahhhhhhh!*'

I think it's Deep Voice. I hope it's Deep Voice and not Wilson.

Scarface looks at Monkey-boy. 'Watch him,' he says. He grips his knife and runs towards the screaming.

Monkey-boy stands up. He flexes his fingers, then he wanders a few steps in the direction Scarface took. It's gone quiet. He peers into the trees. Something tickles my left wrist. I imagine a beetle crawling over my hand so I shake it as much as the cords will allow.

'Nylons are condensation copolymers,' comes a whisper from behind the tree.

Wilson.

Wilson is cutting the cords. Oh wonderful, clever, poor, mad Wilson. He's trying to cut the cords. I can feel the vibrations as he saws with something. Where did he find something sharp? How did he get away from the dog? And the boys?

248

Monkey-boy looks back at me. From this angle Wilson is hidden behind the tree. I keep my face blank and stare into the fire. Monkey-boy goes back to his position, listening out for the others. One of the cords goes slack and drops to my feet. What am I going to do? I'll have to just make a break for it as soon as Wilson gets through the second cord. We'll have a slight start on Monkey-boy.

Then everything happens at once.

I hear movement through the trees and Scarface calling to Monkey-boy, 'That efwurding brainer hit him with a big thing! You carry him with me.'

The second cord drops to the ground.

I step away from the tree, but Monkey-boy hears me and turns, open-mouthed.

I wish I had a stone to throw, but I remember that my pockets are full of metal. I take two handfuls of nuts and bolts and fling them at his head. They fall short, but as I turn to run he says, 'Shrap!' and falls to his knees to gather it up. I guess even out here Specials value shrap.

I follow Wilson running through the trees. I half hear Scarface's strangled rage when he finds I'm gone.

'Get them!' he shouts at Monkey-boy.

'But I'm getting *shrap*!' says Monkey-boy.

I fix my eyes on the back of Wilson's head and keep running. Soon I can hear the boys behind us. We come out of the trees and pound back towards our shelter. I wonder if there's anything there that we could use as weapons. There are only two of them now; maybe we could take them on.

We run and run. By the time we reach the lip of the rubbish pit, I'm exhausted. Wilson pulls me down into a crouch. I'm panting for breath. The boys are getting closer.

'I propose a tactical diversion,' Wilson gasps out.

'You want me to divert them?' I can hardly speak.

'I will lead them off,' he says.

'No! That's not fair. Let's fight them together.' I stand up, but Wilson lays a hand on my arm.

'In times of emergency the greatest minds must be protected,' he says. He gives me a smile like the old Wilson used to before he told a joke.

And then he punches me in the face.

I'm thrown backwards over the precipice and land on my back on something soft. I hear Wilson running. Then a cry goes up. They've seen him. I try to shout, but I'm completely winded. I roll on to my front and retch. I try to get to my feet, but I can't find my footing. Whatever I've fallen on is uneven and slippery. I hear my blood rushing in my ears and the ground seems to be tilting. It swings up and smacks me on the side of the head.

I wake up. There's a terrible smell. Like maggoty fish and rotten eggs. I try to turn away from it, but it's thick around my head. My brain feels like it's throbbing against my skull. I'm cold and I'm lying on something lumpy. I try to open my eyes, but they're stuck shut. I lift a hand and rub away a thick crust of what turns out to be blood. When I peel open my eyes, the bright light makes me squint. I'm surrounded by black refuse sacks spilling with garbage. Wilson knocked me into the rubbish pit. Wilson. He whacked me down here to save me while he . . . An awful image of what they will have done to Wilson comes to me and I vomit into the rotting rubbish.

I slowly scrabble my way out of the pit. My arms and legs are weak and floppy. Finally I roll over the lip of the hollow. The air is fresher up here. And colder. The decomposing rubbish was giving off heat. That stinking pit has kept me alive.

I've got to look for Wilson. Maybe he managed to get away from those boys or maybe they've kept him tied up till this morning. Neither seems likely, but I've got to hope. I hug my arms around myself and try to rub some warmth into my arms. I'll start by looking in the woods.

'Blake!' someone shouts.

For a moment my heart rises imagining that it's Wilson, but it's the wrong voice and the wrong name. I turn back in the direction of the shout. The gate in the fence next to the Academy is open. Enforcer Rice is calling to me. My exclusion is over but I don't want to go back without Wilson. I start to run towards the woods.

'BLAKE!'

I risk a look back. He's following me. And there's someone else. I try to increase my speed but my breathing is already ragged. I can hear them behind me. I scan the ground ahead for a weapon. I stumble to a halt and pick up a stick. I turn to face Enforcer Rice and one of the impeccables.

'Don't come any closer,' I pant. I raise my stick.

Rice sniffs. 'Take him,' he says to the impeccable, already turning away.

The impeccable eyes my stick and snorts. He steps towards me and I focus all my energy into thrusting the stick into his eye.

He bats it away like he would a fly and pins my arms behind me. I'm forced on to my knees.

'You don't understand,' I say. 'I've got to find my friend. He needs help. They were going to . . .'

'We see'd him,' grins the impeccable.

'Where? Is he all right? He needs a doctor. Show m—'

'Shut up, Blake.' Rice yanks me up. 'It's touching that you're making "friends" out here in the Wilderness, but there's not much a doctor could do for him now.' He leans in so his face is close to mine. 'Looks like wild dogs got him.' He smiles. 'Horrible mess.' He pushes me in the back and smacks me around the head. I don't feel it. All I can think about is that now Wilson really is dead and everything is my fault.

The impeccable half drags me back to the Academy, all the time cursing me for the way I stink. Once we're inside Rice looks at his muddied boots and tuts.

'I don't like dirt, Blake,' he says. He makes a fist and punches me in the stomach. I double over. I feel like I'm going to cough up my intestines.

'That's why I don't like you,' he says.

I can't speak.

'Should've left him,' says the impeccable.

'As we are approaching a day of scrutiny it doesn't do to have too much wastage,' says Rice.

I look up through my hair. Scrutiny? I suppose that when The Leader arrives for his visit it will be up to Rice to make sure that the Academy appears in a good light. Just you wait, Rice. There are a few things I'd like The Leader to scrutinise.

'Get clean,' Rice says to me. He does a little jump kick and sends his boot into my shin with a crack. I grasp my hands around my leg, but I manage not to cry out. The impeccable grins as Rice walks away. It's the jump that makes me hate Rice most.

I drag myself upstairs. It seems odd to me that the dormitory is still here unchanged. It's empty; everyone is downstairs in the morning grid session. I sit on my bed. I lean forward and place a hand on Kay's pillow. I don't know how long I stay like this but when I hear footsteps on the corridor I hurry into the shower and let the tepid water pour down on my bowed head. I can feel the blood pulsing painfully in my hands and feet as I start to thaw out, but there is a frozen space inside me that I don't think will ever be warm again.

I know that I should go downstairs and into the grid, but when I get out of the shower I'm overcome by a wave of tiredness. I get into my bed. If they want me, they can come and get me. And what can they do anyway? Actually, they can do anything they like. But I just don't care any more.

When I wake up, someone is stroking my hair. I blink. It's my mother.

'Mum!'

'Shh,' she says, but she wraps me in her arms anyway. We stay like that for a long time. 'It will be all right,' she says. I try to believe that it's possible for anything to ever be all right again.

Eventually I pull away. 'You shouldn't be here. What if someone else comes?'

'I know. I just had to see that you were okay. When I heard that you'd been excluded I didn't realise what it meant. My roommate said something this morning. You know, I think she enjoyed shocking me, and then I didn't know what to do. I couldn't get out of that stupid door to come and get you and . . .' She catches her breath. 'But you're okay. You *are* okay, aren't you?'

She's searching my face. I don't have the energy to tell her about Wilson now.

'I'm fine,' I say.

We hear a door slamming somewhere out on the corridor.

'I have to go.' She kisses my forehead and leaves.

When I wake again there are students coming into the dormitory. I roll over and watch the door, waiting for Kay. I see her white-blonde head peer around the door; she looks straight to my bed.

'Blake!'

'Kay.' In spite of everything my heart lifts.

'You came back,' she says.

'Yes,' I say. But Wilson didn't. Wilson will never come back. I look at Kay. No one is going to take her away. A wave of desperation rises up in me. 'Listen,' I say. I stand up and grab hold of her hand. 'Kay, you have to promise me that you'll come with me and Mum when we escape.'

'I'm not talking escaping more times. Specials can't escape,' she says, pulling hand away.

'Why not?'

Kay throws up both her hands in frustration.

'Why won't you just talk to me about it?' I say.

'Because it's an efwurding stupid idea.'

It's like she's slapped me in the face. She brings her arms back down to her sides.

'I don't want to have bad words with you,' she says. 'I want you tell me about all things that happened to you outside.' She touches me gently on the arm.

I want to tell her everything.

255

'Hey Kay,' Lou yells from the other end of the dormitory. 'Rex wants you.'

Kay looks back at me.

'You don't have to go,' I say.

'Blake,' she says. Already she's tensed up, looking after Lou; she can hardly bear to still be here when she could be dashing off to her precious Rex. 'I want to talk. I do. When I come back?'

'It's fine. You don't have to talk to me. I just don't see why you have to run because Ape-boy has called you.'

She touches my arm again, but this time I pull away.

'Because I want to be Dom. Rex chooses who is Dom.'

A wave of anger washes over me. 'Why is that? Why does everyone have to listen to Rex and do what he says? He's not smart or brave . . . It's just because he's ginger and his name is Rex.'

'Blake, don't! Some people could hear you,' she says. 'Anyway Rex isn't real his name—'

'I like to think he's called Pig-face,' I interrupt.

'—that's what they're all called.'

I stop fiddling with the label on my blanket. 'What do you mean, that's what they're all called?'

'You know. The top Red. He's always called Rex.'

I feel a rush of cold in my chest. 'Oh, that's just lovely. You know what Rex means don't you?'

'Yes. I said it. The top Red.'

'I know, I know, but in Latin – that's a language they spoke a really long time ago – it means king.'

256

'What's "king"?'

'An important person. He tells everyone what to do.'

'Oh.'

'Those Reds fancy themselves, don't they?'

Kay shrugs her shoulders. She won't say anything against the Reds.

'Wait a minute,' I say. 'Is Dom really called Dom?'

'No, it's the littler word for, you know . . .'

'Stop saying "you know", Kay. I don't know, do I? I haven't grown up here and if I'm ever going to work out how to get out of here then it would help if you could tell me things without treating me like an idiot for not knowing in the first place.'

'Don't bad talk me like that. Just because I can't talk satin—'

I snort. '*Latin*, Kay, it's Latin.'

'You won't laugh at me when I'm Dom.' She glares at me.

What a mess. A moment ago she was pleased to see me. I can't bear to fall out with Kay on top of everything else. 'I'm not laughing,' I say. 'Look, what is Dom short for?'

'Domina. What does that mean in . . . Latin?'

'Lady or mistress.' This is weird. 'It's like someone has thought this out. Tell me some more names for things,' I say.

She thinks for a moment, 'Sometimes Reds are called Rufus – does that mean red?'

'Sort of. It's more like ruddy. Seems like someone is mocking the Reds.'

257

'What's "mocking"?'

'Making fun of them, laughing at them.'

'You'd have to be stupid to laugh at the Reds.'

'I do it.'

'I know.'

I pull a face at Kay.

'Why are you all –' she clenches a fist and grits her teeth '– like this? We knowed that Rex is the king.'

'But who thought up these names?' I ask.

'I don't know, people a big time back. Maybe the first Rex.' Her eyes are on the door. She thinks I'm a waste of time and can't wait to run to him instead.

'I know you don't like it when I question what Specials know,' I say. 'But let me ask you this: have you ever been taught any Latin?'

'No,' she says.

'Do you think that they have ever taught Latin at the Academy?'

'No. They don't teach us any words, do they?'

'So it seems unlikely to me that a Special made up those names,' I say.

'Who did then?' She can't help it, she's interested.

'I'd guess an enforcer, probably Rice. He's got a pretty sick sense of humour.'

'Rice? No, it was before him. From when the Academy beginned.'

I stand still. I feel as if I'm falling backwards and that the room is rushing away from me, but when I look at my feet I'm still here. It's like a series of tumblers falling into place in a lock. My growing uneasiness about everything suddenly makes sense.

A thousand snippets of information, lingering doubts, unanswered questions and little clues have suddenly joined up in my mind. And the big clues that I've just been trying to ignore: a police force who don't want to investigate certain crimes, an education system that mistreats children, and a government that makes sure no one really questions anything.

'When you think about it, it's obvious,' I say finally. 'It's all the Leadership, all The Leader.'

'What is The Leader?' Kay asks.

'Everything that is wrong. The leader is controlling everyone'

I lift a hand to push my hair out of my eyes and it shakes. Kay looks at the hand and then at my face. She puts an arm around me and leads me into the bathroom and into the cubicle in the furthest corner and locks the door behind us. She sits me down. 'Tell me,' she says.

'But Rex . . .'

'Efwurd Rex. Tell me everything.'

And for the first time I tell her exactly what has happened to me. Everything from the moment the men attacked me and Wilson in the factory block. What the old woman said. Having my records wiped. P.C. Barnes telling me to change my name. Finding Wilson again and what those awful boys will have done with him.

259

Afterwards I realise that I've been crying and that Kay is holding my hand.

'Oh, Blake,' she says when I'm finished.

'All my life I've behaved exactly as they wanted me to. They train the Academy kids to man their factories and they train the Learning Community kids to use their brains to further the system, but we're told not to think about what it's really all about. I'm an idiot for not realising before.'

But in a way I did realise. I can see now that a part of me knew something was wrong. Learning Communities are supposed to encourage questions, but there were certain questions we knew not to ask. And then there were the rumours about terrorists who wanted to bring the Leadership down. We were made to believe that they were evil people, but now I see that I should have tried to find out why they wanted to remove the government.

Kay reaches out with her other hand and strokes my hair. 'Blake, you're all no colour,' she says.

'I knew, Kay. I knew that there was something wrong with the way Academies are hidden away. I knew it was wrong to separate factory workers from everybody else. I knew that there wasn't enough criticism of the Leadership. I even knew there was weird stuff going on at the Learning Community. I just chose not to think about it.'

'How is all this coming from Rex's name?'

'Because the Specials thought that they had something that was theirs. They thought that even in this horrible place that they could make their own little gang with its own little names. But they were wrong. Even *that* is something they were made to do. And it's the same with the kids in the Learning Community – they're not in control either. They've got to grow up to be good little Leadership team members. And if they don't . . .'

Efwurd. What about that rebellious boy, Fisher? And that enforcer they said had killed him and been sent to the Wilderness. Maybe they just didn't fit in with the Learning Community's plan for them. And now that I think about it, they weren't the only two to leave without much of an explanation. I slam my palm against my forehead.

'I've been having these thoughts about the Leadership for weeks. Why didn't I put it all together?'

Kay gives me a lopsided smile. 'Because you didn't want to.'

It's true. My throat is tightening. 'You don't seem surprised. Did you already know all this?' I say.

'It's easier to see the bad when bad is happening to you. When you have nice things you can look at the nice things and not see the bad.'

'And that's the problem isn't? How will things ever change when no one wants to look at what's happening?'

'I don't know,' she says.

'Neither do I. But I swear to you that somehow I am going to *make* people see what's going on.'

Kay stays with me that whole night. She doesn't even send a message to Rex. We go down to the salon, which is warmer than the bathroom, and sit in the same chair together. We don't talk much. Just being next to her makes me feel better. Later, when we're in bed, just after the lights flick off I hear Kay roll over to face my bed. 'I will come with you on Saturday,' she whispers.

'Thank you,' I say. And I don't just mean for agreeing to escape.

As the week goes on I start to think much more clearly. Now when Wilson comes into my mind I'm filled with anger instead of sadness and the anger powers me. I know that we will get out of here and I am determined that once we do, I will expose this whole rotten, corrupt system and things will change. Things have got to change.

The days pass in a blur. I avoid looking at my mother

in class. Once during an afternoon session Rice appears at the door, causing my heart to ricochet around my chest. I expect him to pull me from the grid, but he just lingers in the doorway watching my mother deliver a lesson on microchips. She pretends not to notice him and in the end he leaves without a word.

On the day of our escape I'm so afraid of accidentally giving the game away that I spend most of my time with my eyes fixed on the floor. At dinner time Kay leans into my pod. 'I said to the Specials no reading classes, so do you want to teach me?' she says.

It's like she's asked me on a date. I can't help smiling. She smiles back.

'Is that a yes smile?' she says.

'Yes.' It will be good to have something to do other than worry.

'We could go to a Making room.'

I don't know what to say.

'It's quiet there and no one will see,' she says.

I stare at her.

She leans closer. 'No one will see the book,' she whispers.

'The book, yes the book. I'll, um, get the book and meet you down there.'

Kay nods.

I go upstairs. It's only a reading lesson, I tell myself. But I'm still smiling.

*　　*　　*

When I get downstairs I see lots of Specials pairing up and disappearing behind doors. As the throng parts I see Kay standing outside a cubicle. Talking to Rex. The butterfly that was in my chest turns into a rock. Kay looks up and sees me; I think that she's going to say something, but she turns back to Rex. He follows her gaze and spots me.

'It's Blakey-boy!'

He's in one of his jolly moods. I hate it when he pretends we're mates.

'You getting some Making?' he asks. 'It's been a big wait for you! What girl is it?'

I look at Kay. She looks at her feet.

Rex laughs. 'Oh, she's a good girl. She fights hard. I bet she Makes hard too.' He turns to leer at Kay. 'Maybe I should Make with you one day.'

I expect Kay to punch him, but instead she just smiles up at him, as if that's exactly what she'd like. Then he pats her on her bottom and swaggers off to talk to a bunch of Reds at the other end of the corridor.

'Are you going to let him get away with that?'

'Blake—'

'Because we both know that you wouldn't let anyone else speak to you like that. You certainly wouldn't let anyone else touch you like—'

'Blake, it's Rex. I don't want to make trouble. I don't want him to start thinking a thing is going on. We have to be careful.'

'Don't give me that. This is a perfect opportunity for you to tell him what a pig he is, but even though we are leaving—'

'Shh,' she hisses.

I lower my voice, 'Even though we're going, you can't help yourself, can you? You think he's so crimson that you just have to suck up. You couldn't even bring yourself to tell him that you were with me, could you? You don't want to spend time in a Making room with me when you could be with Rex.' I finish up out of breath and glaring at her.

She doesn't deny it.

Eventually she sighs and takes a slow breath like I'm this immature little kid that she's got to try to explain things to. 'Blake—'

'Don't,' I say and storm off to the salon.

The room is empty when I get there and I slump down in one of the chairs.

I think of all the bad things anyone ever told me about Academy girls. I thought Kay was different. Obviously I was wrong.

Later I go to see Ilex to talk to him about tonight. 'Remember, I'll meet my mum and then I'll come and get you two,' I say.

'What about Kay?' Ilex asks.

'I don't think Kay is coming.' Before he can start asking questions about that I remind him that they need to

265

wear both their uniforms and bring the food we've been hoarding, then I go back to my own dormitory.

I've been lying in bed for about an hour when the senior Specials' buzzer goes and the door is locked, but Kay is still not in her bed. She must be somewhere with Rex. I'm not sure I care any more. I'm getting out of here and if she wants to stay with her precious Rex then that's up to her.

I wait for what I hope is several hours. Most of the Specials seem to be asleep. Someone turns over and the bed creaks. Further up the dormitory there is some whispering. I slide out of bed and tip-toe towards the bathroom. Out in the corridor, I stop and listen. I can hear the impeccables' patrol lumbering their way down the stairs. I press myself into the shadows and wait until their heavy footsteps fade away.

Once I'm in the classroom, I look up at the clock on the wall. Its digital display glows green in the darkness. 00.38 – I've got a while to wait. Time drags by.

At 1.50 I start to watch the door. I'm twitching in anticipation.

Two o'clock comes and goes.

2.09.

2.16.

I'm panicking. What if my mother's roommate has caught her? What if her fake name has been discovered?

2.24.

She's not coming. Something must have happened. My stomach lurches and I start to imagine the worst again. I mustn't panic; perhaps she's just waiting for the coast to be clear. I sit with my mind in a whirl for over an hour. The last time I look at the clock it's 3.23.

The next thing I know I'm waking up with a crick in my neck from where I've fallen asleep hunched up in a compartment. The grid door is hissing open.

It's Ilex.

'Blake,' he whispers, 'you didn't come. Ali is in the LER.'

I look at the clock. It's gone five. She didn't come. Something must have stopped her. I rub my face and try to take in what Ilex is saying. 'I didn't come because my mother never came. What did you say about Ali?'

'I was awake and you didn't come. I went to see Ali and she wasn't in her bed. I woked up a little Special and said "Where is Ali?" He said Rice put her in the LER for the night.'

Everything is going wrong at once. 'Why?'

'He didn't know it. Why didn't your mum come?'

'I don't know. There must have been a problem.'

'I thought a problem. I came to find you.' He looks around the room. 'No Kay?'

Just her name is like a stab in the chest. She didn't even bother to tell me she didn't want to come. 'No Kay,' I say and Ilex doesn't ask any more questions.

I rub my aching neck. 'I won't know what happened till I get to speak to my mother. We'd better get back to bed. As soon as the morning buzzer goes we can look for Ali.'

He bites his lip, 'I have to get her away from Rice. Will we go?'

'We will,' I promise him. 'One day, soon. We're going to get out of this place.'

Back in the dormitory, Kay's bed is still empty. What the hell has she been doing with Rex all night long? But when I look up the dormitory I can see Rex's auburn head on his pillow. Where can Kay be? I climb into bed and my mind fizzes with all the horrible possibilities of what could have prevented my mother from turning up. When the buzzer sounds, I rush to splash my face with cold water before Ilex comes to get me. When I come back from the bathroom, Kay is waiting for me.

'Blake,' she says.

'I'm not interested,' I say, and turn away. 'And where the hell have you been? You know, if you didn't want to come that's fine, but you could have told me, you could have put the whole thing at risk—'

'LER.'

'You haven't even asked why I'm still here . . .' I register what she's said. 'You were in the LER too?'

'Yes, Rice put me there for the night.'

'Is that what happens when you Make with Rex these days?'

'Efwurding hell, Blake, stop about Rex. I have to tell you a thing you have to know—'

'I don't want to know anything you've got to tell me. Why would I be interested in what you've got to say? You know, Kay, I used to respect you because I thought you were different to other girls in here, but I'm not sure that's true any more.'

'Blake, it's your mother.'

Fear runs through me. 'What is it? What's happened?'

She pulls me closer to her so she can whisper.

'Some person told Rice that your mother gave Ali food one time.'

'What happened?'

'Rice came to get Ali and was all questions. I saw it. I tried to help it. I said it was me. He took us to the LER and got your mother and he was all angry that Ali was no talking. He was going to give Ali a shock and . . . your mother stopped him.'

'How?'

'She punched him.'

A laugh escapes me. But it's not funny. It's not funny at all. Hitting Rice is a serious mistake. This is why she didn't come last night. 'What are they going to do to her?' I say, trying to stop my voice from trembling.

'Rice has done it. He sent her on sick leave,' Kay says.

'Sick leave. That's okay, isn't it? Anywhere that isn't here would be better . . .'

Kay is biting her lip.

'What?' I say.

'It's maybe a lie—'

'Just tell me.'

'They say that when enforcers go on sick leave that they . . .'

'What? Come on!'

'That they go out into the Wilderness,' she says in a rush.

They've sent my mother out into the Wilderness where feral boys eat people.

'But they can't! She was a teacher!' I say.

'I don't think they . . . What-do-you-say? . . . care. I don't think they care about the enforcers, like they don't care about the Specials.'

'How long for?' I say.

'How long?'

'How long is this "sick leave" for? I mean if you can avoid those freaky boys it is possible to survive for a few days out there.'

'I don't know.' Kay is screwing her hands into a ball.

'Well, think! What about the last time? When enforcers go on sick leave how long is it usually before they come back?'

'Listen, Blake . . .'

I can see it in her face before she even finishes her sentence.

'No one has ever come back.'

271

'I'm going out to get her,' I say.

'Blake, that's a no-bad-shouldn't,' Kay says.

'I have to. I've got to go after my mother.'

'They'll eat you.' She clenches her fists and for a moment I'm pleased because Kay doesn't want me to be eaten. I laugh at how ridiculous that sounds.

'It's not laugh-y,' she says.

'Funny. No, it's not funny.' I wonder if it's still freezing outside. 'I've got to help my mum.'

'You can't get out. We still don't know how to get out that door.'

'We won't need the code if I get thrown out,' I say.

I pull on my boots and head for the grid. Kay follows me. 'I wanted to come last night,' she says. 'I wanted to tell you about your mum, but I couldn't. Rice kept me in the LER.'

I stop in the middle of the empty corridor. 'Thank you for trying to help my mum. I'm sorry you were in the LER.' I don't know what else to say. I've got to think.

'I want to help,' Kay says. 'Maybe we should wait for the night then we can try to get out the door.'

I don't know how to feel about Kay right now, but I can't help feeling a rush of warmth that she says 'we'. She tried to protect my mum and Ali and I haven't even asked what Rice did to her in the LER because of it. Some of my anger from last night dissolves. 'I'm sorry but I can't wait till tonight. When did she get sent out?'

'I don't know. It was late, after big Specials bedtime, when Rice took her away.'

I bet he chucked her straight out. 'So she's probably already been out there for hours.'

Kay nods.

I've got to get thrown out again. I need to misbehave, and fast.

Outside the grid other Specials arrive and gather around us and when the door hisses open we cram into the room. At the front, the cage is already occupied. Wearing a thunderous scowl is Enforcer Rice himself.

An Hon Red girl pushes past us. 'Carma's not here. She's having her baby,' she tells Rice. Kay is in front of me and I see her give a tiny shake of the head. Rice sees it too.

'I don't know why you're shaking your head,' he says to Kay. 'At least Carma knows her duty.' He looks down his nose at Kay. 'Not like you, you disobedient little tight-legger.'

I'm instantly consumed by a wave of anger that shoots up me like electricity. I shove my way between Specials up on to the platform and hurl myself at the cage. How dare he? The bastard. The low, miserable, efwurding bastard. I throw myself at the cage again, my fingers scrabbling through the gaps, trying to get hold of his arm. He flinches back into a corner. 'Don't you *ever* speak to her like that!' I say. His eyes are wide with fright. Bloody bars, if he was out here I'd break his nose. I try to shake the cage, but Rice has gone for his baton, he lunges at me and presses it on to my arm. Electricity jolts through me. I'm thrown backwards and land in a heap. I struggle to my feet, glaring at Rice. Kay helps me up. Her hand is so small and so smooth. I want to destroy anyone who tries to hurt her. She gives me a half-smile. 'Now he'll exclude you like you wanted,' she whispers.

I'd forgotten all about that.

Rice is too shaken to enjoy himself lording it over me. 'Send him out. Now. Two days,' he says to the two impeccables he's called in to 'handle' me.

As I'm bundled out of the door I look round at Kay. She's looking back at me.

The impeccables push me down the corridor, past the dining hall and round to the back door.

They push me outside and march me straight down the path towards the fence. As soon as they bundle me through the gate, I run in the direction of the woods. I get all the way to the trees with no sign of my mother, or anyone else. The wind is still cold, but weak sunshine is filtering through the branches. Snowdrops are pushing up through the ground. Spring's finally coming.

I move further into the woods, past a pond and on to where the trees are thicker and less light penetrates. In a clearing I find the remains of a fire. I have to force myself to scan the ground for bones. There are none. But I do find a knife. The blade is dull and it's half buried. I don't think anyone has been here for a while, but I can't really tell.

I slide the knife into my belt. Something rustles behind me. I spin round. Probably a bird I tell myself, but there's the sound of dead leaves crunching and branches breaking. Something big and heavy is making its way towards me. I can hear panting. I look around. My best bet is to get up a tree. I turn and grab at a branch, but I'm arrested by something crashing into the clearing and falling at my feet.

It's my mother.

Her clothes are torn and her face is so pale that I'm afraid she's just dropped dead, but then she takes a ragged breath and opens her eyes. I crouch down beside her.

'Mum? I'm going to get help.' My mind is racing; where can I get help? 'I'll be right back, I promise.'

She grabs my wrist.

'No,' she says. 'Don't go.' She tightens her grip on me and I look down and see that her hand is covered in blood.

'Mum, what's happened to you?'

She lifts her head a little and looks down at her stomach. I realise that the dark material of the enforcers' uniform is even darker there. She's bleeding.

'It's not as bad as it looks,' she says dropping her head back. 'Stomach wounds always look messy.'

'Those boys stabbed you?'

She nods.

'I've got to get you a doctor,' I say getting to my feet.

'No! You've got to listen to me.'

'But . . .' I'm almost sobbing.

'I'm all right.' She heaves herself into a half-sitting position against a tree. 'It's fine. It's not getting any worse. I want you to listen to me for ten minutes then you can go back to the Academy and get someone to come and help. Okay?'

'Okay,' I say.

'I'm sorry about last night. Rice—'

'I know. Kay told me.'

'Kay was brave. I wanted to get you out, I really did . . .'

'It's okay. Don't worry, you'll get better, we can make new plans. We can still escape.'

She fixes me with her gaze. 'I don't know, darling. I don't know if that's the best thing for you. I'm afraid that you're still in danger.'

I still haven't told her what I found out when I was excluded. 'Do you mean those men from the factory? When I was out here before, I found Wilson; he told me that it was me they meant to kill.'

She nods. 'I was afraid of that. I should have told you about all this before. We never had any time. I thought

276

that if I could just get you out of the Academy there would be plenty of time to explain.'

'Explain what? Do you know why those men wanted to kill me?'

'I . . . I'm not sure. I need you to think. That day they attacked, was anything different? Did you do anything unusual?'

'We went on the metro. Facilitator Johnson wanted us to deliver a package and those men were waiting for us.'

'What about the day before?'

The day before was a Wednesday. I used to spend my free session on Wednesdays working on my computer skills. Actually, now I do remember something different about that day. That was the day I tried to find out about my father. The day I hacked into the Register and looked at my details.

Mum's eyes are fixed on me. I can't see how this is important, but I want to tell her everything she asks.

'I . . . I got into the National Register,' I say, bowing my head. 'I tried to find out who my father was.'

Mum sucks in her breath.

'I'm sorry, Mum. I don't even care about my dad, I really don't—'

'It's okay. It's perfectly natural that you have questions about your father. It's my fault. I should have handled this differently.' Her lips are horribly pale.

This is stupid; we're wasting time on things that really aren't important.

'But that's got nothing to do with those men attacking me and Wilson,' I say.

Mum pulls herself up a little more. 'I'm afraid your father sent those men to kill you and then he wiped your records from the Register.'

'My father? But he died . . .' Before I even get the words out I can see from her face that he's not dead.

'You lied to me! Who's my father? Why would you think that he'd want me dead? Besides, you'd have to be someone really important to fiddle about with official records like that.'

My mother looks at me with a trembling lip. 'Someone really important like The Leader,' she says quietly.

I stare at her.

She gives a tiny nod of her head.

My father is The Leader.

'No. No!' I say.

She blinks a yes.

I feel like someone has drained all the warmth out of me. 'How could you . . . be with someone like that? Do you know what that man has done?'

She nods. 'When I met him he was different. Or at least I thought he was. I was so young. I met him at a political meeting before he was The Leader. He thought like me then. Or at least he said he did.'

'What happened?'

She looks down. 'I only saw him that one time. And then . . .'

'You were pregnant.'

'And I'm so glad. You're the best thing that ever happened to me, sweetheart.'

'Did he ever come back? To see me?'

'He didn't know about you.'

'Why not?'

She looks down. 'I found out he was married.'

Without meaning to, I gasp. I can't believe my mother would do something like that.

'I didn't know what to do for the best. Then he joined the Leadership and they seized control of the country and brought an end to the war and all of a sudden he'd become this important man who I'd hear about on the news. Not long after that he was made Leader. I started hearing rumours about some secret policies of the Leadership and I wasn't so sure that I wanted him to be a part of your life.'

My head is spinning. 'I don't understand. If he doesn't know I exist then why do you think he's trying to kill me?'

'The Leader's security team spent a lot of time checking out any potential threats from his past. Your father must have mentioned me and when they found you on the records they sent a man to see me. He told me that The Leader was going to be the saviour of this country and that it was important that people trusted and respected him. He said people looked to The Leader for moral guidance and his marriage mustn't be compromised. They didn't want an error in judgement . . .' She shakes her head. 'Those were the words he used, "an error in judgement" from his past coming out and upsetting people. He said I must never tell anyone or . . .' She sucks in her breath. 'Or it would be the worse for you.'

'But that was years ago.'

'Yes, but then you looked at the Register.'

'I don't understand why that's significant,' I say. 'I just had a snoop around my file. I didn't find anything out about my father. There was way too much security round the file. I didn't see anything.'

'Exactly. I'm sure there isn't normally that much protection surrounding parentage. Who do you think put that security there? He was waiting. You tripped his warning system. As soon as he knew someone was taking interest in your parentage he decided you had to go.'

'Is his name on my records? Surely someone else would have noticed?'

'It doesn't work like that. I didn't give his name, but when a child is born a record is created that includes a genetic portrait of both parents. He's the only possible match as your father. Someone would only need to see his medical records to prove it. He doesn't want you turning up and spoiling his impeccable reputation.' She sighs, her face is growing paler by the second and I know that she needs help, but I need to understand what she's telling me.

'How do you know all this?' I ask. 'Maybe it's a mistake. When Wilson told me they wanted to kill me he wasn't exactly right in the head. Couldn't we just have been mugged?'

'Mugged and then wiped from the records? When I couldn't get in touch with you I went to the Willows and Facilitator Johnson denied you'd ever been there. It was like you'd just disappeared.'

281

I roll a leaf in my hand until it splits. 'He did that to me too. He'd known me for all those years and he deleted me just like that. Wiped all my records.'

'I'm afraid there aren't many people who'd dare to disobey The Leader's orders.'

'He could have done something! He could have tried to contact you. Or told someone or—'

'I think it's more to the point that he didn't tell anyone. If they had learned about your reappearance at the Willows they would have tracked you down.'

'Johnson sent me and Wilson off to be killed! Don't go thinking he was protecting me by not telling anyone I'd shown up again. He was protecting himself. I bet he didn't want anyone to know that he'd messed up.'

She acknowledges I'm right with the smallest of shrugs. She's resigned to the idea that a teacher would throw away a student's life just like that. This is the kind of world we're living in.

She squeezes my hand. 'Once I knew you were here I just had to get inside.'

'Can't be many people trying to break into an Academy.'

She gives a slow smile and I hear her lungs wheeze. 'It's a good job they take volunteers. And it's not a bad place to hide. You know, maybe you should think about staying here. There are worse places you could be.'

Surely she doesn't mean that?

'It's true. I've probably been safer here than anywhere else,' she says.

'What do you mean, safer here?'

She looks off into the trees.

'What happened after you left me that message telling me to stay here? They said your account was terminated,' I say.

'They switched my account. They said it was a technical fault, but I felt like they were watching me.'

'Did they threaten you?'

'No. Nothing happened. I just . . . I've been waiting for it. I suppose I've been waiting for it for a long time. It doesn't matter now anyway.' She struggles to pull a folded piece of paper out of a pocket sewn into the inside of her shirt. 'You should take this.' She hands it to me and I open it up.

It's my birth certificate.

'If you need to, use it to bargain. If you find yourself in –' she closes her eyes and takes a breath. '– in a difficult situation, tell them that you've given it to someone and told them in the event of your disappearance to hand it to the press. Do you understand?'

My mouth has fallen open.

'This is important, darling, do you understand?' she says.

'And you'll do the same thing?' I ask.

She nods her head and smiles. 'You take it. Put it somewhere safe.' She leans back against the tree and breathes out heavily.

'Mum, you really need help. I've got to—'

'Don't go, darling; I just need to catch my breath.' She closes her eyes. 'I'm sorry I've made such a mess for you.'

'Why didn't you tell me?'

'It was too dangerous a piece of information to give you.'

'Even if you didn't tell me The Leader was my father you could have told me what sort of man he was, you could have told me that the whole stupid system is corrupt.'

She opens her eyes. 'And how would you have fitted in at the Learning Community then? Do you know what they do with promising young learners who start to question the system? They send them to Academies. Or worse.'

'I'm in an Academy anyway and I can't see how things can get any worse.'

'I know, I know,' she says and she stares hard into my eyes. 'I should have told you the truth. I was just trying to keep you safe. I just want you to be safe.'

'*AHHHHHH!*' someone screams from the direction of the pool.

My mother's eyes widen. 'Run!'

I won't leave her. I can see someone running through the trees; they're almost on us. It's one of those boys. One of those boys that stabbed my mother. I'm on my feet and I'm hurtling over fallen tree branches. We come face to face just outside the clearing – it's Scarface. He hesitates for a moment, surprised that I am running towards him.

But he's too late to stop his momentum and he rushes to meet the knife as I stab it into his chest. He looks down at the hilt still sticking out. Then he staggers backwards and falls to the ground.

I've killed him.

The sunlight hurts my eyes. I lurch back through the trees towards my mother. I push back the branches and then stop like I've hit an invisible wall. She's lying completely still.

'Mum?' I say.

Her eyes are staring blankly.

'Mum?'

I can hear a bird singing in the distance.

'Mummy?'

She's dead.

50

I'm awake, but there is something wrong with my eyes. In the shadows I can see bodies. The trees are running with blood and in their branches hundreds of crows' eyes stare down at me. A hand is reaching out of the ground. Its bony fingers grasp at my feet. I curl into a ball. The whole world is pulsing with death and dripping with blood. I smell someone's fetid breath in my face. The Leader. My father. In front of me, Scarface rises up and pulls the knife from his chest. He points it at me. 'Just like your father,' he says. 'Just like your father,' join in the birds. And the leaves. And the dead bodies crawling towards me.

'No.' I say 'NO!'

Then the heaving bodies blur into blackness and so do I.

In the morning everything is clear to me. I've seen all the evil that The Leader has brought. He has made everything bad. It's his fault that my mother and Wilson are dead. It's his fault that I am a murderer. His fault that no one sees how poor Kay and the rest of the Specials suffer. He is responsible for *all* of this.

And I must make him pay.

After some time staring into the leaves it dawns on me that I don't even need to escape to get at The Leader. Soon he will be coming to the Academy to do his publicity stunt for the new Academies. What I'll need to be able to move around the Academy freely is an enforcer's ID card. I've never managed to get close enough to an enforcer to steal one, but now I realise that I don't have to steal. There's one right here in the forest.

I make my way back towards the clearing. I'm struck with a horrible thought and for a moment I freeze and then I break into a run. I should never have left my mother there. What if the rest of those boys came back for her and . . . ? My mouth goes dry. I burst through the trees. She's still there. She hasn't moved.

I move towards her as quietly as I can, as if I'm afraid of waking her. I crouch down at her side.

'Mum, I need your ID card,' I say. It feels like it would be rude to start fishing about in her pockets without saying anything. I try the pocket on the front of her shirt. It's there.

'Thank you,' I say. I don't want to just leave her in case those cannibal boys come back, or someone from the Wilderness. I need to bury her. I scan the clearing. There's a natural dip beneath one of the trees. I carry her as gently as I can and lay her in it. I use my hands to scoop earth over her at first, until I find a flat piece of bark to use instead. I work hard at it for a long time. My face runs with tears and sweat. When I'm done, my mother is well covered and my arms are quivering with fatigue.

I kneel down and press my lips to the mound of earth. 'I'm going to get him, Mum,' I say out loud. 'I'm going to put an end to all this blood and fear and cruelty. I promise.'

Then I walk back into the shade of the trees.

I spend the night hiding in the rubbish tip, clutching a sharpened piece of metal in case another one of those boys or anyone else from the Wilderness comes near me.

When Rice and two impeccables arrive at the gate in the fence, I'm sat waiting. Enforcer Rice seems surprised to see me, but he doesn't say anything. He doesn't even give me a lecture about my behaviour. He rips a bit of skin near his thumbnail off with his teeth. When we get inside one of the impeccables accidently brushes against him as we walk along the corridor.

'Watch it, you idiot!' says Rice. 'I haven't got time for this.' And he rushes off.

'Why are all the enforcers all . . . ?' The taller impeccable makes claws out of his hands and bares his teeth.

'They're scared of a thing,' says the other one.

'What thing?' I ask. What on earth would scare an enforcer?

289

The impeccable shrugs. 'I don't know. They're scared, so they're bigger mean.'

The impeccable takes me to the grid. I stumble to my seat and the rest of the day passes in a haze. Kay tries to talk to me, but I can only shake my head and turn away. After dinner she takes me upstairs and puts me to bed like a baby. I'm shaking with tiredness, but I can't sleep. Images of my mother and Wilson dance in my mind.

Ilex and Ali come and talk in whispers to Kay. The light fades. I stay where I am. Staring. Thinking. Other students come in chatting and arguing. Then it's late and the lights are switched off and everyone is asleep and I'm still staring.

'Blake?' whispers Kay.

I want to answer but somehow I can't break my stillness. I wonder if I'll just lie like this till I die.

I hear Kay getting out of bed. Then she climbs on my bed and lies down behind me, wrapping her arm around me.

And everything still hurts, but she is here with me.

When I wake up, Kay is still lying behind me. Her arm is around my waist. It feels nice. Warm. I'd like to just stay here and go back to sleep, but I start thinking about The Leader. My father. He'll be here soon. I don't have to go out and get him; he's coming to the Academy. I struggle to remember what day it is. The last few have run together.

I try to recall exactly when Tong told us he was coming. If Rice is twitchy it must be soon.

Kay stirs. I freeze, willing her to drift back to sleep and hold me for a bit longer. She stiffens. She's definitely awake. She lifts her arm gently and rolls away, so that I can no longer feel her warm softness pressed against my back.

'Blake?' she whispers.

I turn over so that we're lying side by side.

'Mmm,' I say.

'What happened?'

The woods. My mother. The boy. The knife. A horrible wave of redness washes through me bringing back that crazy blood-dripping night and I'm afraid I'm going to be sick. I breathe in slowly. 'She's dead,' I say.

And then I tell her. How my brave mother came to find me, how she worked out what happened to me and how she finally told me the truth about who my father is. I don't tell Kay about Scarface. I don't think I could bear her knowing what I did to him. When I get to the end, Kay slips her hand in mine.

'Kay, everything awful that has happened: my mother, Wilson, those crazy boys – this whole efwurding system – it's all The Leader's fault. And he won't get away with it.'

Kay doesn't say anything.

'All I need to know is when he's coming and where he's going to be.'

'Rex will know.' She looks at me questioningly.

I don't care about Rex any more. 'Ask him.' I say.

In five minutes she's back. 'Tomorrow,' she says. 'He's coming tomorrow.'

At lunchtime Kay takes me to the empty dormitory bathroom.

'What are you going to do?' she asks.

'I've been thinking about this; do you know what would hurt him most?'

Kay shrugs.

'If I ruin everything he's worked for – his career and his reputation. We're going to do what I said we would. We're going to expose the Academy system and make sure that everyone knows that he's responsible.'

Kay nods.

'And then I'm going to kill him.'

I stare at the hinge of a cubicle door. I'm angry at myself for not having planned this out better. When I first knew that The Leader was coming I suppose I imagined the sort of school visit we used to have at the Learning Community. I thought there would be an opportunity for Specials to talk to him. I thought he'd want to talk to me and hear about everything that has happened and that he'd be able to help. I was such an idiot. Of course now I realise that they'll be keeping him as far away from us as possible. In fact, Kay says that Rex says that the press conference will take place in the older part of the Academy, where Specials rarely go.

'What time will he be here?' I ask.

'Nine o'clock.'

'How are we going to get out of the classroom?' We're expected to be strapped into the grid by seven a.m. We could just not turn up in the morning. But then they'd be looking for us. Tomorrow, Rice is going to want everything to run smoothly. 'Maybe it would be best if we go to the grid as usual and then somehow slip away,' I say.

'We need a thing for all people to look at so they don't look at us.'

'A diversion?'

Kay makes a noise like a contented cat. 'Does that word say all those words?' she says. 'I love words. Diver-sion. We need a diversion. We should think of a diver—'

'Okay, okay. Who's going to do the talking in this diversion?'

Kay nudges me in the ribs. 'No person is going to be diversioned by talking, Blake. We need a fight.'

Finally. Something it will be easy to organise in this place.

52

At the end of the afternoon session I grab Ilex. We go up to his dormitory and I explain to him what I want to do.

He goes quiet.

'You don't have to be involved,' I say. 'I mean, you don't have to do anything. I don't want to get you into trouble.'

Ilex's face is creased in thought. 'You do a lot of trouble things. Do you want trouble?'

'I don't like trouble. I have to do this. The Leader has done so many wrong things.' I drop my voice so the other Specials in the room can't hear me. 'It's his fault my mother and my best friend are dead. I've got to do something.'

'Is stopping The Leader stopping Rice?'

'I hope so. I hope we'll get rid of Academies.'

'I want to stop Rice hurting Ali.'

'Does that mean that you want to help?'

'Yes. What things do I do?'

* * *

I force some dinner down. I've got to keep my strength up. Then Kay and I go to the salon. Rex and a pack of Reds are sitting on the best chairs, surrounded by their followers. It's so noisy that it feels safe to talk to Kay about tomorrow. I tell her the same thing that I told Ilex, that she doesn't have to be involved, but she pretends that she hasn't heard me and gets straight to planning.

'If you want a fight diversion you need Rex,' she says.

'Rex isn't the only person in this place who knows how to fight.' I try to pull a tangle of metal-legged chairs apart.

Kay laughs. 'Blake, you fight little-more-good now, but I don't think—'

'I'm not suggesting that I start the fight. I'm going to be doing the really difficult bit, in case you hadn't noticed. But there are a large number of students capable of starting a fight other than your precious Rex.'

'We need the goodest, I mean the best. We need the best brain, so we have you. We need the best fighter, so we should have Rex. I'll talk to him.'

I pull the chair so hard that it comes free and I stagger backwards. 'Fine. That's fine. Just don't use any of the new words you've learned when you're talking to him.'

But she's already gone.

I sit on the plastic chair and try not to look at Kay, who has joined the swarm of girls around Rex. I need to think about what I'm going to do. I'm imagining myself bursting in on the press conference and describing exactly what happens in an Academy in front of the cameras, but

I don't think that will work. What would be best is if I could get a camera into the Academy proper to let people see what it's really like in here. I want to show how all this goes right back to The Leader. And the horrible way that he doesn't just want to crush these students, he wants to control them too. It's so underhand. Letting them think that they've got their own rules and their precious gangs, but all the time they're being run by the Leadership. And those Latin names. It's like an extra insult. I bet The Leader thinks it funny.

Which makes me think about Rex. Maybe The Leader's influence goes as far as the Reds' leader. Maybe he's in their control too. Now that I think about it, it's always seemed strange the way Rex never seems to be in trouble even though he claims to do as he pleases. And there was the time that Rice found out about the bowls, Rex was the one who actually provided some of the Specials with empty margarine tubs to use as bowls, but I was the one who got into trouble for it. How did Rice know? And how did Rex manage to get hold of all those tubs? I look up at Rex's porcine face and a wave of revulsion washes through me. He grunts with laughter and I'm taken back to that night when Kay and I were trapped in the kitchen. I remember Tong telling someone to spy on the Specials and I remember her informer agreeing.

By grunting.

I spring out of my chair.

Rex is sprawled in the least beaten-up armchair, with a

gaggle of girls surrounding him. Kay is sat opposite him. I imagine it's taken her all this time to work her way to the front. He leans forward to say something and Kay laughs. I hate him. As I'm striding over, they get up and go out into the corridor. I follow. They get to the door of Rex's room.

'Hey, Kay!' I say.

She turns and looks at me with her lips pressed together.

'Hey, Blakey. Kay can't talk you now,' Rex says, strutting into the toilets.

'I need to speak to you,' I say to Kay.

'Not now, Blake,' she says and follows Rex.

'This is important,' I say, stepping in the tiled room.

'This is 'portant,' mimics Rex.

'A childish repetition suggests that you've failed to understand what has been said,' I say.

Rex's smile fades. He steps so close to me that I'm forced to look up at his ugly face. 'Don't do that brainer stuff on me.'

'Why? Does it scare you?'

He grabs me by the collar. 'Shut up, you efwurding brainer.'

'Well if you've finished demonstrating the full extent of your vocabulary I've got something important to say.' I pull his hand off my shirt.

'Blake, don't be stupid. We need Rex,' Kay says.

'You don't need Rex! I mean, *we* don't need Rex,' I hiss.

297

Kay takes a step towards me and says right into my ear, 'Stop this little-boying. I'm doing this for you.'

'I've got to tell you something,' I say.

'Tell me later,' she says.

Rex puts his hand on Kay's shoulder. I clench my fists.

'She doesn't want to hear you,' Rex says. 'You think you're so crimson with your words. Words don't mean nothing here.'

'Yeah? Okay, maybe this is a case of actions speaking louder than words,' I say.

Rex scrunches his face in disgust. Kay looks away.

'You tell me, Kay,' I say. 'What does this *say* to you?' I grab Rex by the right hand and yank up his shirt sleeve. On his wrist is a livid purple scar. It's the sort of mark a butter knife might leave if it was plunged into your arm in the middle of the night that you betrayed everyone who looked up to you.

53

'I got that in a fight,' says Rex. But he knows we don't believe him.

Kay's mouth is open. Her eyes are boring into Rex. He spreads his hands, palms up.

'What?' he says.

Kay takes a step towards him.

He pulls back. 'What?' he says. 'Stop looking at me like that.'

'*Urrargh!*' Kay screams. She pulls back her fist and it's like she sucks all her anger into a blistering point and then powers it into Rex's face. The punch sends him sprawling against the sinks. He ends up sitting on the tiled floor.

'You efwurding bastard!' Kay shouts. She kicks him in the stomach. Rex just stares at her. 'You're supposed to help Specials,' Kay says. 'You're supposed to be our leader.'

Rex gets to his feet and shrugs his shirt back into place. 'It got us stuff. It was just little talk to Enforcer Tong. She's gone. I didn't tell her all things.'

'You told her the bowls were my idea and she told Rice,' I say. 'I bet you've told her a load of other stuff too. And now she's gone, you're probably telling it all to someone else. Did you tell someone that my m— that Enforcer Williams gave Ali food?'

'No.'

I don't believe him. 'You're scum,' I say and I throw a punch, but Rex blocks it and pushes me away. He pulls his cuff back down over the purple mark.

'It's not for you to talk about,' he says to me. 'It's not for you to say I'm good or bad. You can't do that. I'm Rex. I'm in charge.'

Kay shakes her head. 'You're not. You're not in charge. *They* are. It's all them. Just like Blake said. There's nothing for us.' She raises her fist to strike him again, but this time he catches her hand. Kay tries to shake herself free. 'How could you do this?' she says to him. 'How could you do this to all the Specials? How could you do this to me?' She stops struggling and fixes Rex with a glare. 'You are a . . . a coward and you're stupid and cruel and . . . ugly and bad and bad.'

'I don't know your stupid words. Stop your stupid words. It's about Reds and I'm the big Red,' says Rex.

'Words aren't stupid. Words can do things. You used words to hurt everybody.' She wrenches herself out of his grasp. 'And I can use them to say to the Specials what you did.'

'No!' says Rex and he slams out both his arms and

pushes me and Kay back against a cubicle door. 'You don't tell!' he shouts.

'Don't you touch her,' I say and punch him in the stomach. While he's bent over Kay leaps on to his back and smacks him around the head. He twists around, trying to pull her off. Just as I knee him in the face, the door to the corridor slams open.

It's Enforcer Rice and three impeccables. He's holding a taser.

'LER room. NOW!' he says, glaring down his nose at us. 'And you can stay in there tomorrow too.'

This is terrible. This is awful. The Leader will be here in less than twelve hours and Kay and I are both locked in a high-security padded room with a stunned Rex in the isolation space next door. Worse than that, Kay is crying and I don't know what to do. She's huddled in a corner with tears running silently down her face.

'All the time from when I was a little girl . . .' she says.

'I know,' I say. Poor Kay. She's been holding on to this dream about Reds and being Dom for her whole life.

'I worked so hard,' she cries.

'I know.'

'All that fighting, all that getting in with the Reds, and getting shrap, and saying things that are not the things I think.'

'You've done really well.'

'Do you know a thing, Blake? I didn't like the fighting. *Ha!*' She throws her hands up. 'I don't like hitting people just for people to see. Some of the times . . .' She drops her voice. 'Sometimes I was scared.'

'I was scared all of the times,' I say.

She gives a hiccup of laughter. 'But I did it,' she says. 'Do you know why I did it?'

I nod my head. I do know. I know exactly how poor, brave Kay has worked all her life to try to feel special. Truly special, not Specials special.

'I wanted to be the best. I wanted to know how it feels to be someone.'

She is the most amazing someone in the world. I want to say, *You are the best.* I want to say, *You are incredible and the other Specials, the enforcers, all the students at the Learning Community – none of them will ever be as brave and as strong as you are.* But I can't. Instead I say, 'You are someone to me.'

Then somehow I've wrapped my arms around her and she leans against my chest and all I can think is: *I won't let anyone hurt you again.*

We sit in silence for most of the evening. I can't see any way out of the room. It's empty apart from a couple of sleeping mats. To the left of the door is a tiny hatch. On the right-hand wall there's a barred door through to the Isolation Room, where Rex is still passed out on the floor. He tried to punch one of the impeccables so Enforcer Rice stunned him with his taser.

Kay hasn't spoken for hours. She's stopped crying. She's even stopped looking angry. Her jaw is set and her

303

eyes stare into the distance. Her world has crashed down around her like mine did when my mother told me the truth.

There's a clanking sound outside the door and I spring to my feet. I've got some crazy hope that they're going to let us out. But it isn't the sound of the door; it's the hatch. I slide up its little door. In the space behind is a tray with three cups of water on. I lift the tray out, place it on the floor and then feel around the interior space. There are no gaps. Obviously this is set up so that when the little door on our side is open, the door that opens on to the corridor is covered. No way out there.

'Kay,' I say, 'do you want some water?'

She doesn't answer. She draws her knees up to her chest and rests her cheek on them. I remember her cheek on my chest and I'm filled with this ache that hurts and feels sweet at the same time. I shake my head. I've got to concentrate.

I slide a cup towards her and she looks down at it as if she doesn't know what to do with it.

I pick up my cup. My mouth is dry. As I'm about to drink, Kay knocks the cup from my hands. The water splashes out and the cup spins across the floor.

'Don't drink that,' she says.

She's right. It's not like the enforcers to think about our well-being. I bet it's drugged. I try to work some saliva around my mouth. At least Kay seems alert again.

'We've got to work out how to get out,' I say.

'Yes,' she says. 'Yes, let's go.'

Kay paces around the tiny room. The door is the only way out. There's no code keypad on this side. Kay runs her hand over the door. Halfway down on the right-hand side a box-shape sticks out. 'This is where the lock is,' she says.

'Can you open it?'

She bends down and peers into a tiny gap between the plastic casing and the door. 'I'll get it open,' she says. 'I need something . . . metal.'

I look around the room yet again, as if a tool box is going to suddenly appear. There are only the cups.

Kay walks over and takes out the tray from underneath them. It's metal. She goes back to the door and pulls a piece of shrap off the thread around her neck. She eases its thinnest edge under the lock casing and starts to pry it off.

'What do you need the metal for?' I ask.

She keeps pushing the shrap, trying to wriggle it further into the crack.

'Is it a magnetic lock?' I say.

She doesn't answer me. While she's working, I look through the bars at Rex. He's still out of it. His mouth is hanging open. He's such an ugly, dribbling pig. I look away. Kay keeps working. Easing the shrap up and down.

Then she starts screaming.

'*Ahhhhhhhhhh!*'

'What? What is it?' I rush to her.

'*AH! AH! AHHHH!*'

'Kay!' I get hold of her face and turn it to me. She's not crying. Or in pain. She's just screaming. 'What is it?' I say.

The door opens. A terrified-looking impeccable peers in. Kay smashes him over the head with the tray and he slumps to the floor. Kay stops screaming. She gestures to the door. It's now propped open by the motionless impeccable. She gives me the first smile in what feels like weeks.

'I thought you were going to get the lock open,' I say.

She shrugs. 'I was, but then I heard someone outside. I thought he would come to look if he heard me scream.'

'My ears are still ringing. I think everyone heard you,' I say.

'I heard you,' says a voice behind us.

Rex is awake.

55

'Don't even look at him,' I say to Kay. 'Let's get out of here.'

'Kay, my girl,' Rex starts.

'She is not your girl!' I spit at him. 'And when everyone hears what a lousy traitor you are I don't imagine anyone will want to be your girl.'

'Don't tell,' says Rex. He grips the bars with both hands and pulls his face up against them. 'If you tell, you efwurding brainer, I'll kill you.'

'It's all right,' I say. 'I won't tell anyone . . .'

Rex's forehead creases.

'. . . I'll let Kay do that.'

'My Kay won't tell it, will you, babe?' he says. He switches on his wide smile.

He's leering at her. I'm going to smash his face. I walk towards him and he takes a step backwards. Kay puts her hand on my shoulder. He's not fit to speak to her.

'What do you think you can possibly say to Kay that would stop her telling everyone what a nozzle-scum bastard you are?' I say.

Rex looks away from me. He peers up through his eyelashes like he's suddenly shy. 'Babe,' he says, stretching an arm through the bars and trying to reach Kay's hand, 'I'll make you Dom.'

'As if that . . .' I start to say, but then I see Kay's face. She's thinking. 'Kay!' I say. 'Tell him. Tell him you don't want to be Dom any more.'

'He doesn't get it, does he?' Rex says to Kay. 'You and me, we're Academy. We work hard. You're a good girl, Kay, you should have the good things. I can give you things, look after you.'

Outrageous. 'Kay, look at me,' I say. 'Don't trust this back-stabber. You don't want to be connected with him.'

But she doesn't look at me, instead she turns to Rex. 'All right,' she says to him. 'I'll be Dom.'

It's like a punch in the stomach. How can this be happening? Kay with Rex. I'll kill him.

'Good girl. I'll make it all good for you,' Rex says. He looks at me with a sneer. 'She wants to be with me.'

'I want to be Dom,' she says to me.

'Why?' I say. 'It's all nonsense, remember? The enforcers made up those names and it's all controlled by the Leadership and Rex is working for the enforcers and . . . and . . .'

Kay shakes her head. 'You don't understand.'

308

'No!' I shout. 'No, I don't. Are you forgetting every-thing that we've found out? Are you saying—?'

'I'm saying I don't care,' Kay says. 'I want to be Dom.' She presses her lips together.

This is ridiculous. 'But, Kay, we're going to bring down the Academies.'

Rex snorts. I turn away from him and take hold of Kay's hands. 'We're going to escape to where they can't control us,' I say.

'Oh, Blake!' she says. 'Do you think that's not a lie? That it's more better outside? They wanted to kill you.'

'All people want to kill him,' says Rex.

'It will be different,' I say.

'It *won't* be different.' She pulls her hands away. 'It's all the same.'

'But we have to try, Kay. I want you to have something better than this.'

'I don't care,' she says. 'I don't care if this is the most bad place. I want to be at the top.'

I can't believe it. Kay doesn't want me. She's choosing the most despicable, idiot scum I have ever met instead of me. Everything is ruined.

'I'll go then,' I say.

'I'm sad for you, Blake-boy,' Rex says. 'But Specials have to be with Specials.'

I look at him. I hate him. He lowers his gaze. Then jerks his head back up.

'You can't tell,' he says. 'It's not for me. All the

Specials will be sad if you tell,' he says. 'Don't say. Tell him, Kay. Specials need Reds and Rex. Don't take it away.'

Rex is a lot smarter than I realised. He's a manipulative bastard.

'How are you going to stop me?' I say and I spring forward and punch through a gap in the bars into his stomach. Then I step back so he can't reach me. 'If you don't want people to know you're an efwurding bastard, Rex, then you shouldn't act like one.'

Kay puts a hand on my arm. 'Please don't tell, Blake.'

This is too much. I feel like I might explode into a million pieces because to continue existing is too much to bear. But I don't explode. Or hit Rex again. Or fall at Kay's feet. I just turn around and walk away.

I ought to go and find Ilex and work out how to organise a
diversion, but instead I stop at the top of the stairs and sit
down. I don't know what to do. I don't know how to do this.
I don't even know if I care any more. I want my mother. I
want to turn back time to how it was before. When I was at
the Willows and didn't know any of this. Why should I try
and change everything when no one else is bothered?

Someone taps me on the shoulder. It's Ali.

Blake, she signs by drawing a capital 'B' on the palm
of her hand. She gives me a huge smile. *Where have you
been?* she asks. *I looked for you.*

'I'm sorry, Ali. Enforcer Rice . . .'

She steps closer to me.

'We got in trouble with Enforcer Rice,' I say. 'What are
you doing out here? It's late. You'll get into trouble if
they see us.'

*I had to find you. To say sorry about your mother. Your
mother was good.*

'She was. She was a really good mother.'

Ali leans against me. *What are you doing, Blake?* she asks.

I look at her peaky little face.

'I don't know, Ali. I don't really know what I'm doing.'

She looks back at me solemnly.

'What I want to do is get rid of this place,' I say. 'Get rid of all the Academies and get rid of The Leader.'

Ali nods.

'But I don't think I can,' I say.

She pats me on the shoulder. *You can,* she signs. *Blake can.*

So we wake Ilex and in one of the cubicles in the bathroom we form as much of a plan as is possible, given that we don't know exactly how things will happen tomorrow. Very early, before they notice I'm missing from the LER room, we need to try and get some of the other Specials onside. Then, I'll go down and hide somewhere in the oldest part of the Academy, which is where The Leader will be giving his speech, ready to jump out and have my say. Ali will be my messenger. Once I've used my mother's swipe card she can take it back to Ilex and that way he can bring in anyone who is prepared to help us make our point more forcibly. It's not much, but it's all we've got.

I get into bed. My insides seem to be heaving about like choppy water. Kay's bed is empty. She stayed with Rex in the LER room. I picture them together, then dig my nails into my palm to take the image away.

I hardly sleep. The lighting switches to dawn setting and I allow myself to think of my mother and Wilson. Instead of getting upset, I'm furious. It's like cold liquid metal pumping through my veins. I'm going to do this.

Ilex appears by my bed. 'Are we ready?' he says.

'Well, we're not going to get any readier,' I say. The phrase makes me think of Kay. 'We'd need to speak to as many Specials as possible. Ali's dormitory is probably the safest place to talk. Start waking people up, quietly. No Reds.'

We get Specials out of their dormitories through their bathroom doors and in through Ali's to her dormitory, where none of the Reds sleep. Soon there are several hundred students crammed into the room. I stand on a bed and look down at them. I remember when I arrived. Nobody would have come to listen to me speak then. I raise my hand for quiet.

'My name is Blake—'

'We know it. You're all times saying it,' someone says.

My face gets warm. I was a bit of an idiot in the beginning, always going on about my AEP score. 'I know that you've heard me talking rubbish before—' I say.

'Yeah, why are we listening to this no-ranker?' somebody says.

'He isn't a no-ranker,' says Ilex. 'He's a one-two-er.'

'I'm proud of that one,' I say. And even though I don't think that most of them know the word 'proud' they get the gist and they laugh.

'That Special got us bowls,' says someone at the back.

There's a murmur of agreement.

'He's teaching Specials to read,' Marn says. 'He knows things. He can help us.'

Some of the Specials from the reading classes start clapping. I have to gesture for them to be quiet.

'What do you want us to do?' a black-haired girl asks.

'Listen,' I say, 'I'm not trying to get you to do something for me. I want you to do something for all of us. This place is wrong. Bad. Kids should not be beaten or given electric shocks or made to sleep in dirty beds. We should have a proper education. And choices. *Everybody* should have choices. If you don't want to work in a factory then you shouldn't have to.'

They're staring at me. I should have got Ilex to speak. I don't think they understand half of what I'm saying.

'It's a fight,' says a voice from the bathroom doorway. It's Kay.

The Specials crane their necks around to see her.

'It's a fight to get out of the Academy. It's a fight for food and a fight to stop EMDs and the LER room. This is Specials against the enforcers. Specials against The Leader and Specials against the Academy.'

Everyone starts to talk at once.

'The Specials will win,' calls out Ilex.

'If you want us to win,' Kay says, 'you have to fight. You have to do the things that Blake tells you.'

I can hardly bear to look at her. I need her. Nothing

works, nothing makes sense without her. She makes everything right. The Specials are looking at me expectantly.

I swallow. 'Today I'm going to show everyone how bad the Academies are,' I say. 'And I'm going to punish The Leader. I need you to fight the enforcers and The Leader's . . . enforcers. When Ilex tells you.' I nod to Ilex to take over. I look back at the door, but Kay has gone. 'I've got to get into the old part of the Academy before someone notices I'm missing from the LER room,' I say.

I reach out to Ali and she takes my hand. We walk towards the bathroom and I hear a tapping sound. It rises to a clattering. I look over my shoulder and I see that they're clinking their shrap together.

For me.

I turn back to the door and square my shoulders. I've got to make this work.

It's still early and there's no one about. Ali and I slip quietly down the stairs. When we reach the door that I first entered the Academy by, I type in RECEPTION and swipe my mother's card. For a moment I worry that it won't work, that they've taken her off the system, but the door clicks open. We creep past reception and the lift and take the corridor that leads to the older part of the Academy. I peer through one of the doors leading off; it looks like a disused classroom.

At the end of the corridor the doors to a hall are propped open. There don't seem to be any locks in this old section.

'Let's have a look,' I say to Ali.

The hall is like something out of an old film. There's a polished floor, covered with rows of wooden chairs, and a stage with steps leading up to it at the far end. Ali skips over to some French windows looking out at a lawn. It must be a long time since she's seen the outside, but we haven't got time to admire the view. It's clear that someone from the Info has been here already because there are lights set up on towers and cases of equipment lying about. We need to find a hiding place. I take Ali's hand, but before we can move I hear voices coming up the corridor.

I scan the hall. They'd soon spot us if we duck into a row of chairs. Behind us, back towards the entrance, is another door. I run to it, pulling Ali behind me. I fling open the door and we rush inside. I was expecting another classroom, but this is a much smaller room. There's a desk with a computer in one corner and a bucket and a mop in another. On the floor is an open tool box and on the wall is a cabinet of keys. It's a maintenance room. More of a caretaker's cupboard really. I gesture for Ali to sit down at the dusty desk.

Now we'll just have to wait.

For a long time we listen to the banging and clanking of what I assume is the crew setting up. Then I hear a new set of voices in the hall. I wonder if this is the journalists arriving for the press conference. The voices are getting closer. I squeeze the door open a crack to take a look out. Through the gap I see the red uniform of The Leader's guards. They're heading towards the cupboard. I close the door. *Hide!* I sign to Ali. She ducks under the desk. I spin around, uselessly looking for somewhere to hide myself.

The door crashes open. 'Get your hands in the air!' a man shouts. He points a gun at me.

I slowly raise my hands.

'It's a kid!' he says to another man coming through the door. They're both dressed in red guards' uniforms.

He's going to hand me over to Rice. I'll never get The Leader now.

'Sorry, sir,' I say, dropping my eyes to his ridiculously shiny boots.

'What the hell are you doing, boy?' says the second guard. 'This is a premium security area. Civilians by invite only.' He's massive.

I slacken my facial muscles and make my eyes blank. 'I don't know your words,' I say.

He rolls his eyes.

The first guard steps towards me. I flinch. I hope he can't see Ali.

'What are *you* –' he points to me. '– doing *here*?' He points to the ground.

'They said The Leader is coming here,' I say. 'The Leader is . . . good. I want to see The Leader.'

'Gree, we're supposed to be out front,' says the tall one. 'Just find a teacher and hand the boy over.'

'I have to go?' I say.

'Yes! C'mon Gree,' says the tall one.

'Sorry, kid, we've been told to clear the area.'

'I go to my enforcer,' I say. I walk towards the door.

The tall one's radio buzzes. 'Let's go,' he says.

We walk down the corridor to reception.

'Now you go straight back to your teacher,' Gree says, patting me on the shoulder.

'Yes, sir,' I say and start walking back towards the other part of the Academy. I can feel them watching me. I walk slowly, hoping they'll move on by the time I reach the door. When I can bear it no longer I look back. They're gone. But there's a whole crowd of people in their place.

I've got no choice. I'll have to cut through these people. I walk back down the corridor looking about for enforcers, but there are none. There's the wire-haired receptionist that I saw when I first arrived. She's sat at her desk signing people in, with an impeccable sat on either side of her. I make sure the throng of people is screening me from them and move back into the passage leading to the hall. There's a trickle of people in suits moving down it. I try to merge with the crowd. I hope that if anyone notices my uniform they'll mistake me for an impeccable. When we get close to the hall I realise that there are now two guards posted on the hall doors and everyone is having their press passes checked. Great. There's no way they'll let me in. And poor Ali is still trapped in the cupboard.

I drop back and loiter amongst the bunch of people. I can't do this by myself. I'm going to have to convince one of the journalists to help me. I can't get in to confront The Leader, but one of them could. This is too hard. Part of me wishes that I was back in the classroom with no difficult decisions to make. Then I think about all the Specials that are sat in the grid. And will be stuck in the grid until they're sent to the factory. All those Specials who were banging together their shrap because they believed that I could help them. I'm not going to get another chance.

'Excuse me, are you a journalist?' It's out of my mouth before I can stop myself. The man I asked looks back at me and gives a slight nod, but he's caught up with a group of people moving towards the hall and he doesn't stop. I look back to see who else is coming and I realise that someone is watching me. It's a young woman with hair in waves that are so black and shiny that they look painted.

'Don't I know you?' she says.

With a jolt of recognition I realise she's right. It's the woman that interviewed us on the Info when Wilson and I won the Moritz Prize for Outstanding Research, Janna Mason. I nod vigorously. 'Yes, you do, I—'

'You were that Science genius at the Learning Community.' She looks down at my Academy uniform. 'What on earth are you doing here?'

'That's a long story,' I say. Now I've got a journalist I want to grab her by the wrist and force her to listen, but I've got to be smart. 'It's a long story that would sell you a lot of papers,' I add. I look over my shoulder, afraid that an impeccable is about to appear. 'Do you mind coming in here while I explain?' I open the door to one of the empty classrooms and we slip inside.

'You're The Leader's son?' Janna runs her fingers through her glossy hair. It swings immediately back into shape. 'Do you expect me to believe that?'

'You don't even have to mention that part,' I say. 'It's not like I care if anyone believes I'm his son. It's not like I want to be his son. The important thing is that you tell people what goes on in Academies.'

Janna folds her hands in her lap. Her nails are a dark shade of red.

'Did they really put your class in cages?' she says.

'That's nowhere near the worst of what happens in here.'

Her forehead puckers.

'So, will you help me?' I say. 'Will you ask The Leader some questions in there? About the use of electric shocks or why the food is drugged . . .'

She smoothes her hair behind her ears and shakes her head.

'Of course, you're the journalist, I'm sure you can think of the questions,' I say.

'No.'

'What do you mean no?'

She fixes her gaze on me. 'You've been very brave, Blake. But you're an intelligent boy and I think that you have experienced enough to know exactly what I mean by no and why.'

'But this is an incredible piece of news! Guaranteed headlines for weeks. It's what every journalist wants,' I say.

'Hmm. Most journalists just want to stay out of trouble.' She sighs.

Do I detect contempt? Maybe this is a way in. 'But not you,' I say. 'You're clever and . . .' I try to feel my way to what she wants to hear. 'And . . . smart and different.'

'I can't afford to be associated with heresy.'

'Are you scared? Don't you care that it's the truth?' I say.

'There are all kinds of truth. I like the kind that makes me popular with my editor.' She twirls a strand of hair around her finger.

'Really? Because it looks like it bores you to tears.'

She looks up at me. I've got her attention.

'Go on then,' I say, 'get off to the press conference. I'm sure you'll have a great time writing up your report and including exactly what The Leader tells you to.'

322

She's scowling. I'm getting to her.

'I don't know how you stick it,' I say. 'It must be mind-numbing just copying propaganda down like a robot.'

She takes a step towards me.

'Really, you might as well be working in a factory. All you're doing is carrying out orders.'

She purses her lips.

'You should join the Academy. They like them obedient like you. I thought you were clever. I thought you might even be a dare-devil, but you're not are you? You're a good g—'

She shoves me in the chest. I go sprawling backwards.

'Don't you dare tell me what kind of person I am,' she says. 'You don't know anything about me.'

I get slowly to my feet. I shrug my shoulders as if I'm unconvinced.

'Oh, all right!' she snaps.

'So you'll do it then?' I realise I'm breathing heavily.

'No. I'm not going to ask those questions, Blake.'

My shoulders sag. I was sure I had her.

'*You are*,' she says.

'Me?'

She leans in so her face is close to mine. 'It's true that I'm bored to tears with playing it safe. But whatever psychology you use on me, I'm not a moron. I don't want to end up in a cage. If there's going to be risk, then you –' she extends a finger till it's pressing into the centre of my chest '– can do the risk-taking.'

323

'But I haven't got a press pass,' I argue.

'Stop whining. If you want a press pass, I'll get you one. Wait here.' She disappears.

I lean against the wall behind the door. Is she going to be able to get me into the hall? Then what? Will they just shut me up as soon as I open my mouth? I drop my chin on to my chest and my mother's face comes into my mind. 'I'm trying,' I say out loud. 'I'm really trying.'

Janna reappears. She's got someone's press pass in her hand.

'Won't –' I squint at the card '– Mr N Morris mind?'

'He doesn't know he's lost it yet.' She rummages in her bag and takes out a tiny camera. 'Smile.' She clicks a button. Then she prints the image out. 'I'm wasted in journalism,' she says. She folds the edges and neatly tears them off so it's the right size to cover the photo of N Morris. 'We need glue,' she says.

I riffle through the drawers at the front of the classroom. There are yellowing pieces of paper and several pens, but no glue. Janna scrabbles in her bag again. She takes out a tab of gum, chews it and then uses a tiny blob to attach my photo to the card. 'It's not perfect,' she says. 'I'll distract them and you just flash it.'

'Thanks.'

'Then you're on your own. You get caught, you don't mention me. Got it?'

'Okay.'

She shrugs off her black suit jacket and hands it to me.

324

It's not a bad fit. A little short in the arms. Her red dress is tight. She's watching me from under hooded eyes. I swallow. 'Why are you doing this?' I say.

'Because I feel like it.' She laughs and shakes back her hair and wriggles her shoulders with pleasure. For a moment she reminds me of Carma.

'Come on, they'll be starting soon,' she says.

I follow her meekly, even though I'd like to shake her. She's behaving like this is a game of dare. She's not interested in abused children, but she likes the idea of being a bit naughty. A nasty thought strikes me: was I ever that selfish? But I have to push it away because we're out in the corridor and I need to concentrate.

I try not to slink along or look over my shoulder. I walk tall and pull together my jacket so that my Academy shirt doesn't show. As we approach the hall I see the two broad guards standing just inside the doors. My heart races. *I've got a press pass*, I remind myself. When we pass through the door both the guards' attention is fully fixed on Janna and her swaying hips. 'No recording equipment,' one of them says. He waves a scanner over me and then starts on Janna. 'Steady on!' she giggles and bats away the scanner as he brings it closer to her chest. She hands him her communicator to add to a pile already confiscated. He grins at Janna while he takes her name. 'You can collect it afterwards,' he says.

The hall is rammed. The rows of chairs go all the way from the back to the foot of the stage with only a narrow gap down the middle. We sit near the back at the end of a row. We're close to the maintenance room. The door is still closed. I hope Ali is okay.

I'm surrounded by a sea of suited journalists. Because only the official cameras and microphones are allowed, they're all clutching old-fashioned notepads.

A man with silver hair comes on stage and the audience rustle into silence.

'Good morning, ladies and gentlemen,' he says. 'In a moment we will go live on the Info and, following a short speech from our esteemed leader, there will be an opportunity for questions from the press. But first I would like to thank you all for attending. Today we are lucky enough to witness a great leap forward in education. Today a dozen new Academies will be opened. Let me introduce to you the man who has built up a system which has eradicated teenage unemployment and bolstered the production power of our factories . . .'

All around me the audience clap.

'. . . The Leader.'

The curtains at the back of the stage part and there he is.

My father.

He looks like he does on the TV. He doesn't seem right for real life. His tan is too deep and his hair is too shiny. Like he's impersonating himself. *That's my dad*, I tell myself, but it means nothing.

A whippet-thin man in trainers bobs in front of the camera and gives a countdown. The Leader snaps on a smile. 'Ladies and gentlemen,' he says, 'we're here today to celebrate. We're here to celebrate success.' He pauses like he's about to give us the punchline of a joke. 'Not my success in instigating a more effective Academy frame-work and not your success in supporting a system that guides young people to realise their full potential, but the success of those young people themselves.' He turns to the audience and widens his eyes. People are always talk-ing about what great presence he has, but actually in the flesh he seems a bit . . . intense. Creepy even.

'Seventeen years ago this country had just come out of the Long War. Times were hard.' He bangs his fist on his hand. 'Our young people were without guidance or prospects. They were low, they were useless, they were without *purpose*.' He stamps his foot to match his raised voice.

I have to bite my lip to keep from laughing; he sounds ridiculous, but everyone else is listening intently.

'Today we have a system that teaches young people to work. A system that shows them there is a reward, yes, a sweet reward *if* you work hard and contribute to the country. We have let our children know that we don't tolerate slackers or non-conformists.' He pauses to sweep the audience with his flashing eyes. 'We have to teach the children that idleness leads to destruction. And do you know what, ladies and gentlemen? They thrive on it. We have given these children boundaries and expectations and they have stepped up to the mark and taken their place as useful members of society.'

I almost shout out: *As slave labour*. But I choke it back.

'Academies don't just give these children an education –' he raises both hands like a conductor '– they give them a future.'

The applause is deafening. Bile rises in my throat. What is wrong with everyone? They're taken in by his glaring and pointing. They're only hearing his stamping and shouting. None of them are listening to what he actually says.

The Leader is reaching out his arm to draw an Academy student on stage.

'I'd like you to meet someone special,' says The Leader. 'This is Carma.'

Carma appears on stage. It's the first time I've seen her since she disappeared to have her baby. Her stomach is flat again, but she's walking a little stiffly. She tosses back her hair and smiles to the camera.

'Carma, can you tell us what your life was like before you came to the Academy?' says The Leader.

'My mum had a morph addiction and my dad hitted us. It was ef—' Carma catches his eye. 'It was big bad.'

Janna looks at me. I shake my head. Kay told me that Carma was born in an Academy. She's never met her mother.

'Tell us about your life at the Academy,' says The Leader to Carma.

Carma takes a deep breath. 'I've been given inspiration, education and aspirations,' she says in a rush.

Janna snorts. She's right. Inspiration, education and aspirations? King Hell. The scriptwriter could at least have given her something to say that sounded like her. But nobody seems to care. They're all clapping again.

'And soon Carma will be ready to continue her contribution to society by joining our factory workers.'

The audience clap again. The Leader gives Carma a gentle push off stage, but she walks slowly, waving and blowing kisses.

The Leader spreads his hands 'Any questions?' he says.

Before he's finished the words I'm on my feet. 'Why are electric shocks used on Academy inmates?'

The hall goes silent. The expression on The Leader's face doesn't change. His eyes flick sideways to his aide with the silver hair. He pushes his smile out even further. 'The Academy system provides a package of sanctions and rewards,' he says. 'Discipline is an essential factor in enabling children to fulfil their potential—'

'Are you saying it's acceptable to use electric shocks? And beatings? To starve children? To drug them—'

'These children have a history of violent non-conformist behaviour. It's disappointing when we have to listen to these so-called liberal protests. Do you really think our children, our country, would benefit if we allowed them to run wild? Maybe you're too young to remember a time when violent students terrified their enforcers – the very people trying to assist them?'

'Enforcers don't assist anyone,' I say. 'Enforcers encourage unmarried sex between students and allow brutal fights to take place. They stand by while malnourished children are kept in filthy conditions and if anyone dares to speak up about this treatment, what do you think happens to them? They're thrown out into the Wilderness.'

There's a sharp intake of breath when I mention the Wilderness.

'You are mistaken,' The Leader says. 'Enforcers are

trained to get the best from their students.' His smile has gone.

'I don't think you should beat children to get what you want from them. I don't think young people should be imprisoned in Academies at all.'

People are muttering and turning round to try and get a look at me.

'We *need* Academies.' The Leader clenches a fist. 'We need to be tough to get the best.'

The audience are still nodding their heads, but there's an air of unease.

'Children need discipline.' He slaps his hands together. 'It's discipline that's got us where we are today.'

'He's getting angry,' Janna whispers. She's right. He's waving his hands even more than before and a flush is creeping up his neck.

'No one said that getting back on our feet would be easy. There are always sacrifices to be made. Every difficult decision I make, I make for the good of this country.' He's glaring out at the audience. 'If you only knew—'

The Leader's aide touches his arm, but The Leader shakes him off.

'Are you saying that Academy enforcers do use electric shocks and drug the kids?' calls someone from across the hall.

The Leader grips the side of the lectern. 'Let me tell you what this comes down to. We need every citizen's efforts just to endure. Criticism does not sting me, but this soft and weak attitude could be our undoing. I urge you not to be taken in by this feeble talk. Academies are the backbone of this country.'

I'm angry now. 'Don't try to explain it away.' I raise my voice. 'Don't use your rhetoric. There's nothing that you can say that will make it right to mistreat children. You are *wrong*.'

'No, young man, *you* are the one who misunderstands. You have no idea how important it is that our children learn. We can't survive without their contribution and they must learn their duty and if we have to beat that into them—'

'CUT!' shouts the aide.

We've got him. He's admitted it.

The Leader is red in the face now, jabbing his finger at the audience. 'It's for their own good!' he shouts. 'It's for the good of all! You can't begin to appreciate just how tough life is. I am trying to help my people. And anyone who gets in my way will be—'

'Ladies and gentlemen,' one of the suits from The Leader's party interrupts.

The aide leads The Leader away. The journalists have all started talking.

'Let's not get overexcited,' the suit continues. 'The Leader is following a punishing schedule at the moment and I fear it may have taken its toll on his health. I think we should avoid taking remarks out of context.'

'Is it true Academies use electric shocks?' a man with a booming voice yells out.

'He said the kids should be beaten. Is that official policy?' calls a woman.

'No,' says the suit.

'But he said it. He said it live on the Info,' she says.

The aide reappears. 'The Leader said that appropriate sanctions were used.' He glares accusingly into the crowd. 'And we were not live.'

I turn to Janna. Not live? I don't believe it. After all that. None of this has even been heard by the public. What a waste.

The aide goes on, 'You should be aware that The Leader's "live" performances always have a fifteen-minute delay period to safeguard from any unfortunate incidents.' At this point he looks out with laser eyes to where we are standing, but I've already dropped to my knees to hide behind the row in front.

'But is it true?' repeats the woman.

'It *is* true,' says a tiny voice.

The whole hall swings round to see who said it.

It's Ali.

Ali spoke.

Ali keeps talking. 'Academies hurt kids. The enforcers electric shock us and hit and burn and scare us. We're dirty and hungry and sad. All the times.'

My chest swells. She's such a good girl. I try to make my way towards her, but there's a crush of people surrounding her and the hall fills with sound. The journalists are yelling out to the aide. Some of them are on their feet. One of the men in suits powers through the crowd towards Ali, but she is swept up into the arms of a journalist who cradles her on her knee. A journalist with a beard grabs a camera from the container of confiscated items and tries to take a photo of Ali, but he is rugby-tackled by one of the guards. In the confusion Janna sidles up to the container and retrieves her communicator.

The aide flicks the switch on his microphone. A wail of feedback silences the room. He gives us a tight smile. 'Obviously there are a lot of questions to be answered. We will transport you all to the Leadership building where we can have a thorough debriefing and we can address any queries on Academy policies.'

Janna edges back along our row and crouches down beside me.

'How long is this going to take? I've got an interview at two,' someone says.

'It didn't work. The whole thing is ruined,' I say to Janna.

'How about you give us some answers now?' says Booming Voice.

Janna gives me a long look then she reaches down the front of her dress and pulls out the smallest AV bug I have ever seen. 'It's all on here,' she says.

My heart lurches. That device will have copied all of the footage recorded by the official cameras. We can still show the public what he said. If we can get out of here.

We're not the only ones who don't want to be taken to the Leadership building. Lots of journalists are complaining.

'I'm leaving,' the man next to me says.

'This is a disgrace,' calls someone near the front.

There's a rush towards the door, but the guards are blocking it.

I start pushing my way towards Ali again.

'You can't keep us here,' the bearded man says. 'I'm not going with you.'

'Attendance is compulsory,' the aide says.

More guards swarm out from the stage wings and start rounding people up.

Janna's eyes dart about the room. She flicks her hair impatiently out of her eyes. 'Oh efwurd,' she says.

She's finally realised that this isn't just for her entertainment.

The guards are almost on us.

'Don't let them take you,' I say. I stand up and pick up my chair and hurl it into the aisle. Janna stares at me. There's a guard heading straight for me. I pick up another chair and whack him with it. Janna stops staring and picks up her own chair. She's not the only one. The hall descends into chaos. The journalists are yelling and throwing punches at the guards, who are trying to restrain them and pull them out of the hall. Chairs are flying and one of the lighting towers topples with the sound of crunching metal. I reach the place where Ali was sat on that woman's lap, but there's no sign of her. I pick up a broken chair-leg to use as a weapon.

'I'm getting out of here,' Janna says. She pushes her way between angry journalists. She lifts a chair and hurls it through the French windows. People duck and scream as the glass shatters. Janna heads straight for the gap and some of the other journalists follow. But a surge of guards swarm up behind, grabbing at arms, clothes and hair.

They can't reach Janna. She's out first and she doesn't look back. She sprints across the lawn with a guard in pursuit.

I weave away from the window where the guards are concentrated. I feel a tug on my jacket. I spin round, chair-leg raised.

It's Ali.

'What—?' I say, but she pulls me three steps back into the maintenance room. She pushes the door shut and drags a stack of dusty chairs in front of it.

'No people saw us,' Ali says.

'Ali . . . you're talking.'

She nods her head as if I'd said it was time for dinner.

'How are you talking?'

'I had to. They were listening to that man telling all the wrong things. All the things he said were . . . were . . .'

'Untrue?'

She nods. 'I heard so many untrue things that I had to say the true thing.'

'But—'

There's a shriek from outside.

'Blake,' Ali says, 'when they have got all the people they will look to find us.'

She's right. They heard me asking questions and they heard Ali telling the truth. They're not going to let us get away with that. I've put Ali in danger. This was a stupid idea. How did I ever think that we could take on The Leader? How could I be so deluded as to think that I could do something to help the Specials?

'The people are fighting good but there are too many enforcer ones—'

'Guards,' I say.

'Too many guards.'

'We need more people.'

337

'We've got more people,' she says. 'We've got hundreds of Specials. They're ready to fight.'

'But we can't get to them. We can't tell them,' I say. I stare at the computer. 'And that's no use to us,' I say. 'I already know there's no way of contacting the outside world. I checked out the computer system on my first day and there was only an internal . . .' I dash to the computer.

'What is it?' Ali asks.

'There's an internal comms system. I'm going to send the Specials a message.' I switch the computer on.

'How?'

'The computers are connected. I can write something on this and send it to the Specials' computers in the grid and it will flash up on their screens.' I pull up the communications menu and check *Message all student terminals* with my forefinger. Enough of the Specials can read now that I hope the message will get passed around.

'What should I say?' I ask Ali. 'I don't know what to say.'

'Say: *Time to fight. Go with Ilex and Kay. If you fight you get food and you get free.*'

I type as fast as I can then I tap the send icon.

There's less banging and crashing coming from the hall. They're subduing the journalists. I wonder if some of them are already on their way to the Leadership building. What will they do to them?

I listen for the sound of the Specials. Nothing, but some thumping and cursing. Those poor journalists. I just keep making things worse for people. And The Leader is getting away with it. I want him stopped. I want him to run into a pack of angry Specials and then I—

'King Hell,' I say.

'What?'

'The Specials won't be able to get to us. They won't be able to get through the door. We've still got the door card.'

Ali bites her lip. 'They will come. Kay will think how to come to us.'

I groan. 'We're all in big trouble. I should never have started all this talk about stopping Academies.'

'Blake, we have to get ready to fight.'

'What's the point? It's all over.'

'No. No giving up. You don't give up. You said Specials should read and now the Specials can read. You said I can talk and I can. And all the time you say Academies are wrong and we should get out of the Academy. You're right. Let's get out. Let's fight.'

I look at Ali. She's clenching her little fists ready to take on a pack of guards.

I nod my head and I pick up my chair-leg again.

Then we hear it.

A rumbling.

Ali opens the door a crack and we peer out. There are still a number of journalists putting up a fight against the guards. In between the scuffles, crew members from the

Info are hurriedly packing up equipment. One by one they stop still to listen to the rising sound. It's like the rush of water getting closer. But it's not water.

It's Specials.

I can hear shrieking and the pounding of feet. They're coming. From the sound of it, they're all coming. The door is flung open and there's Kay.

'No more Academies!' she shouts. 'No more electric sh—'

The rest of what she says is drowned out by the screaming and growling of hundreds of Specials as they pour through the door. It's chaos. The guards try to grab hold of students, but there are far too many of them. The remaining journalists break free and try to fight their way out. A wave of enforcers arrives, but the Specials don't care any more; they fight them too.

It's wonderful.

I step out of the cupboard. Kay rushes up to me and throws her arms around me. I press my face into her sweet hair.

'We've got to find Janna,' I say.

'Who?'

'She's got what we need to show everyone that The Leader is bad. I think one of the guards got her.'

Kay nods and we start to work our way through the crowds. When we get close to Ilex I yell above the noise.

'Blake!' He beams at me.

'They'll send more guards soon. Get the Specials outside. Use the door card.' I make to hand it over, but he holds up his own. 'Kay took it from Rice.'

'Nice work!' I say. 'Open all the doors and tell them to run for it.'

Ilex nods. 'Where are you going?'

'I've got to find someone.'

He turns back. As we push on, the word spreads that it's time to get out, and the flow of the crowd turns. Now everyone is surging down the corridor back towards the newer part of the Academy.

In reception Ali is standing out of the way, up on the desk. When she sees Kay she climbs down and takes hold of her hand.

'Where would they take the journalists?' I say.

'Vans,' Ali says. 'The man said, "Go to the vans". What's "vans"?'

'Ali—!' Kay says in amazement.

'Vans are a vehicle,' I interrupt. 'Like a car. They must have gone down in the lift. To the car park.'

We fight our way across the reception area to the lift. Kay is squeezing Ali and telling her how pleased she is that she's talking. The place is rammed with Specials all

342

pushing back to the newer part of the Academy. I can hear a guard's whistle, but I can't see any of The Leader's men. They're completely outnumbered. We weave in and out of the Specials. Some of them are cramming bread into their mouths. They must have broken into the kitchens.

We reach the lift and I press the call button.

'What's the door?' Kay asks.

'It's a lift.' I press the call button again. 'You know, like the enforcers have.'

The door opens. Kay peers in. 'Is it not-dangerous?'

'It's safe, but you two should stay here.' I press the close doors button and the button marked *B* for the basement car park, but before the doors slide shut Kay and Ali step in.

'No,' I say. But the doors have already closed behind them and I've got to be quick. 'You can stay in the lift,' I say.

We wait.

'Is it going?' Kay asks.

'No, it's efwurding not.' I hit the basement button again and the lift hiccups downwards and then stops.

Waaaaaaarrrrrrrruuuuunnnnn!   Waaaaaaarrrrrrruuuuu-unnnnnn! A siren starts wailing somewhere outside the lift.

'It's the noise.' Kay turns pale.

'What noise?' I say, stabbing at the lift controls again. We've got to find Janna before she's taken away.

Kay is frozen.

'What does it mean?' I say.

'The noise for everybody get out. You know, the hot-hurt noise.'

The hot-hurt? 'Do you mean the fire alarm?'

She nods.

We're in trouble. I hit the emergency button. It flashes, but nothing happens. The alarm shrieks on. I press every button on the controls in turn. Still nothing. Ali's eyes dart from side to side. 'Get out,' she says.

'We will,' I say. I reach past her and pull open a tiny door. Behind it are another set of controls labelled *manual override*. I hit the down arrow, but nothing happens. Next to the arrows is the outline of an old-fashioned lock.

'It needs an override key,' I say.

As well as the controls there's a simple communicator. I flick the switch for a connection. The screen crackles into life. It's an efwurding recorded message. A woman with hair like a helmet says, '*We are aware of a malfunction in lift ML17, location A34. Please remain calm and wait for an engineer. We will now connect you to the service person in your building.*' The screen blinks and shows us an empty office. I don't know what room it is, or who is supposed to be in there, but right now they're probably running away from the fire.

'We're trapped,' I say. 'No one knows we're here and—'

Kay glares at me. Ali's eyes are stretched wide.

'It's all right,' I say to her. 'Everything will be all right. It's fine.'

We stare at each other. Under the screech of the alarm comes the thumping of feet. Everyone is running. The lift shakes. We're going to die. My muscles stiffen with horror. The lift is going to fall, to plummet down. We'll be hurled around and when we land I won't even know which way is up. The idea of being imprisoned like that, buried in a metal tomb without even the sense of which direction is the way out, makes my stomach contract. I can't bear it. I can't be trapped like that. I don't want to suffocate.

'Blake.' Kay shakes me. 'Lift. Ali. Up.'

She's staring up at a hatch in the ceiling. I bend down. My legs are shaking. Ali clambers on to my shoulders and I stand up. We've got to get out.

'Push harder, Ali,' I say.

I brace my legs to take the strain.

'Try twisting it,' Kay says.

Ali tenses with the effort.

'It's no good,' Kay says. 'It's maybe locked on the out-side.'

Ali gets down. Kay clicks the buttons again and flicks the switch on the communicator.

There's nobody there. There's no way out.

Something bangs against the door. Near the top, but right outside. I hammer my fists against the smooth metal. 'HELP!' I scream. 'WE'RE TRAPPED.'

Kay and Ali join in with the thumping till I hold up my hand. We listen for a response. Nothing, but the alarm.

I look round at the walls. We're sealed in. I feel the weight of the building above us and imagine it collapsing on the lift. Leaving us buried, but alive. I've got to get out. I need to get outside, to be in the open, to see the sky. I thump the *B* button with my fist. Then I lean into the communicator and scream, 'WE'RE TRAPPED! GET US OUT!' My breath is coming in gasps.

'Blake . . .' Kay says.

I jam my fingers into the crack where the two doors meet and pull.

'Blake! That could be dangerous.'

I keep pulling. I have to know where we are.

'Blake, it won't help.'

Something gives and I can drag the doors apart. I'm staring at the concrete lift-shaft wall. We're wrapped in concrete and metal. I can't breathe.

Ali tugs my sleeve.

I try to pull the flailing fear tight inside me so that I can look at her without screaming.

She points upwards. There, in the concrete wall, is the bottom of a door. *Oh, thank goodness*.

'We only went down a little bit,' Kay says. 'I think it's the door where we came in.'

She's right. The lift barely moved before the power cut out. That's our way out. We can get out. I need to be calm.

Ali makes to climb on me again.

'No, let me,' Kay says and she pushes me into a crouch so that she can climb on to my shoulders.

I put my hands on the shaft wall to steady myself as I stand up. 'Open it,' I say. 'Get it open.'

She wriggles on my shoulders. 'There's a no-lock lock.'

'A what?'

'A thing that opens the door.'

'Like a catch? Just open it, will you?'

'Ali, give me your shrap.'

Ali slips off a piece of copper piping that is strung around her neck and hands it up to Kay.

Kay struggles. 'It keeps slipping. The catch has got slipping stuff on.'

I sniff. I think I can smell smoke.

There's a click. The door opens. I look up to see a strip of light. The alarm blares louder and a wave of smoky air blows in. At the top of the lift, in front of Kay's head, is a gap, about twenty centimetres high, leading on to reception. Kay hooks her hands over the edge and pulls herself up. 'HELP!' she shouts. 'HELP US!'

There's no response.

'I can't see a person,' she says.

'Can you get out?' I ask.

She pulls herself up with her hands till she's standing, bent over, on my shoulders. She turns her head and slides it through the gap; when she gets to her shoulders she stops. 'It's too little.'

347

Ali taps my arm. 'I'll, do it.'

'Let Ali try.'

Kay scrambles down.

'What do I do? How can I get Blake and Kay out?' Ali says.

I take a deep breath. My teeth are chattering. I've got to look after Ali. 'If there's a fire, Ali, or if there's danger, then you get out of the Academy,' I say.

'I want to get you out,' she says.

'Only if there's no danger, go back to the maintenance room. There's a key cabinet. Like a little cupboard, a door. See if you can find the override key,' I say.

'What's "key"?'

'Like shrap. Like lots of sticks of shrap hanging up. Look for one that says "lift". L-i-f-t.'

She nods. Kay helps her on to my shoulders and I stand up. She slides out through the gap smoothly.

Her head appears back at the gap and she smiles. Then she's gone.

I look at Kay. 'At least she's out.'

Kay nods.

'Could you see the fire?' I ask.

'No. Nothing. No person. Just a mess. Broken things.'

'Do you think it was Info equipment that started the fire? One of those big lights? Because Ali was heading back in that direction.'

'It could have started any place. Maybe in the kitchen. There were Specials getting into the kitchen.'

She's right. One of Rex's Reds and a gas cooker wouldn't be a good combination. I touch the side of the lift. 'Does it feel warm to you?'

'Should we close the door?'

'No.' Closing the door would be like closing the lid on our coffin. That strip of light is keeping me from screaming. 'We should leave it open so Ali can hand us the key.'

She looks at me and says, 'Okay, we'll leave it for Ali.'

She's being so nice to me after I've been such an idiot.

'Kay?' She looks up at me and I can't stop myself from reaching out and pulling her into my arms. 'Thank you for coming to fight. And for talking to the Specials this morning. You were the one that convinced them to help me. I'm sorry I got you into this mess and I'm sorry that you didn't get to be Dom and to do all the things that you wanted to do.'

She shakes her head and puts a hand on my cheek. 'All I wanted, Blake, was to be not just a Special. I wanted to know how it feels to be someone.' She looks up at me. 'And I do. You make me feel like someone.' She rises on tiptoes till her face is close to mine. 'This is how it feels.'

Then she kisses me and my head fills with rushes of colour and my knees shake and I hold her in my arms and wait for the world to fall down around us.

62

The longer we stand here, the less likely it seems that Ali is coming back. The alarm is still moaning on. I can definitely smell smoke. I keep my eyes fixed on the gap.

'Do you think all the Specials will get out?' I say.

'Ilex will open the doors. And the enforcers too, they'll open all the doors.'

I raise my eyebrows at her.

'They will. The enforcers need to get out and then the Specials can get out too.'

Maybe she's right. Maybe the enforcers will forget about hating us while they're running for their lives.

'Blake, I don't understand a thing.'

'What's that?'

'Why did The Leader try to get rid of you?'

'I told you, I'm his son.'

'So? You're a good one. You were Learning Community, not some Academy scum.'

I flinch when she says 'Academy scum'.

350

'It doesn't matter. He's ashamed of me. He was married to someone else and he . . . got my mother pregnant. You've got to realise that he pretends to be so moral and the perfect family man.'

'All the Academy babies are born with no marrying.'

It's so hard to make Kay see that things are different on the outside. 'It's not the same. People care about rules and the proper way of doing things.'

'They don't think Specials are people.'

'They don't realise. They need to see—'

Someone is shouting down the hall. Using the protruding lip of the control panel as a toe-hold I haul myself up to look through the gap. Down the corridor, part of the wall has collapsed. Clambering over the rubble is Ali.

'She's come back!' I say. 'She's come back for us.'

Kay scrambles up beside me.

Then I hear more shouting. 'STOP!' a man bellows, followed by something else I can't hear above the alarm.

'ALI!' I shout.

The man is The Leader's aide. He's got a gun. He grabs Ali and spins her around. He's shaking her. I try to push my head out through the gap, but it's too small. He's shouting in her face. She shakes her head.

'STOP IT,' I shout. 'LEAVE HER ALONE!'

He can't hear me over the alarm. I scramble with my legs, trying to walk up the concrete. I thrust forwards. I scrape the skin off my temples and I feel the wetness of blood, but I can't get my head out. He's waving the gun at her.

'LET HER GO!'

Ali's shaking her head again. She's just a child, why can't he leave her alone? He's angry. He raises his hand and smacks Ali hard across the face. She falls to the ground. He leans over her and holds her by the hair.

'GET OFF HER!' Kay screams.

Now the aide is right in Ali's face. Ali stares back at him. He's shouting at her again, but she won't answer. He pulls her to her feet by her hair. He's obviously furious. Then a shower of plaster rains down on them. He ducks back out of the way. Ali makes a break for it, but the man sees her. He fires his gun. Ali falls face down.

He's shot her.

He kicks the wall in frustration then climbs back over the rubble.

'Oh no, oh no, oh no no no,' Kay says.

The alarm keeps shrieking.

'COME BACK YOU EFWURDING BASTARD! YOU CAN'T LEAVE HER. SHE'S HURT.' I'm screaming my throat raw.

'Ali, Ali,' Kay sobs. 'He's killed her. Why did he kill her? Why?'

We hang there, crying.

This is all my fault.

Then Ali raises her head.

And she starts to crawl.

'She's moving,' Kay says.

She is moving, but she's moving very slowly.

352

'You can do it, Ali!' I shout, but she's still a long way down the corridor and I don't think she can hear me. She slowly drags herself closer to us. When I can see her face I can tell that she is looking at me. I shout again. Nod my head to encourage her.

'I should sign to her,' I say to Kay, 'but . . .' My arms are taking my body-weight. I can't move them.

Kay drops back into the lift and I feel her shoulders under my feet. I try to keep some weight on the top part of my arms, which are stuck out of the gap; I only move them from the elbow down, to sign to Ali. *Good girl* I sign and *well done* and *keep going* and *I will look after you*. I repeat them again and again.

She keeps her eyes fixed on me and inches forward till she's close enough to touch. She doesn't stop. I don't think she can.

'Let me down,' I say and I hit the floor just in time to catch Ali, who rolls right through the gap and drops into my arms.

Kay closes the door behind her. The sound of the siren is slightly muffled. Ali has been shot in the shoulder. Her clothes are drenched in blood. I kneel down with her in my arms.

'It's all right, Ali,' Kay says.

Ali opens her hand and I see the key. Kay takes it.

'I got it,' Ali says.

'You're a clever girl,' I say.

'I didn't tell him, Blake. I didn't tell him where you were.'

My breath catches. The aide was looking for me. Ali was protecting me. She should have told him. She shouldn't have come back for us. She should have escaped.

'You've done really well, Ali,' I say. 'Just hold on. Everything is going to be all right.'

There's the sound of another shot outside.

Kay springs to her feet and inserts the override key. She presses the *down* button. We don't move.

'Blake,' she says.

I turn round. There is smoke seeping through the crack at the top of the door.

'It won't go down,' she says.

The smoke is getting thicker. There's another shot. It wasn't supposed to all end up like this. I look down at Ali. Her breathing is shallow. She's tried so hard to get us out of here and it was all for nothing.

'What about up?' I say. 'Will it go up?'

Kay presses the arrow and suddenly we shudder upwards. It doesn't stop at the floor we've come from. I hold my breath, imagining that we might just go up and up till we're stuck at the top of the shaft, but then we stop and the doors jerk halfway open. Wide enough. I stagger out, carrying Ali.

I look about. Immediately to the left there's a security

door. Kay takes my mother's card from my pocket and opens it. We're on the first floor in the middle of a corridor of dormitories. 'Come on,' I say. 'We've got to get out before the whole place goes up.'

We run along the corridor. I've never seen the place so empty. As we speed down the main stairs I smell smoke again. We turn the corner to see black clouds pouring out of the dining hall. Ali coughs weakly. I step back.

'Get down low,' I say to Kay. 'Can you see down the corridor?' Can we get to the door?'

Kay drops to the floor and crawls forward in commando style. She's soon back.

'Can't get to the door. I can't see it. It's all hot and fire.'

My violent urge to be out where I can see the skyline returns. 'We've got to find another way out,' I say.

And that's when we hear the screaming.

It's coming from one of the dormitories. 'Take Ali,' I say, handing her over. I run up the stairs and into the dormitory.

There are twenty or so Specials riffling through the lockers at the ends of beds. Closest to me, Rex is shaking a girl who is screaming. I pull him off her.

'She's got my shrap. She's stolen my shrap,' he says.

I look round at the Specials. They're all draped in bits of metal. They've been looting the dormitories.

'It's all stolen, you idiot,' I say.

Rex pushes the girl away and turns on me.

'Don't,' I say and when he sees my face he drops his fists.

356

I pick up the lid of one of the lockers that has been ripped off its hinges and smack it against a bedstead. The metal makes a ringing sound. The Specials turn to look at me.

'We've got to get out of the Academy. Come with me.' I stride towards the door.

'We don't want outside,' Rex says. 'We can stay here with no enforcers.' The Specials cheer. They're so used to following Rex.

'There's a fire! You'll be killed. Come on!' I shout at them.

'Let's get food! Rex'll get you food!' Rex cries.

More cheering.

There's the sound of something crashing from somewhere below us. It sounds like another wall collapsing. The Specials are shocked into silence.

'We need to get downstairs now,' I say moving across the dormitory.

Kay appears in the doorway, holding Ali. She shakes her head. 'We can't get downstairs any more.'

64

Out on the corridor, even Rex can't deny that things look bad. Everyone can see the smoke curling up the stairs. I run to the top of them. I can feel the heat of the spreading fire and hear crackling and hissing below me.

'Blake,' Kay says, 'we've got to get Ali outside.'

'But there's no out,' a blonde girl says.

I knew it. I knew this place was a death trap. This is the only staircase. There should be safety features. There should be an efwurding fire escape. And then it hits me. There is. I saw it when I was excluded.

'Kay, we have to go up again,' I say. I turn to the Specials. 'Listen to me. You've all got to come with us. We're going to the roof, to the top of the Academy. And then we're going to climb down.'

From the back of the rabble, Rex forces his way through.

'That's stupid. We can't get down from big high.'

'We can. There's a ladder.' I realise that they won't

358

know what a ladder is. 'There's a kind of steps . . . stairs. I've seen it.'

'How?' sneers Rex.

'I've been outside.'

They know that's true. Exclusions get talked about. They know I've been out and come back again.

'You can come with us or you can stay here with the fire,' I say to everyone.

I take Ali back from Kay. 'We're going to get out of the Academy, Ali. You can see the trees again.'

Ali's eyes roll open and she gives me the smallest nod.

'I'm not going with this no-ranker,' Rex says.

There's an almighty bang. I'm thrown backwards off my feet, taking Ali with me. I cushion her fall but she lets out a terrible moan. A pulse of hot air passes over us. I struggle to lift Ali again. At the far end of the corridor I can see sky. And flames. Something in the kitchen below has exploded, creating a hole in the wall.

'OUT! NOW!' shouts Kay and starts pulling Specials up by their collars and shoving them up the stairs. I follow with Ali. Rex tails behind me, muttering.

At the top of the stairs Kay opens a security door. One of the little Specials finds a storage space full of boxes and stacks of chairs and a door with multi glass panels leading out on to the roof. I tell Kay to type ROOF into the panel and then she swipes my mother's card. It works. The Specials pour out.

'Now we're stuck all high,' Rex says.

359

Kay glares at him.

Outside it's a beautiful spring day. A bright blue, cloudless sky. To the rear of the Academy, black smoke is streaming skywards.

'Look, Ali,' Kay says.

I turn round. In my arms Ali struggles to lift her head. To the front, filling the wide driveway, are hundreds of Specials. They keep coming. Pouring out of the Academy. My breath catches. They're out. That could be the whole Academy. Out. Free. Ali smiles. *Take that!* I think. *You can't keep us prisoners.*

We cross the roof and I find the top of the fire escape.

'How are you going to . . . ?' Kay looks at Ali.

'It's fine,' I say, but my arms and my back are already killing me. I can't see how I can carry her and hold on to the ladder.

'I'll take her,' Rex says.

'No,' I say. I don't want him to help. I don't look at Kay. I know her eyes will be telling me to change my mind. Instead I look down at Ali. She looks up at me. She doesn't say anything. Just looks right into my eyes. She trusts me.

I hold Ali out to Rex. 'Be careful with her,' I warn him.

Rex hoists Ali over his shoulder and then starts down the ladder. The other Specials queue up to make their way down to the ground. Kay and I drop to the back of the line.

Kay looks at me and for the first time she doesn't try to hide her feelings with a straight face. She's afraid.

I open my arms and she stumbles into them.

'Blake,' she says, 'I have to tell you my sorry.'

'You don't have to be sorry. You saved the day. You were perfect . . . You are perfect.'

She looks up at me and a jolt shoots through my body and out to my fingertips.

'I'm sorry about Rex. I thought I wanted to be Dom. I had a long time wanting to be Dom. Then we found out about Rex and all things were bad and I thought if I could still be Dom then it would be okay.'

I stroke her hair. 'Everything is okay,' I say.

She looks down at the shrieking Specials surging around the front of the Academy and laughs. I laugh too. She wraps a hand around my neck and draws me down to her. She presses her full lips against mine. Oh, she is so sweet. I put my arms around her and pull her closer to me. She kisses me harder. It's so good. She is so good. When we draw apart I keep my arm around her. It feels right.

She gestures down to the escaping Specials. 'Look what you did, Blake.'

'It's because of you. I didn't know how to do anything before I met you.'

We've reached the front of the queue. She presses her lips against mine again and then she starts down the ladder.

I follow. My hands are shaking so hard I have to concentrate to grip the rungs. The metal is rusty. Soon my sweating hands are coated in orange-brown flakes. The ladder shakes as we climb. I think about the explosion and hope there won't be another one before we reach the bottom.

On the ground there are Specials everywhere. There's a group fighting over some packets of food and some of the older boys are trying to smash in the windscreen of a parked car, but most of them are surging away into the trees.

My ears are ringing from listening to the alarm for so long.

I look around for Ali and Kay.

Rex has laid Ali on one of the wide stone steps leading up to the grand Academy entrance and is standing guard over her.

'Find Ilex,' I say to him.

To my surprise Rex listens to me for once and ploughs straight into the crowd bawling, 'ILEX!'

I crouch down next to Kay, who is holding Ali's hand.

Ali is staring up at me. She's taking slow, rattling breaths.

'You did it,' she says to me.

'*We* did it. Kay and I wouldn't be here if it wasn't for you.'

'Blake can do anything. You can get rid of all the bad.'

I stroke the hair off her face. A spasm of pain goes through her.

'Just lie still, Ali,' Kay says. 'Ilex is coming and we'll get someone to make you better.'

Ali grips my hand hard. 'Tell Ilex I was brave,' she says. 'Tell him . . .' She struggles for breath. 'Tell him that I said Ilex is the best brother.' She smiles at me.

I try to hold her here with my eyes. I try to keep her blood pumping by willing it. But I can't do it. I can't help her. I watch the sweetness and the brightness and the life run out of her like water through my fingers and there's nothing I can do to stop it.

She's gone. Little Ali is gone.

Kay slumps against my chest and I put my arms around her. We sit like that while the Specials are running around screaming, throwing stones at each other and fighting over stolen food.

Kay breaks away to close Ali's eyes. I stand up to see if I can see Ilex or Rex. They're not there. In the distance I hear a siren.

'We have to find Ilex and get out of here,' I say.

'Out?'

'Away from the Academy.'

Kay's eyes flick wildly between the Academy and the drive leading into the trees. Her lip is quivering. 'I don't think . . .' she says. 'I don't know . . .'

She's afraid to leave. The Academy is awful, but it's all she knows.

'It's okay,' I say. 'I'll be with you.'

'We have to stay with Ali.'

Somewhere down the drive, men are shouting and Specials are screaming.

'Kay, they're coming to round us up.'

'We can tell them. We can tell them about the Academy and how The Leader is bad.'

'Kay.' I hold her by the shoulders and force her to look at me. 'The guards are coming. The guards work for The Leader. They will take us away and they will put us in another Academy.' I fear that what they would actually do is worse than that, but I mention another Academy to shock her into listening.

Kay is shaking. She looks back at the Academy again. 'What can we do? Where can we go? I don't know how to.'

'I'll look after you. We've got to try to get to the entrance.'

She grips my hand and stares into my face. Then she nods. 'What about Ali?'

'We have to leave her, Kay. We've got to save ourselves. That's what she would want.'

I stoop down and kiss Ali's forehead.

'We have to tell the Specials. They need to run away too,' Kay says.

The forecourt is no longer jammed with Specials, but there are still hordes of them milling about.

'Listen!' I shout.

No one can hear me.

Kay climbs to the top step. She puts her fingers in her mouth and gives a piercing whistle. A lot of Specials turn round to look at us.

'SPECIALS!' I yell. 'The guards are coming to lock you up. You've got to run. Run this way! Try to get out of the gates.' Some of them don't hear. Some of them look around wildly, paralysed with fear. But once the running starts, most follow.

I take Kay's hand and we join the stampede into the trees.

'When I arrived, I came from this direction,' I say. 'There must be a gate up here.'

We stay off the drive where we'll be easily seen and instead fight our way through the overgrown bushes. I aim for where I think the entrance must be. Up ahead, we can hear Specials clashing with guards.

'King Hell, Kay, look.'

Through the trees there's an army of red advancing.

Kay sucks in her breath. 'We can't get out.'

What the hell are we going to do? Should we try and slip past the guards in the crush? Maybe we could try to hide.

'Blake,' Kay says.

I look up. There's a guard ripping through the greenery on a motorbike. The Specials scatter on either side to avoid being hit. He's heading straight for us.

I grab Kay by the wrist and run in the opposite direction. We stumble back through the trees.

I look over my shoulder. The bike is twisting and swerving, but it's hard for the rider to make a path through the undergrowth. We move further away from the gate and the rest of the Specials.

'I think we've lost him.' I turn in a circle, scanning through the greenery in all directions.

Something red streaks out from behind a tree and grabs me by the shoulder.

Kay swings a fist straight into the streak's face.

It's not a guard. It's Janna. She reels backwards from the impact of Kay's punch.

'Kay! Stop it. This is the girl I told you about. The one who can help us stop The Leader.'

'What the efwurd are you doing?' Janna spits at Kay. Her nose is bleeding.

'What the efwurd are *you* doing?' Kay says.

'I'm trying to get you out of this mess.'

Kay scowls.

'How?' I say. Hope rises inside my chest.

'Come with me.' Janna looks Kay up and down. 'Not her.'

I step closer to Kay. 'I'm not going without her.'

Janna rolls her eyes. A gunshot goes off up ahead. She flinches back into a tree. 'Just move it.' She strides away.

'Come on,' I say to Kay.

She doesn't move.

Panic tightens my chest. We've got to go with Janna. This is our way out. '*Please . . .*' I say.

Kay shakes her head to herself, but she lets me take her hand and lead her after Jana.

Janna takes us to a van parked in between the trees. My steps slow. I reach out an arm to stop Kay.

The van has got the guards' logo on it.

Janna has double-crossed us.

66

I tense, waiting for guards to appear.

Janna turns back and sees my face. She gives an exaggerated sigh. 'For efwurd's sake, relax,' she says. 'It's not a real guards' van.' She pats me on the cheek. 'Anyone would think that you didn't trust me.'

Kay lets go of my hand.

Janna scans the trees around her and then unlocks the side door of the van. I clamber into the windowless space and gesture to Kay to follow. She takes one last look back in the direction of the Academy and climbs in beside me.

Janna slams the door behind us. I shift up to give Kay room. In front of us a metal grille separates the back of the van from the front seats; through it I see Janna climb into the passenger seat. 'Let's go,' she says to a blond young man in the driver's seat. He's wearing a red shirt, which I guess is supposed to help him look the part, but up close like this, you can tell it's not a guard's uniform. He starts the van and negotiates his way between the trees.

'Thank you,' I say to Janna, 'for coming back for me—'

Janna lets out a shriek of laughter. 'Come back for you? Oh, that's good. I wouldn't have come back to this place for anyone. Since I made my impressive escape out the window it's taken me all this time to get hold of Ty on the communicator and for him to get this van down here to get me out of here.'

'Then why—?'

'I saw you. I thought you might be useful.'

The van lurches on to the main drive. Janna turns to Ty. He's tall and he hunches over the wheel. I wonder why he's taking such a risk for Janna.

'Let's make this as fast as possible,' she says.

The van jerks forward and we pick up speed.

Kay's fists are clenched so tight that her knuckles are turning white. I don't think she's ever been in a car or a van.

If I press my face against the grille I can see out of the windscreen.

'Keep looking for Ilex,' I whisper to Kay.

We must be nearing the gate because up ahead I can see a swathe of guards in red intermingled with the grey of Specials.

'We'll never get through this,' Ty says. He slows the van to a standstill.

'Are they winning?' Kay says. 'Are the Specials winning? Maybe we should stop and help them.'

'Don't stop,' Janna says. 'Just drive right through them. If you hit one, then the rest of them will get out of the way.'

'Don't do that!' Kay says. 'Don't hurt the Specials.'

Janna swivels around in her seat. 'I can see you're going to be an asset.'

Kay lunges at the grille but Janna doesn't flinch. 'Just remember whose van this is, sweetie,' she says.

Ty is talking to himself under his breath. 'We'll never get out of this . . . I should never have . . . The old man's going to kill us . . .'

We're inching our way through the fighting Specials and guards.

'It's not really your van, is it?' I say.

Janna pouts. 'It's my boss's.'

'And her boss doesn't know that I've risked my neck and "borrowed" it,' Ty says.

Janna gives him a devastating smile and places her hand on his chest.

Kay tuts.

'It's a good job you're so fond of me,' Janna say.

'But why has this boss got a guard van?' Kay says.

Janna looks at me, not Kay. 'I know you think journalists don't do anything worthwhile, but actually we do carry out some investigations. My boss has found that painting a van in the guard style has allowed him to get into a number of places he wouldn't normally be welcome.'

'What will he say when he finds out you've got his van?' I ask.

'A lot,' Ty answers.

Kay is watching the fighting out of the window. 'I want to get out,' she says.

Janna scowls at Kay. 'Don't be too effervescent with your thanks for my gallant rescue.'

'Thank you,' I say, before Kay can answer. 'We really are grateful.'

'You can pay me back. I've got plans for you. You know what went on in that place. And there's the matter of your family connections. I'm not sure I've got much use for your girlfriend though.'

Kay opens her mouth to reply, but I interrupt. 'You know, Janna,' I say, 'you're right. I could be useful to you. You could be rich and famous. You could be the person who takes out the Academy system. You could even destroy The Leader.'

A slow smile spreads across Janna's face. 'No, Blake,' she says in a silky voice.

Kay stiffens beside me.

'We've already had this conversation,' Janna continues. 'The Leader can be destroyed, but not by me. It's all up to you.'

'We're getting near the gate,' Ty says. 'You should get down.'

'Blake, what about the Specials?' Kay says. 'They're getting them. They'll be taken to an Academy. We have to help. We have to.' She reaches for the van door.

I grab her arm. 'Kay. We can't. There's nothing we can do now. Maybe we could come back and—'

'Shh. Get down.' Janna says. She drops into the seat-well herself.

I pull Kay down so we're hidden. Her eyes are full of reproach.

'We have to get out of here,' I whisper. 'If we want to really help, then we *have* to get out. I will fix it. I promise.'

The van continues to creep forward.

'Efwurd. We're in trouble,' Ty says.

'What is it?' Janna asks.

'Quiet. Stay down.'

I turn my head a little so I can see through the gap between the two seats. There's a guard stood right in front of the van.

'He wants me to stop,' Ty says under his breath.

There's a rapping on driver's side window. I slither down further, pulling Kay with me. The window hums as it opens.

'Right,' comes a voice through the window. 'I need you t—' The guard sucks in his breath. 'Hey! You're not— Get out of that van.'

'Drive!' shouts Janna.

'Who the hell?' says the guard.

The van shoots forward. I scramble up to see what's happening.

'I NEED BACK-UP!' the guard roars.

We bunny-hop to a halt.

'There are kids everywhere,' Ty says. 'Get out of the efwurding way!' he shouts out of the window.

'Don't stop!' Janna says. She pulls herself out of the foot-well and slams her hand down on the horn.

In front of the van the throng of red and grey figures throw themselves out of the way as we speed forward again.

I press against the grille to look at the dashboard computer, on the rear-view screen there's a mass of red coming up behind us.

'They're following us,' I say.

Beside me, Kay sits up to look at the screen.

'Faster,' Janna says. 'Put your foot down.'

There's a thump as we hit something. I'm thrown off-balance as we skid and the back end of the van swings round. The engine cuts out.

On the screen the blur of red is swallowed up by a sudden wave of grey.

'More Specials!' Kay says.

'See? They can look after themselves,' says Janna. 'Come on, come on Ty!'

Ty starts the engine. He stalls. Janna's door is flung open. She screams. A guard grabs her by the neck. I bang uselessly on the grille. Kay throws the side door open. She shoots out a leg, catching the guard square under the chin. He crashes down. I pull Kay back into the van and she slams the door shut. The engine springs into life. Ty pulls the van round and we pick up speed. Janna takes great grasping breaths. She wraps her arm around the neck of her seat and manages to lean out of the van and pull her door shut. I can see the gate ahead. It's open.

'Drive!' Janna shrieks. 'Efwurding drive!'

And we're through the gate.

For a moment there's silence.

'We're out,' Janna says.

'We're not the only ones,' Ty says. He points to the rear-view screen. A stream of Specials is pouring out of the gates behind us.

Kay breaks into a smile.

'We did it! We did it!' Janna says.

'No need to be too effervescent in your thanks for my gallant rescue,' Kay mimics Janna.

Janna turns around to stare at Kay and then throws back her head and laughs. I join in. Kay and Ty too.

'We're through!' Ty says. 'I can't see anyone following us. We're really through.'

I look at Kay. 'We've escaped,' I say. 'And lots of the Specials too. We've done it.'

'Really escaped?' She bursts out laughing again. 'Oh, Blake.' She throws herself against me and kisses me. Hard. My hands tangle in her hair. She is everything.

Janna makes a vomiting noise. 'You should be kissing me for my genius escape plan.'

Kay and I break apart.

Ty is singing.

Janna puts her arms in the air and stretches out her legs. 'No ugly guard is getting his hands on me! You know,' she says looking round at me, 'we are pretty efwurding good at this. So what do you think, Blakey? Are you ready to take on The Leader?'

I look at Kay. We've made it this far. We're free. Kay reaches out and pushes my hair out of my eyes. Anything is possible when I'm with her.

'You can do it, Blake,' she says.

She's right.

I can.

And I will.

About the Author

C.J. Harper grew up in a rather small house with a rather large family in Oxfordshire. As the fourth of five sisters it was often hard to get a word in edgeways, so she started writing down her best ideas. It's probably not a coincidence that her first 'book' featured an orphan living in a deserted castle.

Growing up, she attended six different schools, but that honestly had very little to do with an early interest in explosives.

C.J. has been a bookseller, a teacher and the person who puts those little stickers on apples. She is married and has a daughter named after Philip Pullman's Lyra. THE DISAPPEARED is her first novel.